JUSTICE for JENNIFER

Linda Hughes

As Lukas waits quietly for the principal parties to enter the courtroom, he considers how to tell Gabriel about his medical condition. He'd known about the cancer for months, hiding it while mulling over the best time to address it. Countless times, he'd wanted to ask Gabriel to attend his doctor appointments—sometimes needing assistance to get there—but ultimately chose not to involve him. It had been a heartfelt decision not to divulge his medical problem any sooner than absolutely necessary, wanting to keep the cancer hidden until after the trial's conclusion. To do otherwise would not only be unkind and insensitive, but just plain wrong.

Life had been in constant turmoil since Jennifer's disappearance, and Gabriel and Michelle were distraught enough. Why add to their misery by revealing his illness before the trial began or speaking of the horrific news received on the same day the jurors began deliberating. Under the already somber circumstances, his illness would create an unnecessary distraction. There would be time to discuss it later . . . most likely, but not too much later.

The doctor's words had been expected but still hard to swallow. "Give it to me doc and don't sugarcoat it," he'd stated at the beginning of that fateful meeting. But when he heard, "After your final test, it's . . . ah, definitely terminal . . . six months . . . maybe eight at best." He recalled gripping the chair tightly to keep from falling forward and briefly staring at the floor. Although apprehensive and expecting the worst, hearing the actual words gave him an imaginary sucker punch in the gut and his nausea returned with a vengeance . . . a common symptom of the disease. Without looking at the doctor, he'd stood, turned toward the door, and exited without saying another word. What else was there to say or ask? Nothing else . . . he'd thought then and still did.

Having asked a myriad of pertinent questions to numerous specialists, he already knew if the results of the latest brain scan turned out as predicted, the tumor was large, now aggressive, and intrusive . . . having grown undetected for years until noticeable symptoms appeared. Only after ignoring the intense headaches for as long as possible, had he finally sought medical attention. He'd done a good job of covering-up the fatigue, the memory loss, and some of his speech problems . . . passing them off as senior moments.

Once fully aware of the far-reaching mass entwined within his brain, chemotherapy and/or radiation were not viable options to fight the uncontrollable cancer. Oh well, he'd accepted the outcome like a man . . . like a man was supposed to do. He'd lived a pretty good life and would be celebrating his seventy-fifth birthday next summer. Well, maybe or maybe not. Well, probably not. Huh, there was "no probably" about it . . . most likely not.

Lost in thought, Lukas was brought back to the present when the bailiff said loudly, "All rise for the Honorable Judge Donald J. Wilkins." Almost immediately, others rushed in from both side doors—like ants converging on a sugar cookie—and the front section of the courtroom was once again full. In spite of the active front area—separated by a short railing—only a small number of spectators were in attendance . . . maybe a handful at most.

When the defendant entered, Lukas turned away but noticed the same two meticulously dressed men sitting directly behind the defendant's table. Often wondering what connection they had to the defendant, they'd sat in those same approximate seats throughout the trial. Perhaps they were friends of the defendant. If they were, then he considered them part of the enemy's camp.

As Lukas watched the jurors file in, he tried to get a feel for their decision. When he zeroed in on each face, he secretly wished more blacks were on the jury . . . not just two. Not a single juror looked toward the defendant but rather looked at the judge or downward. Was that a good sign or not? In his mind there was only one acceptable verdict to be reached, and only one decision that would satisfy him. That smug, smirking piece of crap defendant needed to be found guilty. God forbid and even if Jennifer was never found, he should be locked away forever for taking her.

As the jury foreman read the verdict, Lukas wanted to scream, "What did you say? No, no, no, that's impossible. That can't be right." Dumbfounded, a familiar wave of clamminess and nausea rushed over him. Watching the defendant and his prick attorney shake hands, Lukas was filled with utter disappointment, rage, and a sense of loss for his granddaughter all over again. He wanted to run toward them, and for a split second wondered—then knew—who he'd strangle first. The hopelessness of the situation, combined with a glimmer of self-control, kept him from acting on his animal instinct to hurt the ones who'd harmed not only Jennifer but his entire family. His hate didn't stop with the defendant or the defendant's team of attorneys; he also hated the prosecutor and the entire jury for voting to acquit that rotten son of a bitch. They'd all let Jennifer down and played a part in this unbelievable travesty. If guns were permitted in the courtroom, he'd have shot the whole lot of them on the spot without remorse. Lukas looked over at his son and daughter-in-law as they held each other and openly wept.

How can scum like that be free to enjoy life while his sweet granddaughter is missing and probably dead? It was beyond unfair . . . just downright horrifying. Clenching and unclenching his fists, something needed to be done. If the court system wouldn't do its job to protect the innocent, he'd somehow find another way to give Jennifer and her parents the justice they deserved.

Since the defendant didn't take the stand and testify, Lukas was determined to get answers from him—one way or another—triggering sadistic thoughts and visions to rush through his mind. He'd now found a profound reason for staying alive for as long as possible, as he contemplated how the answers would come slowly and painfully from that despicable human being before he silenced him. His hate for that disgusting mound of crap was beyond anything he'd ever experienced or imagined

before. On second thought—yet vastly less personal—
Hitler came to mind. There were others—serial killers
and the like—just as evil, but they slipped his mind at
the moment.

Beginning with day one of Jennifer's disappearance,
he'd been constantly perplexed with the unknowns . . .
why take her and where was she? As they weren't wealthy
people, it wasn't surprising that a ransom demand hadn't
been received. Realizing only a few months remained to
carry out this undertaking of fact-finding and revenge . . .
whatever it might be; he would again put off the heart-
to-heart conversation with Gabriel. He certainly didn't
want his son getting in his way or hovering about while
he proceeded to do what had to be done. Not sure how
or where to begin or exactly what to do; he did know
what he intended to accomplish—or try to accomplish—
before he died. Regardless of his declining health and
mental sharpness, or whether or not this turned out to be
his last act before dying, he planned on carrying out his
own form of justice and righteousness.

Thinking about righteousness, he would pray to God
for understanding and forgiveness for his upcoming
actions. While praying, he wondered if it would be wrong
to ask for additional time and more strength in the few
remaining months he had left. Since none of his prayers
had been answered so far—especially during the search
for Jennifer—why would he expect God to listen to his
present requests? Undeniably, God will be fully aware of
his every thought and action as he moves forward to sin.

Well, so be it. What was . . . was. What is . . . is. What will be . . . will be. Considering his inability to change the "was" or the "is," he'd be damned if he couldn't change the "will be."

Afraid of throwing up, he cautiously sat down, cupped his hands tightly over his eyes, and began to cry uncontrollably.

Chapter 2

Kenneth Lehmann walked briskly down the courthouse steps before nonchalantly entering the nearby parked car. Per his instructions before leaving the courtroom, transportation had been prearranged by his attorney. Although certain the car would be waiting, he settled into the backseat and sighed deeply with relief.

Leaving the congested downtown area of San Francisco, no conversation was offered or received by either of the front-seat occupants. While the driver concentrated on street traffic, the front-seat passenger stared thoughtfully straight ahead.

As the car moved down Market Street and closer to the Embarcadero district, Lehmann watched the building fronts pass by in a blur . . . like a fast-forwarding movie—seeing them but not clearly. Sitting comfortably in one of his many company cars, he momentarily reflects on what could have been and where he might presently be. At long last and completely free, it is finally time to put the last few months behind me for good, he thought.

When the car slowed in front of his warehouse—conveniently located near the port facilities—Lehmann sat up and appeared more interested in his whereabouts. Moments after entering the empty parking structure, the car stopped abruptly in a space marked "Reserved."

Gordon—the front-seat passenger and one of the two men present in the courtroom throughout the trial—jumped out, opened the rear car door, and nodded. Once standing eye to eye with his employer, he smiled before saying, "Congratulations."

"Thank you, Gordon. Let's hurry upstairs. I've got a lot of catching up to do. And Gordon, I'd like my set of keys."

"Should Ronald stay with the car or go up with us?"

"He's free to do as he pleases but needs to stay close and in phone contact . . . in case needed later."

Searching the inside pocket of his suit coat, Gordon handed his boss a group of keys attached to a stylish gold ring. Stopping briefly to talk to Ronald, Gordon rushed back . . . just in time to enter the private elevator designed to take occupants from the parking area directly to the top floor of the three story building.

As always, their hidden business, The Club, was never discussed outside Lehmann's office unless done quietly in a remote place . . . usually when walking near the water. Even in other parts of his own building or within the private elevator, any discussion or even mentioning The Club was off-limits. This mindset was strictly adhered to anywhere there was the slightest possibility of their conversation being over-heard or recorded. Constant emphasis on secrecy had served them well in the past. These precautions were not only necessary for their own protection and survival but vital to the secrecy of their exclusive clientele of club members. However, as he'd sat in the courtroom—accused of kidnapping—he needed to be more diligent and cautious in the future . . . if that was even possible. There could never be the slightest possibility of this happening again, regardless of any last-minute problem arising.

When they exited the elevator, Gordon walked hurriedly across the small, insignificant hall and entered a security code into a keypad located beside the only entrance into the building's third floor. Pausing a moment, they waited for an extended beeping sound before Gordon's key was used to open the door. Once inside the narrow waiting room, Gordon pushed the all-clear button before resetting the security system.

"It's great to be back in my sanctuary," Lehmann remarked.

Revealing a quick smile, Gordon answered sincerely, "It's great to have you back. What's our plan? Should we get back to business as usual?"

"Not quite yet. Given that I've been preoccupied with the trial and keeping a low profile; I want to first settle into my office and recap your assignments."

Briefly passing several folding chairs, a modest table covered with stacks of trade magazines and numerous antique catalogs, they soon arrived in front of Lehmann's office door. Gordon used the same safety procedures as before on a keypad next to the door. In spite of these security measures, two different keys were slipped into two separate locks before entering.

Lehmann's office—the most secure location within the building—has its own bathroom facilities and an escape hatch hidden in the floor of an adjacent walk-in storage closet. This obscure exit—concealed by a wooden lift-up door and covered with a non-skid rug—hides narrow stairs leading downward to the back of the warehouse's first floor. Across from the bottom of these stairs and opening only from the inside is an outlet door with no handle on the opposite warehouse side. Unknown to anyone except the two of them, this creative escape route was designed to blend in and offer additional protection if or when the necessity arose to secretly depart the premises. Occasionally, during early morning hours—when the warehouse was closed, locked, and security cameras purposely turned off—items had been removed from his office via these concealed stairs and outlet.

Glancing around the office, Lehmann went directly to the ornately carved elm-wood desk—a gift from an appreciative Chinese club member—and sat down. Adjusting into the high back leather chair, he motioned toward the velvet covered settee, saying, "Gordon, have a seat."

Waiting until Gordon seemed comfortable and attentive; Lehmann took a moment to marvel at his employee's dedication and uncompromising loyalty. Beyond the fact that he paid Gordon exceedingly well, they shared a common obsession, but one never discussed openly. Sometimes, unable to keep exciting moments under wrap, they shared flashbacks of special encounters, discussing them in hushed voices while walking on the dock or other safe areas.

Lehmann's official livelihood—the import and export of rare and unique antiques—is a bogus business venue . . . giving the appearance of conducting a legitimate enterprise. In actuality its purpose was to offer cover-up for The Club's existence. The warehouse, delivery trucks, and manifests serve him well in disguising the true operation of his lucrative international endeavor. During the previous five years, he'd been substantially compensated beyond belief for creating and managing The Club's secret parties in San Francisco and around the world.

Once a year—occasionally more often—and always with Gordon's assistance, he hosted The Club's gathering in his own building. Every so often, when the opportunity presented itself, one or both took advantage of this home base hosting. Their personal activities would take place following the completion of a party and after the attendees vacated the property.

Glancing around the office a final time, Lehmann spoke seriously. "I'm assuming you've had the entire area scanned for bugs, the security cameras wiped clean, and the computers destroyed and replaced. I mean . . . ah, above and beyond our normal scheduled cleaning and replacement process."

Gordon's reply was a short and definite, "Yes." As an after-thought, Gordon added, "It was handled by the customary vetted personnel. As always, I closely observed."

Appearing more relaxed, Lehmann inquired, "Was the car flattened and placed on the appropriate tanker?" After receiving affirmation—a nod from Gordon—there was a brief frown on Lehmann's face before he resumed speaking. "I don't need to remind you that our last problem can never happen again . . . regardless of the reason. Moving right along and before I forget, did you procure the burner phones?"

"I did and totally understand what you're saying. Since we're due to host our annual party here in two months, is it still on?"

"Yes, but we need to get a feel for how the Tokyo party goes next month. We should see if negatives exist from the Japanese host or other club members . . . ah, regarding the trial. As usual and this goes without saying, no discussion about anything that pertains to the trial with anyone. While in Tokyo, let's stick to business . . . enjoying as usual but staying tuned-in to side conversations. Be non-committal with your answers and direct any awkward questions to me. Well, Gordon, one thing for sure, we've learned that our safeguards work. I intend to put all of this drama behind me." Pausing for a deep breath, he grinned before continuing, "Okay, I think we deserve a drink . . . don't you?"

Without waiting for an answer, Lehmann opened the bottom desk drawer, removed two shot glasses, and a ten-year-old bottle of Japanese malt whiskey—a gift from another happy club member. Pouring both glasses almost full, he held one out to Gordon and picked up the other. Holding his glass forward, he clicked it against Gordon's and offered, "Cheers and to fun times ahead." After each enjoyed a second shot, they left the office and walked to the other locked door on the opposite side of the waiting room.

Before a club member could attend a party at The Club's San Francisco location, there were several security procedures which had to be precisely followed. All members, regardless of how long they'd attended club gatherings, could not enter the premises without prior approvable, facial recognition, and a secret code at each site . . . beginning outside the parking structure's roll-up metal door. Once a member entered the parking enclosure, no speaking or conversation was allowed—except to answer security questions—until entering the third floor's party room. Each club member had to strictly adhere to the following process: immediately leave the parking area, go up the private elevator, cross the hall, enter the waiting area, and eventually pass through the final door of the party room—the one Gordon was about to open. This access procedure was accomplished under the watchful eye of either Lehmann or Gordon . . . sometimes both.

Club members at international locations were also personally scrutinized and vetted for everyone's protection. Since members were extremely wealthy and influential—including politicians and high-ranking worldwide officials—the utmost security was not only needed but absolutely necessary. Therefore, similar procedures were adhered to at all locations around the world in order to prevent scandalous consequences from occurring.

From the onset of this arduous process, each and every member readily agreed to these stringent terms prior to receiving approval to this elite and secretive group. At any time—sometimes hours before a party—access codes could be changed. Although a daunting and time consuming task, Lehmann took pride in keeping everyone and himself safe, while amassing vast personal wealth, and from time to time joining into the pleasurable festivities of satisfaction.

They stepped into the party room after Gordon entered yet another security code into a similar keypad beside the door. The room's first impression was similar to what you'd expect to see in an upscale hotel's sitting area or lobby . . . elegant and stylish, yet chic and traditional with the exception of a large round lounging structure in the middle of the room. On the ceiling above this odd piece of furniture were several spot lights.

Luxurious chairs, over-stuffed sofas, and a myriad of intricately carved wooden tables were scattered about. Along one side of the room was an elongated marble-topped bar stocked with a multitude of alcoholic and non-alcoholic beverages from all over the world . . . anything imaginable that could be requested by a club member was available at all times. There were no windows in the room but many flat screens adorned the walls opposite the bar area.

Carefully scanning the room, Kenneth noticed its appearance hadn't changed from before or after the search warrant was issued to acquire access. Examining the area more closely—not sure what he expected to be different—nothing seemed altered, disturbed, or out of place since last being there. Since purposely staying away from his property for an extended time, he couldn't help but be curious. It was also disconcerting to know strangers and the police had wandered through his private domain.

Beyond the bar were four doors, opening to rooms arranged in similar bedroom motifs with accompanying bathroom facilities. Each of these rooms had a large walk-in closet containing an abundance of adult and children's clothing and costumes in sizes from very small to extra large. Next to these walk-ins were rows of wooden shelves packed with miscellaneous children's dress-up accessories like: petite high heels, costume jewelry, fancy hair barrettes, twinkling tiaras, small sized cowboy boots, hats, and bandanas. Displayed on middle shelves were baskets of lipsticks, mascaras, eyeliners, scented oils, creams, soaps, and powders. On the bottom shelves were boys' and girls' toys and games. Scattered among these shelves were colorful and playful masks.

Although completely fabricated, but a reasonable assertion used when talking to the authorities, the large room was utilized for hosting parties and entertaining visiting wealthy clients associated with Lehmann's international trade business. Equally untrue, the bedrooms allowed these guests complete privacy and respite after traveling far from home without the need to leave following heavy drinking or the inconvenience of shopping for gifts.

While explaining the need for the party room, bedrooms, closets, and shelves, Gordon had been the one to quickly point out that a section of each bedroom's shelving held an array of gift boxes in miscellaneous sizes—kept there for a guest's chosen gift or gifts. Also, noting that next to the gift boxes were packages of disposable diapers . . . just in case a foreign client brought along a child accompanied by a nanny. In truth but not told to the authorities, these diapers, costumes, accessories, and miscellaneous items were available to members during a hosted San Francisco The Club's party.

Because of his and Gordon's commitment to safety with each and every minute detail, not one single incriminating item had been found during the search. As expected, nothing could be found on the new computer taken by the authorities from his office. Even if the computer hadn't been replaced before it was seized, all names and locations of The Club's members were entered using a complicated code of letters and symbols . . . then immediately wiped clean after each party.

Also, every possible object or place touched by anyone had been meticulously scrubbed and sterilized;

the furniture coverings, plastic mattress covers, and bed linens burned in the warehouse furnace. All remnants to anything or anyone connected to the party were removed and replaced . . . disappearing as if it, she, or he never existed. Most importantly and immediately after each party, if there happened to be human baggage to deal with—like after their last party—it would be taken out to sea and dumped. If not for the one slight mishap with his personal car, a trial would never have taken place. That bitch . . . Carly.

"Well Gordon, all looks perfect. I've ordered a new car. Have Ronald take you to pick it up. It should be ready at Bayside Mercedes. It's not white this time and not a Cadillac. It's silver. Would you bring the new car back to the warehouse unloading entrance by five o'clock? In the meantime, I'll be seeing to our latest antique acquisitions, a group of rare Tibetan Singing Bowls."

Soon after Gordon's departure, Lehmann took a final look around before resetting the security alarms, and heading to the building's first floor.

The first floor or main floor of the warehouse was used for loading and unloading some small but mostly large crates of imported items. Within this large open area was a restroom used by workers and a modest office, comprised of a small metal desk, a couple of metal chairs, and a few filing cabinets.

Adjacent to this unpretentious office was a tasteful sign next to an elevator stating: *Showroom on Second Floor.* This elevator was programmed to travel only one floor up, opening into a large display room featuring unbelievable treasures from around the world. Customers and sales people seeking unique and one-of-a-kind objects would confer here with Lehmann or Gordon on a regular basis. Although this trade business began as a concealment setting, Lehmann had grown to enjoy obtaining and trading these exquisite and splendid objects.

Chapter 3

Placing a small notepad on the kitchen table, Lukas looked through a drawer for a pen. Somewhat unsteady on his feet, he finally located one that worked and sat down. While fresh on his mind, he wanted to start a list of people he hated and wanted to punish. After placing the defendant's name at the top of the page, he stopped writing. Exhausted physically and emotionally, he folded his arms on the tabletop and laid his head down.

Dozing off for a few minutes, his short rest was disturbed by the phone ringing. Off-balance, he pushed himself from the chair, awkwardly turned, and leaned against the sink for support. Trying to hurry but feeling light-headed, he staggered along the countertop before answering on the fifth ring.

Surprised he'd not missed the call; Lukas cleared his throat and said, "Hello."

Without hesitation Gabriel asked, "Dad, are you all right?"

"Sure . . . why?"

"You left the courthouse before we could say goodbye. I wanted to check on you . . . ah, make sure you got home okay. I almost hung up."

"I've been here a little while . . . trying to decide what

to have for dinner."

"About that . . . you're looking thin. I don't think you're eating enough. And Dad, I won't give up on getting you to move in with us. It's awfully lonely here."

Before Lukas could respond, he heard Gabriel making quivering sucking sounds, just prior to mumbling, "Sorry . . . Dad."

"Not necessary to apologize. We'll never stop missing her . . . no matter where we live or who we live with. At least your mom isn't alive to deal with this."

"Dad, are you sure you're feeling okay?' With no answer, Gabriel continued. "Not only are you looking thin, but you seem tired and distracted . . . ah, lost in thought a lot."

Ignoring his son's last remarks, Lukas answered, "Guess I'm still missing your mom's cookin'. Maybe it's an age thing . . . just not hungry anymore."

"I love you, Dad," Gabriel replied thoughtfully. "Please reconsider moving in with us. You won't need to lift a finger. We'll take care of everything."

"I know and thank you . . . but no."

Not liking his dad's response or perhaps not wanting to argue, Gabriel resumed talking but on another subject. "I tried to talk to the prosecutor, but he was late for another trial. He did say, 'Win a few . . . lose a few.' What a jerk. I guess there's nothing more we can do. I don't want to give up. But after today . . ."

After a noticeable silence, Lukas answered forcefully, "I'll never give up. Never! It makes me sick that . . .

that . . . that creep was found innocent. If he didn't do it, he knows who did. I believe every word Carly from the Boys and Girls Club said. And that little shit witness lied under oath. I'm sure of it. It makes me so angry. I should go."

"Dad, the police said they'd keep looking, so maybe we'll still get her back home. I'll be over to see you soon. Please take care of yourself. Bye, Dad."

"Bye, Son."

Placing the old fashioned receiver on its cradle, Lukas found Gabriel's comments enlightening. He'd purposely worked at being quieter and keeping his conversations to a minimum, hoping the in and out memory loss wouldn't be noticed as much . . . if at all.

Taking a moment to look around the kitchen, Lukas tried to remember what he was doing before the phone call woke him. Right . . . starting an enemy list.

Before returning to the table and his mission—or his obligation as he saw it—he stopped to open a cupboard. Gazing up and down the shelves of stacked can goods, nothing sounded appetizing. Knowing that eating was important . . . even necessary, it didn't matter if a food item sounded good or not. If for no other reason, it was now essential to feed his dying body. Now—more than ever—he had to keep his strength up for as long as possible. Being hungry was of no consequence but eating was.

Opening a can of mushroom soup, he wouldn't take the time or trouble to heat it. Why bother . . . he'd swallow it down like medicine anyway. Taking the can to the table, he carefully sat down. Having missed the chair before, he needed to be extra careful and attentive to whatever activity he was doing. Whether it was a balance problem or just not paying attention, completing his quest had to be uppermost on his mind. At least while he had a mind that still functioned. Stifling the urge to laugh, his last thought seemed somewhat funny.

Before beginning his unappealing yet vital food source, he needed to add the name of that no-account witness to his list. However, there was a problem with that. Either he didn't remember his name or never heard it. The bastard was probably paid off. Why else would he change his testimony from what he told the police? For now he'd add him as "witness" some place on the page until more information was available. That thought led to realizing how ill-prepared he was for this undertaking. Okay, he shouldn't let himself get bogged down with the particulars at the moment . . . reminding himself that it was barely day one of his intended objective.

Seeing the soup can beside the writing pad, he'd forgotten to grab a spoon. Damn it . . . was it the brain tumor, old age, or just stupidity? Flipping the page over, he should start another list of things to do, people to call, and things to buy. His head was beginning to throb. While on his way to get a spoon, he'd stop and take a pain pill . . . maybe two.

Chapter 4

In spite of retiring early the previous night, Lukas felt wiped out, yet oddly on-edge when awaking. He couldn't help but wonder if his sleep was consumed by an unremembered nightmare . . . perhaps caused by his brain's deterioration, the hard to swallow potent sleeping medication, or both. The doctor told him—more than once—of this happening and a definite possibility to watch for in the future. But unlike past mornings before the cancer took over, if he woke after a scary nightmare, it would hang on for awhile. Now, he wasn't aware of dreaming at all. The downside of this was the inability to recall the happy and fun dreams of being with Thelma. Remembering her smiling face immediately after waking would somehow make it possible to face the day alone.

Leaving the on-edge feeling behind and going through his regular morning routine . . . starting with getting something into his stomach—the second half of yesterday's mushroom soup would do—he gulped down his first group of eight medications. A creature of habit, he fixed a cup of instant coffee, and then went into the living room to watch the early morning news. Finding nothing on television interesting . . . a predictable happening of late, he returned to the kitchen to locate his address book.

Lukas hadn't talked to his old army buddy in a couple of years but knew if anyone could, he'd be the one to offer good ideas and point him in the right direction. When the call was answered, no introduction was given when he said, "Joseph, I need your help."

"Anything for you, my friend; you know that. What's up?"

"Do you have a minute to talk?" Lukas asked.

"Of course, my man. For you I've got all the time in the world. What can I do for my buddy who lives in the City by the Bay?"

"Well, my granddaughter was kidnapped almost a year ago and never found. She was waiting for her mom, and this guy picked her up. He was charged but got off. Since you worked for the court system, can you tell me how to get some information?"

"That's terrible. I'm so sorry." After an uncomfortable pause, Joseph continued, "I'll give it my best shot. Could you be more specific?"

"Let's see. I've written down some questions. Hang on while I check my notes. Damn it . . . my glasses fell off. Okay, here goes. How do I get the names of the defendant's legal people? How do I find out the name of a particular witness? Better yet, get his address. Does a verdict for acquittal need to be unanimous? Also, is it possible to get the names and addresses of the jury members? Let's see. Information on the prosecutor and . . ."

"Whoa, Lukas, what's this all about?"

"Can you help me with this . . . ah, stuff? I already have an idea on some of it."

"Lukas . . . again, what's going on?"

"Better you don't know. I wouldn't be asking if it wasn't important. Listen Joseph, I'm not asking you to do anything wrong, just steer me in the right direction?"

"Okay, let's see. The first place to start is with the court transcripts. You'll need the court reporter's name to get them. You can learn their name and telephone number from the court clerk where the trial took place. Call the clerk and give the trial date and any pertinent information you have. Ask for the case number if you don't already have it. Once you've got the number, you can give it to the court reporter. Are you following me so far?"

"I'm trying to take notes . . . still on trial date and case number."

"Lukas, you'll need to pay for the transcripts. I'm not sure what the going rate is nowadays. It might take awhile to receive them. It will depend on the reporter's workload . . . perhaps a couple of months, maybe longer."

"No problem. Got more for me?" Lukas asked while doing his best to jot down as much information as possible.

"I'm guessing you already have the name of the defendant's attorney."

"Yeah, but there were three . . . maybe four lined up on his side."

"Really? The guy must be well-healed. You should be able to find him and the name of the firm on their website . . . even pictures you'll recognize."

"I'm not much on web looking up stuff . . . whatever it's called. Thelma meddled in it a little. I don't even know how to turn the darn thing on . . . that machine thing. Gabriel gave it to us the Christmas before Thelma passed."

"Well, I'm sure Gabriel would be happy to lend a hand with that. I bet he can also assist you with answering most of your questions. Have you talked to him . . . ah, asked him?"

"No, and I'd rather not involve him in any of this," Lukas replied sternly.

"Okay, I'm just saying. Moving along with what I jotted down at the beginning of our conversation, some of the information you're after is public knowledge, but some isn't. Juror names will be all but impossible to get—much less their addresses. Now, let's go back to my original question—what the hell is going on? Level with me. It won't go any further. You know you can trust me with anything."

"I know and thank you Joseph. You've been a great help."

"I don't like how this sounds. Lukas, tell me what this is all about . . . please?"

"Justice," Lukas answered plainly. "Justice for my granddaughter, Jennifer. I'll talk to you soon. Bye, Joseph."

As Lukas hung up the phone, he was pleased with himself for taking notes. They would come in handy when making calls later. Not wanting to share his terminal illness with Joseph, he also didn't want to tell him that waiting for months to get the transcripts wouldn't be a practical option; even waiting a few weeks might be too long before getting started.

With the abrupt conclusion of the call, Joseph looked pensively at his cell phone screen . . . call terminated. There had been no time to ask Lukas for additional information. What the hell? He'd been completely caught off-guard by his friend's odd line of questioning. Although curious, he knew if Lukas wanted to tell him more; he would have. It didn't take a genius to figure out Lukas was obviously on a crusade to settle a wrong. If so, there'd be no talking him out of it. He could probably help more but should he?

Thinking back to their conversation, why didn't he ask exactly what happened, ask for specific details about the circumstances surrounding his missing granddaughter, or ask how Gabriel and Michelle were holding up? How awful for them. Chastising himself, he'd not asked Lukas how he was getting along since Thelma's passing, or how he was doing health wise, or how about them getting together for a Giant baseball game.

Returning to his recorded movie, Joseph couldn't rid himself of how strange and thought-provoking the call had been. Pushing back in his worn and tattered recliner, he stopped the movie and backed it up to the beginning.

Before pressing the play button, he remembered Lukas carrying him—unconscious and wounded—out of harm's way in Vietnam. Lukas literally saved his life, and that's something you never forget . . . never. His life would have ended there in that steamy bamboo jungle if not for Lukas. Hell, he wouldn't even be here today to take his friend's call, so he'd be indebted to Lukas forever. How can a man repay another for giving him his very existence? Regardless of the passing years, there was no doubt about it; if he ever needed help again, Lukas would be the first one by his side . . . no questions asked. Although Lukas was black and he was white, they'd be brothers beneath the skin forever.

Having forgotten how the movie began, Joseph started it again from the beginning. A little girl—lively and energetic—was holding the hand of a fragile grey-haired man. As they walked down a narrow street without sidewalks, a car rushed past and loudly honked. Someone from inside shouted, "Get out of the way old man." Okay, that's a sign, he thought. So, regardless of what Lukas wanted or needed, he'd do his level best to make it happen.

Chapter 5

Today, Lukas would concentrate on rewriting the scribbled questions to ask the court clerk. He'd planned on cleaning up the list after yesterday's talk with Joseph but needed to run errands, especially the one to pick up crucial medicines at the drug store. Since every task seemed like a struggle anymore, he'd returned home depressed and too exhausted to tackle the job.

Lukas hated running errands. Whether the errands were important—like picking up necessary medications—or fairly unimportant—like buying new house shoes—the exertion left him warn out. But, like so many things he'd learned to deal with in order to survive, he'd pretty much come to terms with it. As he'd shuffled off to bed the previous night—too tired to take another step forward—he reminded himself that compared to dying; being exhausted was just a small part of the big picture. Besides, it made more sense to deal with the important tasks—whether wiped out or not—than let them slide and be sorry later.

Last night, while waiting for his pain pill to kick-in, Lukas concluded that handling his revenge preparations would be better served when more rested and hopefully more clear-headed. So, fixing the list tomorrow—now today—seemed to make better sense.

Since recently becoming a list person by necessity, every organizational tool became important to his new way of life. When his mind began to slip . . . thinking one thing but saying another, he tried to write down what he wanted to say or do in advance. Naturally, this concept worked better on the telephone than in person. After initiating this new process, his biggest problem was remembering where he'd left the reminders. He often found a grocery list or errand reminder near where he last visited . . . in the closet, in the bathroom, or once in the bread box. After countless searches—elevating his frustration level even higher—he made a concerted effort to place the reminders next to the kitchen sink and directly in front of the medicines.

When notes stacked up into a noticeable pile, most were considered either old or useless. Flipping through them, doubts would surface as to whether he'd followed through with some or perhaps any of them. As this scenario was happening more often of late—either not knowing or not remembering—he began to date them. This helped immensely, knowing that if a particular item hadn't been handled after a few weeks, he guessed it no longer mattered.

Looking at the messy words written during yesterday's conversation with Joseph, many were impossible to decipher. Since Thelma kept their life organized via lists and calendars, he'd never considered the importance of keeping things orderly before. Thelma would have written down the significant words during the conversation just once. Not only that, but when finished, her notes would be clear and readable. Thelma was remarkable at that type of chore, having been his private home secretary during their entire marriage. Never complaining, she was the one who took care of their appointments, paid the bills, kept track of important dates, and reminded him of things he planned to do.

Tearing up, he missed Thelma each and every day in so many ways. She not only made his life easier but filled it with joy. It was difficult to think of her and put the right words together to describe her. He missed her smile, her touch, and even the times when she scolded him. Once she was gone, he was left with the memories, but also the guilt of not telling her everyday how much he loved and appreciated her.

Not sick, Thelma's passing—a mere two years ago—was a total shock, but he was grateful she'd died peacefully in her sleep from a heart attack and didn't suffer. He'd always thanked God for their wonderful life together and never doubted that she was in heaven.

After Thelma's passing, he'd not cared if his life was in order or not . . . spending his time saddened by missing her and feeling sorry for himself. Thankfully, Jennifer stuck by his side like glue and refused to let him be gloomy. She was constantly giggling and replacing the bitter sadness with utter joy. Lukas closed his eyes and saw Jennifer's beaming face and bright eyes as she bounced along beside him . . . always insisting on holding his hand. His granddaughter's words constantly remained with him. "Grandpa . . . Grandma is in heaven. We'll see her when we die." Jennifer's words were matter-of-fact and without fear. He couldn't help but wonder if Jennifer and Thelma were together and holding hands in heavenly bliss. He closed his eyes and wished and prayed this imaginary picture would stay with him until the very end.

Sighing and finalizing the list of questions to ask the court clerk, his thoughts again returned to Thelma. A good Christian woman, no way would she approve of his planned vengeful undertaking. He could only hope to die in his sleep and go to heaven but had little hope of either happening. On a good note, at least his dear wife wouldn't need to watch him turn into a vegetable and crap his pants.

Finishing a late bowl of cereal, the phone rang. Thinking it would be Gabriel checking on him again, he picked up the phone and said, "I'm fine."

Instead of Gabriel, he heard Joseph say, "Long time . . . no hear. I'm glad you're fine."

"Back attcha, Joseph. Sorry, I thought you were Gabriel," Lukas responded quickly.

"I figured. Been thinking about our talk yesterday. I understand you don't want to share anything with me, but whatever you're up against, I'm here for you."

"Thank you, Joseph. It's better that way, so let's leave it at that." Lukas replied plainly.

"The reason I'm calling—other than to say I'd like to help—is to tell you that . . . well, ah . . . I asked my son for assistance. After I explained our connection and that he wouldn't even be here if not for you, he agreed to be all in . . . like he would be for me."

"I don't think it's a good idea to involve your son. As I said yesterday, I don't want to include Gabriel in this."

"Now Lukas, let me finish. The reason I wanted to discuss it with him is because he has lots of expertise in kidnapping cases and crimes along that line. I won't get into his background right now, but he's a former police officer turned private detective."

"Joseph, I can't afford to pay him. I've got a few bucks saved but not much."

"How about he stays with you . . . like rent free? Maybe you could pick up a few incidentals along the way. I'll only ask two things. You'll be honest with him and not put him in a bad situation. What do you think?"

"Let me think about it."

"No, there won't be no thinking on it. It's a done deal. You met him when he was young . . . I think. His name is James, and he's my oldest son. I've told him as much as I know . . . which isn't much."

"I'm not sure," Lukas answered after a long pause.

"Well, I am. He could use a vacation anyway. What better place to visit than San Francisco? Lukas, how are you doing? I'm sorry for not asking yesterday."

"Can't complain. Never does any good anyway."

"Good for you. I'll have James call you soon . . . within a week or so. Maybe we could set up a Giant ballgame. Wouldn't it be fun for the four of us to go if Gabriel could join us? Lukas, take care and call me anytime. Be sure to let me know how things are going. Oh, and please tell Gabriel and Michelle how sorry I am."

"Thanks again, Joseph. I'll keep in touch," Lukas answered, doing his best to sound sincere.

Although glad to get help . . . professional help, Lukas didn't know how to handle Joseph's son. Worse yet, letting him stay at his house would be more than worrisome. What reason could he give Gabriel for James being there? What would he do about hiding the cancer from both James and Joseph . . . much less Gabriel? Although it would eventually come out, he didn't have time to play games. His time was short. Damn, he shouldn't have called Joseph in the first place but too late now. Mad at himself, he'd released a huge can of worms. And, as Thelma would say after a bad decision . . . which he'd made many, "Honey, be careful what you wish for."

Oh well, he'd call the court and see how that goes. Once he talked to the court reporter, maybe he could pay extra to speed up the transcript process.

Let's see . . . I'll talk to the court clerk and then the reporter. What should I do next? What should I say to Joseph's son, James, when he calls? How about, "Hi there, want to help me kill some people?" Suddenly aware of talking out loud to himself, answering his own questions, and pacing through the house; he felt a bit foolish. No . . . like a total idiot. Well, to hell with it. No one was there to witness his actions, and that's how he wanted to keep it. No way could Joseph's son stay with him. That was a given.

Chapter 6

James

It had been three years since James walked out of the Van Nuys, California Police Department . . . vowing to never return. Not an easy decision or one taken lightly; he was giving up a decent living and job security. However, if he stayed another day longer, he was afraid of becoming part of the corrupt environment and losing his desire to serve the public fairly.

Soon after progressing from probationary status to a fully accepted member of the force, he'd been placed in the untenable position of turning his head from various out-and-out wrongs. He was disgusted and tired of supporting his fellow officers . . . regardless of their actions. While his partners blatantly broke laws themselves, he was told to forget what he saw or heard and be a game player. As he watched evidence removed, weapons and drugs placed at crime scenes, and reports altered, it was impossible to dismiss the obvious. Each time this happened, it became harder and harder to differentiate between his fellow officers' actions and the criminals.

The final straw broke during his unplanned last day of service. Prior to being dispatched with three other officers in two separate patrol cars, he already knew what would go down and what to expect when arriving at a nearby apartment complex. According to the received tip, their actual mission was to look for drugs on the target premises. However, he didn't know the real purpose until two blocks before their destination. His partner mentioned the landlord's live-in girlfriend was sleeping with the occupant living in a second floor apartment and how the landlord had placed marijuana in the guy's refrigerator.

They didn't have a search warrant, but the guy eagerly let them in on the pretense of checking out the area and his residence for a missing child. "Sure . . . come on in," he'd said pleasantly. As they pretended to look around, it was hard to listen to the young male saying with a chuckle, "I don't think there's a child hiding in my freezer compartment." Then, he immediately followed with, "Whoa, that's not mine."

James cringed and turned away as the barefoot young male—handcuffed behind his back—was thrown down two sets of short stairs. When the guy complained and yelled out in pain, he was told to shut up and quit resisting . . . which he wasn't. As the guy flailed downward, bouncing off several railings until finally coming to rest on the bottom step, the bloodied young male was told, "Guess that'll teach you not to mess around with someone else's girl."

While James sat quietly with his head down on the trip back to the station, his partner offered, "Don't worry about it. Guess the landlord's a distant relative of the lieutenant. We do what we're told. No skin off our noses."

Curious how the report would read; he wasn't shocked about the guy's broken arm and multiple cuts and bruises occurring while resisting arrest. Later, when discussing what occurred with his sergeant—not mentioning what his partner told him—he received a non-committal shrug and, "Go back to work." By the sergeant's reaction, guess he'd been naive to think others within the chain of command didn't already know what would and did transpire. It was disgusting from start to finish, and all he could think about was getting the hell out of there for good.

Turning in his badge, I D, and service revolver, James left the station three hours before his normal shift ended. Going straight home and pulling into the driveway, he saw his wife's car parked under the carport. Thinking she'd left work early with a problem—maybe sick or something—he'd bounded into the house and rushed up the stairs to their bedroom . . . finding her in the sack with the guy next door.

Did he scream, rant, rave, or punch the guy's eyes out? No, he went to the downstairs guest bathroom and threw up.

After giving the neighbor time to clear out and Margie time to dress; he'd waited for his wife in the kitchen.

"James, I'm sorry . . . okay?"

"Really, that's it. Sorry is all ya got?"

"I don't know what else to say."

"Margie, what the hell? Are you in love with . . . ah, our neighbor? I don't even know his name."

"His name is Greg; and no, I'm not in love with him."

"Then . . . why?"

"I don't even know why. It just happened."

"Sex just doesn't happen. Geez, isn't he married? Christ, they have kids too. I don't know how to deal with this . . . with you. It's not like it's the first time. I can't forgive you again. I won't. Once a whore . . . always a whore."

"I'm lonely. All you care about is your frickin' job. You're always working over-time when it's not necessary."

"Oh really . . . not necessary? Who wants the fancy clothes? Who insisted on the big house when it's just the two of us? Who wanted the expensive car? Do you think all that stuff comes from the tooth fairy?"

"I help out. I work too."

"Right . . . you work part-time at a gym which barely takes care of your daily work-out sessions."

"Don't be so mean," she said pathetically. "After I lost the baby, I needed to feel better about myself. You even said so."

"Don't start with the poor me crap. I've heard it all before. Besides, we're getting off subject. I'll move back in with my dad. The rent's paid 'til the end of the month. I'll give the landlord a thirty-day notice. Guess I'll have to pay for another month. After that, you're on your own."

"What will I do?"

"Not my problem. Ask the neighbor to take care of you. I'll gather my stuff and don't follow me around with your puppy dog eyes again. It won't work this time."

James tried not to look at her. He was hurting but couldn't back down. He'd wanted to believe her the first time, then the second, but no way could he forgive her again. It was over.

When he shut the front door, every rational thought left his body. Not caring what anyone heard or saw, he began to scream incoherently . . . all the while having no idea what he was saying. Somehow, he made it to the car before totally breaking down. Swallowing the nasty bile rising in his throat, he struggled unsuccessfully to hide the tears. He was such a failure. No job and now no marriage. His self-esteem was at an all-time low, thinking he'd never be happy again. But then, maybe he didn't deserve happiness. He not only felt sorry for himself but abruptly alone.

Chapter 7

James first met Margie at a rock concert. He was shy and unsophisticated, attending the concert to try something different, determined to push himself out of his comfort zone.

Margie—pretty and flirtatious—accidentally bumped into him during intermission. She had purple and black spiked hair, a nose ring, wearing a jacket that sparkled, and dark boots that almost reached her knees. Although finding her easy and fun to talk to, he readily accepted they had nothing in common. When they parted, she'd promised to keep in touch, and they'd talked on the phone a couple of times . . . maybe three. He wasn't surprised when the phone conversations suddenly stopped.

Oddly enough—okay, it sounds humorous—but they ran into each other again at a tucked away donut shop. Driving home from work, he'd stopped on a whim for a quick coffee or two, needing the boost to stay up late to assist with his dad's back porch repair project.

Since graduating five weeks earlier from the police academy, wearing the police uniform should have made him feel important and in charge. But no matter where he went, he still felt insecure on the inside and easily embarrassed when entering an unfamiliar establishment . . . or for that matter, a familiar one. When working with another officer, entering a business was somewhat easier. He could stand back and let his partner—even if a female—take the lead.

So, there he was; glad the place was quiet and almost empty. Ordering a black coffee and wanting to appear inconspicuous, he took a seat in a far corner. While checking his phone for messages—perhaps his dad needed something last minute—Margie appeared directly in front of his table. Not recognizing her at first, she stood there—hands on hips—and giggling.

"I knew I'd eventually run into a policeman here. Get it . . . donut shop?" Laughing, she followed with, "Geez, what were my chances of seeing a uniformed officer I already knew?"

Aware of his cheeks burning, he managed to answer a shy, "Hello."

While her eyes locked on his, she seemed to be studying his face for a reaction. Her appearance had definitely changed since last seeing her. Granted, he'd only seen her once and months ago, but the transformation was shocking. As Margie flipped her brown hair streaked with blond back, she must have read his mind.

"I'm different. Right?" she asked with a mischievous grin.

Different didn't come close to describing her. Her hair had obviously changed, and the nose ring had been removed. Her face looked less harsh without the bright red lipstick and black eye sockets. Also, the loose fitting gaudy jacket was missing. However, she was still wearing boots . . . maybe the same or similar. He wasn't sure.

When he shook his head in the negative, her expression said she knew he was lying. And, as if she knew what he was thinking, she offered, "I can tell you're glad to see me. I'll get my order. Don't go away." As an afterthought, she asked, "Can I get you something?"

Still stunned from seeing her again, he barely uttered, "No, I'm good," before she promptly remarked, "Oh, I bet you are."

Was her reply meant to be sexual? That's so crazy, he thought. Good Lord, was she toying with him or flirting? Not an optimist, he hoped . . . even prayed for the latter.

As she walked away, the sensible part of him couldn't believe any of this was actually happening. Not only amazed that Margie remembered him but flattered she'd bothered to stop and talk to him.

His eyes continued to closely watch her, ogling her body from head to toe. While he was pushing mid-thirties, bulky, tall, and out of shape, she was probably in her mid-twenties, slender, short, and appeared fit. Besides the age and physical differences, she had characteristics he'd never possessed . . . funny and vibrant with an outgoing personality. As Margie almost reached the pick-up counter, James found himself checking out her bottom half. Although not large, it swayed softly from side to side. Completely captivated by her, he was practically drooling.

Balancing a small tray on one hand, Margie returned to the table but hesitated before saying, "I got you something."

Doing his best to look calm, cool, and collected, he stood while replying, "That was nice of you. Can I help?"

"No, sit down. I'll serve you," she answered firmly.

Placing a powered donut directly in front of James, she asked, "Do you mind if I sit next to you instead of across the table on the opposite side?"

He wanted to answer with a witty comeback but had nothing. His answer was an affirming nod and then a muffled, "Sure."

Smiling, she bent over to place her coffee and glazed donut on the table beside him. He didn't try very hard to look away as her blouse fell away from her chest, clearly exposing perky breasts unencumbered by a bra.

Aware of being closely observed, Margie grinned and carefully sat down; positioning herself by his side . . . close enough to touch his leg. In fact she was so near; James could easily inhale the flowery fragrance emanating from her shiny hair. While Margie did most of the talking, he was content to sit still—doing his best to not move his leg away—smile, and listen. He was intently aware of every movement her leg made against his. Although confused by her forward demeanor, she was captivating . . . and he was hooked.

Mesmerized, he watched her slowly lick the foam from the rim of her coffee cup. Willing his eyes to look downward at his plate, he finally took a bite of his donut.

Without warning, Margie nonchalantly reached over and brushed powdered sugar off his cheek. Just the stroke of her fingers sent chills through him.

After flipping her hair back, she scanned the room before saying sternly, "Shut your eyes." It was like an order, and he obliged without question.

He felt her hand glide smoothly up his arm sleeve . . . lightly squeezing along the way. Totally unexpected, it was not only surprising but bordered on weird. And, even though the movement was on top of the heavy uniform's material, it seemed beyond personal. A myriad of thoughts rushed through him. First of all, they hardly knew each other; and secondly, they were in a public place. Continuing to keep his eyes closed—his senses in overdrive—he heard her chair move slightly. The situation then became even more bazaar. He soon felt her tongue lapping slowly at his cheek; the strong scent of flowers overwhelming. Shocked, he could hardly restrain his head from jerking away; his eyes fluttering out of control and wanting to open. She made a calming, "Shhh" sound before giggling and reminding him, "Keep your eyes closed tight. No peeking." He could feel his face blushing with heat; the attention and feeling was out of this world. Was this really happening? He couldn't remember if there were customers nearby or not. In fact he could hardly remember where he was. One thing he knew for sure . . . he loved what was happening and didn't want the experience to stop.

Hearing her chair move again, she told him, "Okay,

you can open your eyes."

Speechless, all he could do was close his gaping mouth and smile. When she wouldn't stop looking at him and knowing he needed to say something, he finally said, "Wow."

Margie threw her head back and began laughing . . . almost hysterically. "I was cleaning the sweetness off your face, but it's still sweet. I'm betting that was a first for you."

Taking a deep breath, he answered, "Okay, if you say so but maybe not." All the while, thinking . . . what a dumb ass answer. Really, like this happens to me all the time . . . not. Deciding it was now or never, he asked, "Would you go out with me?"

"I thought you'd never ask," she responded. Quickly removing a slip of paper from her pocket, she said, "Here's my number. Call me. Maybe we can go out for drinks or a movie."

Smiling and again tongue-tied, he carefully tucked away the already crumpled paper she'd handed him. Before he could slide his chair back and stand to help her up, she'd already downed the rest of her coffee—almost as if a mission had been completed—saying, "Gotta go. Be sure to call me . . . promise?"

Not wanting to appear like he was chasing after Margie, she'd already reached the exit and opening the door before he'd completely moved away from the table. Following several steps behind and not getting a chance to say, "I'll call you," he watched until she stepped into her car. It was an older model Ford, dull from sitting in the sun, scattered with dents, and had several poorly patched rust spots.

Taking his time, he walked to his car and waited for her to pass by. When just about even with him, she slowed to almost a stop and waved. He wasn't a hundred per cent sure, but thought he saw a smile and maybe a wink. Perhaps the wink was imagined or a squint from the setting sun. Whatever . . . he wanted to believe she'd winked at him.

Did what just happened inside . . . really happen? Unbelievable. He could feel himself smiling so much that he thought his face would split apart.

Was the phone number in his pocket real? If it was, would she answer or blow him off like before? He also wondered why her number was already written down. Could she have purposely followed him or did she keep her phone number ready in case she found someone to give it to? He'd wanted to ask why she'd stopped calling or taking his calls, but couldn't risk ruining the mood or messing up any future contact . . . if indeed that actually happens. Not really wanting answers to his questions because . . . God, he wanted to see her again.

Chapter 8

It was the beginning of a whole new world of adventure for James. After their next time together—a date to a movie and a brief stop for drinks—the sex was fantastic. Although not his first sexual encounter by a long shot, Margie was the first girl to treat him as if she wanted him above all others. Perhaps some men would have been threatened by her aggressive tactics, but he reveled in feeling special and desired. Sometimes, their lovemaking was so intense; he believed no one anywhere on the planet could have better sex . . . considering himself the luckiest man alive.

Being with Margie made him realize just how much he'd been missing with other relationships . . . now considered casual in comparison. She made all of the arrangements . . . where she wanted to go, and what she wanted to do. It never mattered to him what they did as long as they were together. When they weren't with each other, he felt empty, so concentrating on Margie's happiness became his main thrust in life. He tried to be the perfect boyfriend . . . agreeing to her every wish and dealing with her minor dilemmas along the way. Solving them made him feel vital to their existence together.

Margie never wanted to discuss her past, and that

was fine with him. No way could he have a conversation about his early years either, fearing the revolting details of his childhood would surface and chase her away. In his mind it was all about being happy together in the present. There was never a single moment when he considered being with anyone else or not being with her.

When Margie said she was pregnant, he couldn't wait to get married. He didn't feel the slightest bit trapped and pushed for them to marry as soon as possible . . . even sooner than she did. While anticipating the birth of his first child, it was all about the joy of being a family with the love of his life forever.

Just prior to reaching her fourth month of pregnancy and barely into their second month of marriage, Margie lost the baby. They were both disappointed, but like he told her, "We have lots of time to have children and better yet, we'll have more time to be settled financially."

Within a year, Margie was expecting again. This time, she didn't seem excited, but he was overjoyed. Sadly, within a couple of months, she lost their second baby. He was devastated and began doting on her even more, doing his best to brighten her spirits by showering her with whatever she wanted . . . anything that would make her smile again.

*   *   *   *

After the neighbor fiasco, one of the many difficulties of leaving Margie was his inability to get her out of his thoughts. Physically leaving was one thing; mentally leaving was another. Wandering around in a daze, he seemed lost without her. During the quiet moments—which he had a lot of—he continued to dwell on the fun-times, especially their sexual game-playing escapades. While reminiscing, he ignored the degrading put-downs, the remarks about their boring life, and the problems associated with their credit. Not surprisingly, he'd been unwilling to discuss their terrible financial situation with Margie. Accepting full responsibility for their money predicament, it didn't seem right to involve her. After all, he was the main bread-winner, and it wasn't Margie's fault that he was incapable of telling her, "No."

Whenever Margie tried to lure him back with promises of love and faithfulness, he fought the urge to re-establish their relationship, using whatever disgusting memory he could muster up. The major one—the flashback of Margie and the neighbor's naked bodies together—stifled any notion of that ever happening. In spite of this humiliating vision, he still sought out Margie's new job location—a waitress at a close-by restaurant—often observing her coming and going. Yes, he stalked her. Not to do her harm but to see what she was doing, who she was with, and just to see her . . . if only from afar. Even though being unemployed should have panicked him, all he could think about was Margie.

To say he continued to be obsessed with her would be an understatement. He was excited to hear her voice . . . even if the conversation was about a problem she was having. Although difficult, he did his best not to offer advice . . . reminding himself that her problems were no longer his concern. When she bragged about living with someone and telling him about changing her telephone number, he snickered to himself . . . like he didn't already know her new telephone number, where she worked, and where she lived. Nevertheless, it hurt immensely to learn she was already living with someone else . . . repeating over and over, "Be strong. Be strong. Be strong."

Realizing she couldn't weasel her way back into his good graces, Margie must have wanted to hurt him as much as possible, saying, "I didn't lose the last baby; I got rid of it." Wiping away any lingering guilt from the past—his inability to shield her from that particular hurt—her statement was both significant and freeing. Finally, something crucial snapped inside, and he no longer wanted to know where she lived or anything else about her present life. The best part . . . he no longer cared.

Deciding he was good at surveillance, he applied for a job with a detective agency. They referred to themselves as an investigative service . . . stating a modern approach to a traditional profession. Staying busy delving into other people's lives and problems somewhat helped him move forward.

While employed in his new investigative position, he revisited the case of the young man tossed down the stairs, curious to see how it played out. He easily snooped into various records, discovering he'd been released after a short stay in jail. But by then, he'd lost his job, had his car repossessed, and had a drug related arrest record. He didn't know what happened to him after that, but hoped he was doing okay.

*   *   *   *

Returning home to live with his dad was embarrassing on several levels. The most obvious one . . . ashamed of exposing his marriage for what it was . . . a sham. During that stressful time, he was also concerned about his divorce bringing up past hurts for his dad. Although his reason for splitting with Margie was far different from his dad's, their marriages had both ended in the same place—divorce court. Fearful of creating an uncomfortable atmosphere, he tried to hide his true feelings, acting as if the break-up was no big deal.

Once settled into his childhood home and his divorce clearly out in the open, memories of his parent's yelling matches and his mother's drinking resurfaced . . . seemingly following him throughout the house like a silent ghost. When these visions wouldn't disappear, he tried to remember a time when there was a happy moment occurring in a particular room. Unable to conjure up a single time remotely related to something pleasant, he soon gave up. He couldn't remember his parents ever having quiet discussions, watching a movie without arguing, having an enjoyable meal together, issuing an apology, or uttering a kind word. His memories were all about nasty name-calling and escalating shouting matches. These times were followed by his mother passing out, and his father leaving. Looking at the backdoor, he could almost hear the door slamming.

When his parent's marriage eventually ended, his mother was the one to leave, moving out in the middle of the night. She left without saying a word to him or to his younger brother, Jeremy. He was in the seventh grade; his brother in the fifth. At first, he felt ashamed for not caring—even glad—because his mother no longer stumbled around, cursed, or fell down. Sometimes, she'd stagger through the house naked, mumbling incoherently.

As life with dad calmed down, they called themselves the three "Js." There were no new cigarette burns appearing on the furniture, no hateful remarks said during mealtimes, and no hiding under a pillow to block out the loud arguments. Most of all, there were no more embarrassing moments when his friends stopped by to visit.

*   *   *   *

That James survived the aftermath of his terrible breakup with Margie was a testament to his dad's steadfast desire to stick by him. His father constantly lectured him on how much of a good life was waiting, how much future he had, and how many opportunities of love would come around . . . stressing the importance of being willing to give time a chance for healing. He finally asked, "Dad weren't you lonely when mom left?" With a far-away look, his dad answered, "Son, there is nothing worse than living with someone and being lonely."

Obviously, his dad didn't buy into his indifferent attitude about splitting with Margie. It was at his dad's insistence—using the words, "acting suicidal"—that he sought help in dealing with the end of his marriage. Although he considered therapy a bogus idea and a waste of time, he eventually agreed to go . . . mostly to pacify his father. However, it didn't take long to discover how his feelings were clearly wrapped around emotional dependence on someone else.

The therapist opened his eyes to reality, showing how Margie was the first woman to overwhelm him with attention, while he was too immature to know how to handle the situation. Although an unhealthy relationship, they each met the other's needs. He showered her with material objects; she gifted him with emotional praise and sex. Regardless of what she did or didn't do, he readily over-looked her actions. It was a dance they started at the donut shop, and neither wanted to stop the music. He wanted to spoil her, while she wanted to hold on to him— using any means possible—to make sure the spoiling continued.

When he opened-up to the therapist about coming from a dysfunctional family—where his mom was an alcoholic; his dad strict and rigid about rules—she suggested addressing his childhood issues with his father. "Perhaps have an open dialogue about your family dynamics," she'd offered. His response, "I'm not ready to go there yet. Just not comfortable talking to my dad about how my parent's actions affected me." After that session, he wondered if his parent's marriage could have been helped—even saved—if they'd gotten professional help.

When therapy began, he felt inadequate on so many levels. It took awhile to trust enough to share his innermost feelings and a lifetime of confusion about love and marriage. After breaching several personal hurdles, he talked about his present day uncertainties; finally asking the big question, "Why did Margie cheat if he was sufficient in the bedroom department?" The therapist never directly answered, but did hint how women can use sex for different reasons. She followed by saying, "Let's leave the past behind and concentrate on moving forward with your life in a positive manner."

It took some time before he was able to accept that Margie was never right for him . . . "accept" being the key word. As the therapist pointed out, saying, "Although not as devastating, the loss of a relationship is similar to the passing of a loved one. It is important— even necessary— to go through the same grieving steps: Denial (shock and numbness) Anger (why me) Bargaining (attempting to undo damage) Depression (loneliness and hating life) and Acceptance (the realization that the person is gone and the will to embrace life again)."

James couldn't help but wonder if he'd ever find true love built on friendship and a mutual caring of each other? Time would tell and as the therapist said, "James, you've got it all backwards. It isn't worrying about how to make someone like you and want you, but whether you like them for all the right reasons. You are a good, kind, and considerate man. If a woman doesn't want you for these traits, then she isn't worth having."

When he began therapy, he was in a self-imposed isolation pattern . . . not knowing how to reach out and socialize—perhaps never knowing. By the time he left therapy and closer to a sense of normalcy, he was somewhat in control of his emotions and better able to see his marriage for what it was . . . an immature dependence on each other and doomed to failure. It was never sustainable, because it had no solid foundation to build on.

Eventually, his hurt was replaced with the knowledge that he had no clue or understanding of what a normal relationship was all about. He'd believed incorrectly that his happiness began with Margie and ended when he left, but now knew it would be up to him to go forward and find his own happiness.

Before leaving his dad's house and moving into his own apartment, Jeremy and his family came to visit. They sat around the dining room table, talking and laughing about present day sporting events and current happenings affecting their lives. Nothing negative about the past was mentioned. He was delighted that Jeremy had a great family and appeared happy.

Sometime during the meal, James said he'd like to

make a toast. Clearing his throat and looking serious, he stated, "Dad, thank you for taking care of me and Jeremy and thank you for always loving us. I appreciate your guidance in pushing me in the right direction. I love you . . . Dad." When the group touched glasses, he saw all smiles around the table, but his dad's smile was accompanied with watery eyes.

Going forward, James planned on being the best darn investigator he could be, deciding to enjoy female companionship and have fun whenever the opportunity presented itself. Nothing heavy and for sure, no involvement until he was ready . . . if or when the right person at the right time showed itself.

Chapter 9

Lukas went to bed with a headache and woke with a headache. Nauseated, he couldn't decide what to do first . . . take a couple of pain pills with his regular medicines or get food into his stomach. In all probability, if he took the medicines on an empty stomach, he would throw them up. If he ate something first and waited for his stomach to settle down, his headache would continue to pound—like a hammer with a sharp pointed end—and most likely throw up anyway. He was stuck in a catch-22 dilemma. Unsure of either outcome, his decision was to take the medicines with two pain pills, downing them with peppermint tea. That's what Thelma would do when feeling sickly . . . wondering why he'd not thought of the tea before. Remembering the tea was not only interesting but encouraging; noting there were still a few brain cells still functioning. His new problem . . . where would peppermint tea be? Feeling hopeful the tea would calm the nausea, he rummaged through the cupboard, finding old cereal boxes but no tea of any kind.

New decision, take the medicines after forcing down dry crackers. This had sometimes been successful in keeping the queasiness at bay. He would hope for the best but prepare for a quick trip to the bathroom. Regardless of what the prescription's small print said, if he threw up the pills, he'd take the whole lot again, even the pain pills. After all, this wasn't his first rodeo.

On his way to fetch the crackers, Lukas recalled the conversation he'd had with himself after leaving the last, ominous doctor's meeting. He'd decided then and there to save as many pain pills as possible, eventually swallowing them all at once when life became impossible to control. As the headaches were becoming more intense—like today—it was difficult to set pills aside. Occasionally not taking them as prescribed, he'd been able to save a dozen or so in a plastic bag. Not kidding himself, he would need to come to a decision on what to do with them and when before his memory completely vanished . . . either not remembering where the pills could be found—or worse yet—not knowing what they were. Also, he could fall back on what the doctor said months ago when handing him a script. "Lukas, you're not presently taking the highest dosage of pain medicine. I can increase it whenever you ask. Also, there are other pain medications—the strongest pain medicine available outside a hospital setting—that I can prescribe." It was uplifting to know stronger medicines were available. But with them came drowsiness and a fog-like existence. Would he know if it was pressure from the brain tumor or the medication removing him from reality? At that point would he care which? They'd also discussed the strong possibility of him becoming a drug addict. Really . . . like why would that matter? By the doctor's demeanor,

Lukas assumed the doctor didn't care either.

Sitting down carefully . . . still a tad disorientated and unsteady, he broke a cracker in half. Placing the half-piece in his mouth, he felt himself frown. Not because of the cracker's taste, but because no matter how hard he tried, he couldn't dismiss the fear of Joseph's son coming. Regardless of what he was doing, it continued to bug him. At first, he considered not answering the phone. But then, what if Gabriel called? It had been almost two weeks since talking to Joseph; perhaps his friend's son had changed his mind.

During the previous week, he'd finally spoken to the court reporter but didn't like how the conversation went. "Sir, I'll do my best to get the transcripts to you within a couple of months," he'd offered. While trying to justify the importance of receiving them as soon as possible, Lukas was unable to offer a legitimate reason. He almost told the reporter he was dying, but afraid the guy would think he was bullshitting and delay the transcripts even longer. Frustrated and unable to disclose the real reason, he asked if the transcripts could be speeded up if he paid an additional fee. The reporter then went on and on about being extremely busy, saying apologetically, "No extra fee will get them to you any sooner. Sorry."

Giving up, Lukas finally answered, "Okay."

After talking to the court reporter, what could he do in the next two months? He'd not lost his desire for revenge but again felt lost on how to proceed. It seemed like he was back to where he started, and time was fleeting. Still wondering if Joseph's son might eventually call; he'd answer the telephone with pre-planned answers ready . . . but what. Okay, he'd write down the key words for his reply and place them beside the phone.

*   *   *   *

The dreaded phone call came exactly two weeks to the day after talking to Joseph.

"Hello."

"Is this Lukas?"

"Yes, who's calling?" Lukas asked but already knew.

"My name is James Allen. My dad, Joseph, asked me to give you a call . . . perhaps assisting you with some answers or something like that. I'm not exactly sure."

Scrambling for his note of answers but not finding it, he said, "Thanks for calling, but I don't want to put you out. I know you're busy with your life. I'm handling it."

"Actually, I want to be of assistance. Besides, my dad gave me strict orders to lend you a hand. He said if you rejected my offer, I was to let him know. I would have called sooner but needed to clear my calendar. I'd like to sit down with you and visit about the case and see if I have any ideas."

Waiting for a response and after a period of silence, James asked, "Are you still there?"

"What exactly did Joseph tell you? Lukas asked, still fumbling for the piece of paper with his written reasons to keep James from coming and getting involved.

"Not much . . . just that your granddaughter is missing, and the man charged with taking her was acquitted."

"That's true, but I believe with all my heart he took her. I'm seeking the truth . . . and desperately want to find Jennifer. Just because his fancy lawyers got him off doesn't mean he's not guilty."

"Lukas, I'm pretty good at digging around into places that others can't go."

"I'm sure the police had access into everything, but I don't think they tried very hard. The worthless prosecutor seemed like he could care less. When I talked to your dad, I was angry. Guess I'm more resolved to the inevitable."

"How about we meet for coffee? You can tell me everything you know. We can brainstorm. It's better to talk in person while it's fresh on your mind. By the way were you able to get the court transcripts?"

Without answering his last question, Lukas asked, "Don't you live in Los Angeles?"

"Yes, but I like San Francisco. I've actually put in for vacation time, so I'll be all yours when I get there."

"How much time," Lukas asked; his voice full of hesitancy.

"I'm taking two weeks off. Two weeks paid so don't worry about that. I'm certain we can learn something by then. Don't you?"

"I won't have the transcripts for months, so what is there to dig into?"

"How about we talk about it when we meet? I'm

thinking we could get together Monday. Does that work for you? I have your address or would you prefer to meet somewhere else?"

"So soon? Are you talking about this Monday? Can't we do it over the phone?"

"Yes, this Monday. It would be difficult over the phone, well . . . not really."

"I'm pretty sure Monday won't work; it's too soon," Lukas said in a panic.

Confused by his reluctance, James replied, "Hum, I got the impression from Dad you wanted to pursue this right away. Actually, it's a good idea to discuss a case while the testimony is still fresh, especially since you don't have the transcripts." After a noticeable silence, James inquired, "Lukas, do you not want me to come? Just be honest. I'm in a bad position here. My dad says I've got to help you, but you seem hesitant."

"Okay, I'll be honest. I don't want Gabriel—that's my son—to know anything about this. If he knows you're at my house, he'll start asking what's going on. I think he's having the neighbors spy on me. I do want answers; I surely do."

"I understand. Give me a name of a close restaurant and a time to meet . . . this Monday the 3rd. I'll see you there. This will stay just between the two of us. You trust me, and I'll trust you. Okay?"

"Okay," Lukas answered, wondering why he'd not put up more of a fight.

After working out the particulars, Lukas hung up but

continued to stare at the phone. He'd been eager to begin his mission, but suddenly the job seemed too daunting to accomplish before dying. In the beginning he had big plans: buy a gun, find the person who took his six-year-old granddaughter, find anyone involved in setting him free, and kill them all. Now his strategy of revenge seemed foolish. So, here he was . . . moving forward but feeling disheartened. When it was just him, it seemed fairly simple. With Joseph's son involved, it had become complicated. How could he expect to involve another person in his tangled web of vengeance? Sliding his chair back, he looked down and saw the paper with his prepared notes resting on the floor. Oh well, too late . . . it's now a done deal, he thought.

Chapter 10

Sitting in his car, James knew Lukas was waiting inside when he arrived at the "Coffee and More Diner," a few blocks from where Lukas lived. He knew this because he'd already checked out the location of his house, and its proximity to the restaurant. He also knew the make and license number of the car Lukas was driving. At present he was parked three cars down from it.

He'd arrived yesterday in San Francisco to check out the area, hoping to find an inexpensive hotel centrally located. Not an easy task but found a place that would work. Although San Francisco is noted for being an expensive place to visit, he was looking forward to a change of scenery . . . combining his first vacation since joining the company with doing a good deed. While not understanding why Lukas didn't want to involve his son, he would follow his dad's friend's wishes to keep the circumstances quiet.

James entered the restaurant; his eyes squinting before adjusting to the inside lighting. A familiar smell of BBQ dominated his senses; realizing he'd been too busy to have breakfast. Locating Lukas was easy. He was the only patron sitting alone at a table and facing the doorway but seemed thinner than described.

Lukas had arrived at the diner early . . . twenty minutes before the meeting time. His plan was to be there when James walked in. Although wanting to appear calm, he'd already had two regular coffees instead of his usual cup of decaf. He recognized his friend's son immediately when he entered for a couple of reasons. First, few whites frequented the small neighborhood restaurant. Secondly, James had a striking resemblance to his father. And thirdly, there was the fact that he was exactly on time.

Half out of the chair, Lukas did his best to stand. Before fully upright, James was already in front of his table, motioning for him to remain seated. Extending his hand, James said, "It's a pleasure to meet you, Sir."

After shaking hands, Lukas offered, "Have a seat."

"Thank you for meeting me," James answered before sitting.

Lukas hollered at the waitress, "Selma, bring a coffee for this gentleman."

"Okay, Lukas. Hold your horses. No need to yell. Besides, it's already on its way."

Awkwardly waiting for the coffee, James briefly checked out the surroundings . . . an old habit as a policeman; a new habit as a civilian detective. Adjusting his chair closer to the table, he nonchalantly placed a notebook and pen directly in front of him.

Selma placed a full cup of coffee in front of James before saying, "Honey, do you take cream with your coffee?"

James replied courteously, "No, ma'am, but thank you for asking. This is good like it is."

Looking toward the opposite side of the table, Selma asked, "Lukas, do you want a fill-up? Before you answer, don't you go being so bossy. I don't move as fast as I once did. I'm old."

"Selma, you aren't old. You're a spring chicken compared to me."

"Spring chicken or old hen?" she asked with raised eyebrows.

"Either one but still a lot younger than me," Lukas uttered.

"Younger and better lookin' too, I'm thinkin'. How about I get you both some blueberry cobbler? I made it fresh today."

"No thanks," Lukas answered, but James said, "That sounds great to me."

Selma nodded before saying, "I'll bring two, cuz Lukas, you looking down right puny."

"Go about your business," Lukas answered in a dismissive manner but smiled.

"So Lukas, will she bring you a cobbler or not?" James asked quietly.

"Of course, she will. It doesn't matter what I say; she does what she wants anyway. She's been here for as long as I can remember. She and my wife were best friends. I got the names mixed up a few times and caught a lot of flack about it too. Sometimes, it got me in a whole lot of trouble."

"Sorry about your wife's passing," James offered, lowering his head momentarily.

"Yes, I miss her every day. Sure loved that woman." Pausing and looking at the ceiling, Lukas blinked before beginning to talk about the reason for their meeting. "So James, let's get right to it and talk about why you're here. Let me say from the get-go and like I told your father, I don't want to put you in harm's way."

"Not a problem. I'm a big boy, so let me worry about that. Lukas, can you explain . . . as best you can . . . what exactly happened."

"I guess I'll start with the day she's missing. Jennifer goes to—went to—the Boys and Girls Club, usually once a week . . . sometimes twice. She does arts and crafts . . . girly stuff. It's an afterschool program where she meets her friends to play. Her mom picks her up but that particular day, she was running late. Not sure why but it doesn't matter. Jennifer's mom was told, when signing her up, not to worry about being late. The activity person would stay as long as necessary." Lukas stopped talking and took a deep breath.

"Take your time; I know this is difficult for you," James interjected.

Before continuing, Selma appeared beside the table holding two bowls of cobbler.

"We'll, how about that . . . two cobblers," Lukas volunteered. "Woman, you never listen to me."

"Oh, I do. I hear ya . . . just don't pay no never-mind to what you say. You eat every bite . . . ya hear, old man.

That's an order." Selma answered back before chuckling.

After placing the second cobbler in front of the man across from Lukas, James looked up and smiled before saying, "Thank you. It sure looks good."

Waiting until Selma walked away, Lukas continued, "Let's see, what was I saying?"

"Jennifer's mom was running late," James answered plainly.

"That's right. According to what Carly said—she's the Activity Director—Jennifer was real excited about something she'd made and bolted outside to wait for her mother. When Carly noticed Jennifer left her pink purse—she carried that little purse with her everywhere—Carly ran outside to give it to her. When she wasn't sitting on the bench, she looked up . . . just in time to see her get into the guy's car. When Michelle—that's my daughter-in-law—shows up, Carly was surprised and confused, thinking Michelle made arrangements to have Jennifer picked up. She said all this in court . . . just like she told the police. Jennifer's been gone ever since. We called the police, put up fliers, and walked the area . . . everything to try and find her."

"How did . . . ah, Carly know it was the guy's car?"

"She said she recognized the car. Guess he was a big contributor to the Boys and Girls Club. Said he often brought gifts for the children . . . even had an ice cream truck stop to give them treats now and again."

"Was she able to identify him?" James asked, leaning forward.

"What do you mean? She'd seen him lots of times," Lukas responded but frowned.

"Did she actually see his face . . . like driving the car?"

"Well, not exactly. She couldn't say for sure she saw him. She said it was definitely his car, and Jenny wouldn't get into a stranger's car."

"Then what happened?" James asked but already knew how the lawyers would pick her testimony apart."

"The attorneys started saying awful things. I can't remember exactly, but he was mean to Carly. She was feeling bad enough, cuz she didn't stop helping the other kids pick up and chase after Jennifer right away. That asshole attorney asked if there weren't other white cars, and how would she know what Jennifer would do?"

Noticing Lukas was getting upset, James offered, "You're doing great. I'm impressed with what you remember."

"Lots of stuff slips my mind these days, but I've gone over and over this a hundred times. I get so angry. Poor Carly, she kept saying it happened so fast and started to cry. It was awful the way she was treated. The lawyer made her seem like a terrible person who wasn't paying attention to her job. I believed her and thought the jury would too."

"Were there other witnesses?"

"Yes, just one other person. There was a man who told the police he saw a black kid's face against the back window of a car—a white car—going into a building down by the water. He gave a statement but when he testified in court, he changed everything . . . blew it off, before admitting to being on drugs at the time. Then, he said, "I guess I must have dreamed it." That's why I wanted the transcripts to get his name. That bastard was paid off."

"Interesting," was James's only comment, writing down several words on the tablet.

"Lukas, I'll start looking into a few things tomorrow. I have your phone number. I'll call you, and let you know what I find out. My plan is to get some answers for you as quickly as possible."

When James looked up, Selma was hesitantly approaching the table. Somewhat like she was lurking, she embarrassingly asked to no one in particular, "Should I clear the table?" When both shook their heads, she focused on Lukas. "Why is your cobbler not all gone? Looks like you just picked at it. Your friend ate every bit of his. Was it not good?"

"It was fine . . . just don't want to ruin my figure," Lukas answered almost timidly.

"It's too late for that. Besides, you goin' out on the town to show it off?" she asked.

"Now Selma, you know those days are long gone."

"I knows that. Sure fun days . . . fun, fun days, weren't they?"

James reached for the check, but Lukas said, "This is my treat. I'll take care of it."

Waiting for Selma to finish picking up and moving

away, James stood and held out his hand again. "Thank you for meeting with me. I'll do my best to get answers for you. Do you want to keep our conversations just between us? I mean, not discuss anything with my dad. It's your call. I can tell you straight out; he'll be all over me to find out what's going on."

"Lukas seemed pensive and looked away for a moment. "You be the judge of that. You wouldn't be here helping me if not for your dad."

Quickly responding, James said, "Well, the way I understand it; I wouldn't be here at all if not for you. Oh, I almost forgot; where is the Boys and Girls Club located? The general area is all I'll need."

"I'm not really sure. My son lives in Hunter's Point. It must be fairly close to there. I probably have the number at home."

"No problem. I'll find it. If not, I'll give you a call."

James was barely outside the diner before Selma asked Lukas, "What's going on?" I couldn't help from hearing Jennifer's name. Does he have an idea where she might be?"

"Now . . . Selma, have you been snooping about?" Lukas asked.

"Not exactly . . . but maybe."

"He's an old buddy's son . . . visiting from Los Angeles to catch up."

"He was sure writing down a lot of stuff," she replied, seemingly wanting to know more."

"Like I said . . . just catching up."

"I put fresh flowers on Thelma's grave after church yesterday. It was nice and peaceful. I told her you were behaving yourself but looking thin. I think she wants me to keep an eye on you. Why you quit coming in to eat?"

"I don't know. I'll try to do better, so you can report back to Thelma. I saw Steve—that's my next door neighbor—talking to Gabriel. He keeps asking how it's going. I can barely go outside my own house without him wanting to do something for me. Thelma probably has everyone spying on me."

"The Lord bless and keep her," Selma answered.

Chapter 11

Carly

It had been five years since Carly was wheeled from her room to the pickup area in front of San Francisco's Saint Francis Memorial Hospital. Even though it was hospital policy to assist a patient when leaving—for liability reasons—it still felt odd to be helped from the third floor room to the outside. Although in constant degrees of pain after an emergency hysterectomy, she marveled at how kind the personnel had been during her four day stay. Not only had the staff been attentive to her needs, but for the first time in her life, she'd been treated with respect and compassion . . . even pampered.

While trying to distance herself from the extensive injuries throughout her body, she'd spent a lot of time in bed thinking about the past. Since the circumstances creating the surgery, the broken arm, and deep bruises were too fresh on her body and mind to think about, she'd deliberately focused her attention on the preceding years before coming to San Francisco. So, in between blood pressure checks, eating soft foods, sipping liquids, helps to the bathroom, and visits from the hospital doctors, she'd intermittently ventured back in time.

Carly couldn't exactly remember when her nightmarish life began. Maybe because she didn't know how old she was then; or perhaps it was nature's way of protecting her from the reality of her dire predicament. Her memories of living in the jungle in Thailand were becoming vague, so remembering specific details were nearly impossible to recall. One thing for certain and easily remembered . . . as the years passed during that time, each year became worse than the one before.

She had no recollection of parents or siblings, since no one came to mind for as far back as she could remember. When traveling back in time, her memories were centered around sleeping on wet ground, wearing filthy, ragged clothing, and always being hungry. Sometimes, encounters with cobras and scorpions would haunt her dreams. She could visualize being with other children but nothing about their faces.

One day, a group of men chased them into a fenced area, telling them to stay there, or they'd be killed. Within a day or so, other children arrived who appeared better off . . . learning they'd been sold to the bad people by their parents. Their clothes were not as dirty or tattered, and they didn't gobble food with their fingers like she did.

Before leaving the encampment, she was handed a single piece of paper. Unable to read, she was told, "Your name is now Pimchan. You are nine years old." While told to keep the important paper with her at all times, she had no place to keep it safe . . . not even a pocket. Noticing her apparent dilemma, a different man gave her a small pouch, which she tied around her waist. She'd used the listed date of birth from then on but had no knowledge of its accuracy. In fact, through the following years, she wondered if perhaps her age was predicated on her small frame due to years of malnutrition.

Separating the girls from the boys, the two groups were packed into the back of a truck, covered with a tarp connected to four wooden poles, and told to stay quiet. The roads were rough and bumpy. Sometimes, when no road existed, the truck would get stuck. Each time this happened, they were told to get out. Apprehensive and anxious, they would hover together in the muddy water . . . constantly looking for leeches. She had no idea how long the trip took but remembered soiling herself before reaching their expected destination.

Arriving in an industrial area of Bangkok, she was in awe of the surrounding buildings. They were both menacing and spectacular at the same time. The boys were unloaded first; then the truck continued on until reaching its final stop in the garment district. Since arriving in the early hours of the night, the bright lights were amazing. Seeing so many new things . . . like water coming through pipes in walls, inside bathrooms, and people working everywhere . . . almost took her breath away. There were even screens on the windows to keep the mosquitoes out. Although tired, dirtier than usual, and hungry, the difference between her accustomed life in the jungle and Bangkok rendered her speechless. Her life had changed for the better or so she thought back then. It had to . . . it couldn't get any worse, she'd reasoned.

Once cleaned, given a uniform to wear, and fed a small bowl of rice with broth, they were told to go to sleep. She no longer needed to sleep on the wet ground but on a thin mat on the floor in a room with thirty or so other girls.

They were never permitted to leave the garment factory and always told, "It is not allowed. You have no money." They had no money, because they were never paid. Supposedly, their working paid for two meals a day, consisting of rice and broth—sometimes a little meat— their uniforms, and a place to sleep. If anyone tried to escape, they would be chained to a machine or textile loom—of course, done strictly for their own safety.

After being there a couple of months—time was difficult to determine—she considered running away, but where could she go? She had no options. Even if able to escape, they would find her and bring her back. She and the others were prisoners . . . plain and simple. Not only were they kept there against their will but constantly watched, even when stopping to visit the restroom—only allowed after receiving permission.

Every so often, men or women would come though to point out girls who would be sent to a special place to learn English and proper behavior. Those judged favorably were given less time to work and treated to scrumptious desserts. This seemed like an alluring goal to strive toward. Sometimes, girls would leave for lessons and never return. They were considered the lucky ones. Those not selected continued to work at least eight to twelve hours a day . . . six days a week. If their daily quotas weren't met, they were punished by being slapped or kicked—sometimes both—for falling behind. If a worker became ill, they were placed in an unknown location within the building. Sometimes, they came back to work . . . sometimes, never seen again.

Carly remembered feeling proud when finally chosen, wanting to try her best to learn English and good conduct as quickly as possible. Although feeling joyful, she didn't understand a woman bluntly saying, "She can attend classes, but she's too fragile. Fatten her up."

The girls were told many times by their tormenters, "You are a commodity for trade. Each step of the obeying process will ensure you a better way of life." While not understanding the meaning behind the words, most did their utmost to comply, assuming the end result of developing into what was expected would make them worthy of a better life. What a terrible lie was fed to us then, she thought and angrily jerked her head against the bed pillow.

Interrupted by a nurse coming into her room for a blood pressure check, she was asked, "Are you okay? I saw you shaking your head; are you hurting?"

"No, I'm okay. I was just thinking back," she responded.

"I'm so sorry about what happened to you. It must have been awful," the nurse replied.

Carly answered with a nod but thought to herself . . . I wasn't thinking about what just happened a few days ago; I was thinking about years ago.

After the nurse left, Carly returned again to thoughts of Bangkok . . . visited many times while recuperating. Her recollections faded in and out . . . recalling when still working at the garment factory. Since talking openly was forbidden—unless absolutely necessary—it was impossible to become friends with anyone. However, whispers abounded with information during sleeping hours. Fabricated stories were regularly secreted about by many in order to receive favors. When her coveted pouch was stolen, she panicked and expected the worse. Instead of repercussions, she was casually issued another one . . . like it was of no significance. All of her restless nights protecting the pouch were done in vain, she'd thought then. They were constantly told by those in charge to work hard, be subservient, mannerly, and to always smile . . . no matter what was happening around them.

The girls who were considered strong and able to perform hard labor were sold into urban areas as domestic servants. She was glad to learn she was considered too frail to work productively. However, that feeling of relief soon left when she and others were sold into the sex trade business.

So, when did her nightmare begin? Was it when

hungry and lying on the soggy ground in a Thailand jungle, or working long and tiring hours with little food in a garment factory, or when becoming a sex toy . . . used like an animal and locked away without choices? Strangely, the memories of the actual hurtful acts had somewhat vanished but the sensations of hiding in corners and under beds—hoping not to be noticed or chosen—had remained.

While sitting in the hospital room and waiting to leave, she thought about another significant time of leaving. When she was thirteen—maybe thirteen but never certain—she was given a passport with a different name, a little spending money, and travel documents by a seemingly nice lady named Ayand. She could still see her pretty face and sophisticated attitude. Recalling the conversation . . . almost word for word and spoken in perfect English, Ayand told her, "You will soon go far away to a country full of wonderment. You will fly away to a place called America."

It was easy to remember the thrill of going to America—a place full of freedom and hope. A place she'd heard about during her English classes. She recalled the anticipation she'd felt then, thoughts of beginning a new way of life were uppermost in her mind. She was also told by Ayand, "You are very lucky to join other girls from Thailand. You will be placed as a housekeeper for a wealthy family. Your life will be good."

"Can I really go to America? Can I really leave?" she'd asked.

"Of course, my dear . . . it is really true. I have prepared the proper papers for you. Be sure to remember your new name . . . Carly. It is very important. Tomorrow, I will take you to the airport."

"Please don't forget to come for me," she'd pleaded.

Ayand's last words before placing her on the plane, "You must always be obedient."

It was easy to remember that special day . . . a day of leaving the disgust and revulsion behind and beginning a new life in a new land. Not only would it be a new start, but an opportunity to put her entire retched past in the background, hidden away forever . . . or so she thought. Perhaps, it was also easy to recall the day she boarded the airplane to leave, because it would be her last day to be excited or happy about anything. Ayand was added to her list of camellias . . . those who'd lied to her; those who were bad beneath a pretty face or kind word.

Returning to the present, Carly waited patiently in the hospital's pickup area for her ride to arrive. Although relieved Social Services had found her a place to stay while recovering from her injuries, she was filled with a multitude of differing emotions. She still felt frightened and insecure about being outside but glad to be alive. Her life had suddenly changed beyond repair; saddened she would never be able to bear children.

Carly watched as the van pulled up to the curb directly in front of her. Because of everything bringing her to this point; it was difficult to grasp she was actually free. Even before standing from the wheelchair, she tried to look at the driver's face, fearful she might recognize him. She wished she could stay at the hospital until able to run away and hide.

When fully upright—slightly bent over—but fairly steady on her feet, the hospital attendant and driver gently helped her into the van. Even while using a stepstool, the pain was overwhelming with each step upward. Trying to get comfortable on the hard seat, she wondered if fright and helplessness would always be part of who she was.

While the driver concentrated on traffic, Carly purposely kept her eyes downward, focusing on her fingers resting on her lap—one hand mostly covered with a cast. Even though the driver wasn't recognized and seemed agreeable, she still couldn't trust he wasn't part of another evil plot to do her harm again.

Interrupting his singing to the radio, the driver finally asked, "Are you doing okay?"

"Yes," she answered without looking up.

"I'll do my best to drive careful-like. Don't want to hit a bump and jar you. Let me know if I'm going too fast . . . little lady."

Leary of the driver's thoughtfulness, Carly remained quiet and continued to keep her head down.

When the van stopped at her assumed destination . . . in front of a small white house with red shutters, Carly began to sweat and shake uncontrollably. Hesitant to leave the security of the van, she feared being treated well . . . so far, in order to keep her from resisting before being placed in another terrible place.

To Carly's amazement, she was greeted by two smiling ladies, one named Clair and a younger one named Charlotte. They helped her walk slowly down the sidewalk between colorful flower beds and into the modest house. It felt peculiar to notice flowers or other things like red shutters. During her entire life—regardless of where she was, or what she was doing—her main interest in the surroundings was to concentrate on finding a way to escape.

After showing Carly the bathroom facilities and inquiring if she needed privacy; they asked if she wanted to change into sleepwear? Soon, both women helped her carefully into bed. Beginning to somewhat relax, she noticed the bedspread and curtains matched—full of brightly colored birds and butterflies everywhere. The sun was shining through the partially open window, sending rays of light flickering through an outside tree before landing against the wall. Feeling strangely at peace, she took in a deep breath, sighed, and closed her eyes.

Momentarily nodding off, she was abruptly wakened by the sound of the door bell. As she looked for a place to hide, terror rushed through her. Without regard to her incision or arm, she threw the covers off and hurdled off the bed, crouching between the bed and the wall. Expecting the man who caused her injuries to enter the room and take her away; she ignored the shooting pains ripping throughout her abdomen.

To her surprise, she heard the soft spoken words of

the case worker; the one who'd visited her several times in the hospital. Her emotions jumping from panic to relief, she peeked above the bed, thinking she was about to throw up.

The case worker's words were reassuring. "Carly, you are white as a ghost. You are safe here. No one will ever hurt you again . . . I promise." Turning to Charlotte, the case worker asked, "Did the driver bring along her pain medication? Let's hope it's time for a pill."

"Yes, it's in the kitchen. I'll go check."

Carly watched Charlotte leave, and although she wanted to feel safe, she didn't believe it possible . . . not here, not anywhere . . . not ever.

Chapter 12

After weeks of recovery and in spite of her previous insecurities, Carly began little by little to settle down and trust in those around her. When her cast was removed, it was somewhat symbolic of shedding a small part of her hurtful past. However, sometimes while showering, the scar across her abdomen was a noticeable and current reminder.

Carly spent a lot of time in the backyard, reading and watching the birds. As she felt better, she helped around the house, enjoying each day as a new beginning. Realizing she'd had no childhood, a part of her learned to laugh out loud and sing. She also learned to believe in fairy tales, kindness, decency, the sweet smell of flowers, fluffy kittens, playful puppies, and above all . . . freedom. She went with Claire and Charlotte to church each Sunday, listening to words of love and forgiveness. She understood acts of love and kindness, but forgiveness was difficult to do . . . maybe impossible.

As time passed, Carly barely remembered the meager days of scrounging for food in the Thailand jungle or the years in Bangkok. In the beginning of the healing process, the vivid and terrifying flashbacks of being sexually abused were like open wounds, but they too eventually began to fade . . . like a nightmare that wasn't real. After the hysterectomy, she'd been numb and unemotional about life in general. At first, she played games with herself . . . wanting to pretend— even convincing herself—the past never happened. She worked hard at shutting out the terrible memories, replacing them with present-day happy ones.

Keeping busy during the day and feeling exhausted when her head hit the pillow each night, Carly was adjusting to her new way of life. Although lucky and appreciative to receive help from those who seemed to honestly care about her, memories crept back at odd times, often needing to remind herself to be strong.

When bouts of depression set in, it was never an option to revisit a past happy time; there was none to fall back on. With kindness and caring, Carly was pushed to see a counselor who specialized in sexual abuse. She didn't want to discuss her previous life for fear the counselor would be disgusted by what she heard, thus thinking she was a disgusting person.

The counselor began asking what happened prior to going to the hospital. When Carly hesitated, the counselor revealed what she already knew from reading the police report, assuring her that none of what transpired was her fault. "Carly, what I want to accomplish here and my reason behind discussing those events is to help bring you closure. In doing so, our talks should assist you in moving forward toward a productive and happy future. Hopefully, our time together will achieve this."

Waiting for a reaction of agreement but receiving none, the counselor continued, "I'm going to listen and take notes. I don't want to interrupt, so I'll ask you questions later. Take your time and don't worry about anything you say. This conversation will remain just between the two of us. It's no one else's business."

Carly began slowly and reluctantly, starting with her arrival in San Francisco. "I thought it would be a new life for me. I told myself if I was obedient and did as told, I'd reap rewards . . . no matter what I was asked to do. I was beyond excited and happy.

"All seemed fine at first. I was greeted by a nice lady—or so I thought then—who took me to a waiting car. She asked for my passport and told me to get into the car. I thought this was normal procedure in America but didn't like the sinister expression in their eyes of the men inside . . . a somewhat familiar look to me. I ignored them and concentrated on the view outside, soaking in the freeways, streets, cars, taxis, busses . . . anything appearing different from my previous life in Bangkok. They took me to a hotel, demanding that I keep my head down and remain silent. One led the way, while the other followed closely behind. I reminded myself to be obedient and obey.

Knocking quietly, the door to a fifth floor room was opened by an older man in a silky lounging jacket. I thought I was there to be interviewed for my new housekeeping position, but it was not to be. Instead, the older man did not speak directly to me but told the others,

'Prepare her for me.' The driver—the one I followed into the hotel—told me to undress. When I objected, he slapped me before saying, 'Do as you're told, or you'll be sorry.' I knew what was going to happen. So much for a new life, I thought. I began undressing but not fast enough for the older man sitting in front of me on the end of the bed. 'Finish removing her clothes and clean her in the bathroom. Don't help yourself; I want to indulge first.'

"I was beyond distraught and sick at my stomach. It was nothing new—the same awful circumstances—just happening at a different place and time. I was again being used as a commodity for trade, or sell, or whatever. As I was roughly and hurriedly bathed, I thought about how to escape. While knowing I was in a new country without a passport, my only escape was to become numb to everything and everyone around me.

"After I was raped, not only by the older man but offered to the others, he told them, 'She'll do. Take her to my residence and put her in the secure room.'

"Taken quickly from the hotel, I was blindfolded in the car and driven away. After a long drive, I was aware of walking inside a building and riding an elevator down at least one floor.

"I didn't know exactly where I was when the blindfold was removed but was able to see when pushed forward down a dim hallway. I remember hearing a woman or maybe two crying somewhere off in the distance. Then, I was shoved into a stark room with a bed and pot for a bathroom. I still can hear the click of the lock after the door was shut. I finally sat on the bed and wondered what would happen to me next."

Interrupting, the counselor asked, "Would you like to take a break? You've shared a lot."

"No, I'm all right. Once I get the whole story out, maybe it'll be easier to leave behind."

The sessions continued for some time. Initially, Carly went once a week, then every two weeks, and finally once a month. She trusted the counselor, deciding to be honest and not conceal any of the sordid incidents. She talked about getting favors for being obedient and even admitted to playing games to get on her oppressor's good side. She quickly learned not to protest, acting as a willingly participant in order to receive an improved way of life. She even worked at gaining her abuser's affection . . . doing exactly as he wanted and saying exactly what he wanted to hear. When discussing how drugs and alcohol were involved, Carly admitted to being a willing participant . . . using them to hide from the disgusting reality of her plight.

While alone, Carly told the counselor about spending hours reading—acquiring the requested literature for performing as required—but always thinking of ways to escape. Sometimes, she pretended to be a character in one of the books, imagining her life in the book as real, while her real life was imagined. She was told the books came from his private library upstairs. It was puzzling how a person could own great classics by Austen, Bronte,

Falkner, Fitzgerald, and Tolstoy—to name a few—and then be such a sick, freaky individual.

Days into her therapy sessions, Carly finally talked about the time right before she went to the hospital.

"In the beginning, I stayed in the basement for days and only taken upstairs to provide sex. Eventually, I was moved to an elegant bedroom—still in the basement—where I was visited by my tormentor. I was eventually allowed to go outside as long as I was watched . . . never by myself unattended. I was given birth control pills to take. At first, I was handed a pill and watched until it was swallowed. In time and aware of the consequences, I promised to take them on my own. He liked to dress me up in fancy clothes and promised to take me out to a dinner sometime. He told me that he wanted to show me off, and I played along.

"One day, he said he would take me out for a drive. If I behaved, he would let me go out more often. I knew that I'd skipped my period for three months but was afraid to tell him . . . but afraid not to. I'd taken the pills faithfully and don't know what happened. Maybe I was given the wrong ones; I'm not sure.

"That particular afternoon, he had me dress in a tight purple dress—split up the side—and matching high-heeled shoes. As we were going out the door, he said, 'You are looking fat; your stomach is sticking out.' Glad his goons were occupied elsewhere . . . one lagging behind to take a phone call and lock the house; the other getting the car—I whispered my suspicion.

"He told me to speak up. When I said louder I was pregnant, he went into a rage and hit me. Not used to wearing high-heels, I lost my balance, falling down the front steps and landing below. When I tried to get up, he knocked me down, viciously kicking me all over . . . but especially in my mid-section. I was screaming in pain and trying to get up and run away. Out of the corner of my eye, I spotted a lady walking her dog. He must have noticed her too and tried to drag me up the steps and back inside. I was still screaming and trying to get away when one of his men showed up. He grabbed onto my long hair to help pull me inside. I kept screaming with all my might for the lady to help me. He kicked at my face. I think he was aiming for my mouth to shut me up, so I put my arms up to protect myself. That must have been when my arm was broken. Luckily, the lady called the police. I wish I could thank her but don't know her name. Guess you know about the other women—near death—who were found inside his house."

After thanking her for being forthright, the counselor said, "Carly, I'm so proud of you. You've acknowledged what happened. Even better, you've confronted it. I think you've come to understand that none of this is your fault. You've traveled a long way into the healing process, but healing won't happen all at once. You'll have setbacks and times of insecurity. I'll be here for you as long as you need me. Carly didn't hear much after the counselor's words about being proud of her . . . words she'd never heard before.

In time and with the help of many nice people—both men and women—Carly learned to trust in the humanity of good people. Receiving guidance from many . . . therapy counselor, school guidance counselor, Clair and Charlotte, church pastor, and others, she began to feel restored. Even at her age, she had a renewed sense of innocence.

It hadn't been an easy process, but she was determined to survive the past and help others in the future. While attending college, she worked part-time at a nearby day care center, realizing children made her happier than anything else she'd considered doing. Her days of studying and working were hectic and busy yet satisfying and rewarding.

After graduation, she'd had many options for employment but ultimately decided to work with children full-time. Starting out as an assistant and eventually becoming a full-fledged Activity Director; she was living a dream come true.

Each and every day, she enjoyed going to work. Seeing happy faces—full of wonderment when learning something new—and often assuring others who were going through rough times. It was fulfilling beyond her wildest imagination and working became a big part of her path toward feeling secure and embracing life.

That feeling of embracing life and security tumbled down on the evening Jennifer disappeared.

Chapter 13

Even before leaving Lukas and the diner yesterday afternoon, James had decided to personally talk to Carly next. Not having the transcripts to work with, she'd be the logical person to see first. Hopefully, she could shed some light on the events surrounding the disappearance; giving him additional details Lukas may have missed during the trial. After talking to her, he'd move on quickly. There was a lot of fact-finding to do and not much time to do it.

He started to call before seeing Carly, but thought it might be better to drop in cold . . . not giving her time to plan any answers. Best case scenario, she could remember something not brought up at trial. Worst case scenario, she could be involved. He would get a better feel about her after a face-to-face meeting.

Arriving at the Boys and Girls Club sooner than expected, he stopped to check the outside calendar before entering, wanting to determine if he was at the right location. Carefully glancing through the week's daily events . . . concentrating especially on today—Tuesday—he was unable to find anything supervised by Carly, realizing he had no idea what her last name was.

Never having been inside a Boys and Girls Club

before, James expected to sign-in or do something along that line to alert the staff of an outsider entering the building. When no one approached, bells immediately went off in his mind . . . lax security was clearly evident after a missing child occurrence. He searched the room for someone in charge or available to ask about Carly's whereabouts . . . or even if she worked there.

Several groups were doing . . . he wasn't sure what, but the closest group was laughing, holding up their hands, and shouting out answers. Off to the back of the large room was a small kitchen area with adjacent long tables and chairs. According to the outside sign, a free lunch was served to participants every day at noon, except when closed on Sunday. Looking at his watch, it was already after eleven . . . 11:10 to be exact. Not planning his day very well, perhaps he should have picked a better time. Oh well, it shouldn't take long to get quick and simple answers to his questions . . . if indeed, he'd found the right place, and Carly was there.

James had actually gotten up early, checking out a couple of other locations: the property where the accused operated his business and Jennifer's parent's home. He'd made a couple of calls: first to the authorities responsible for conducting the investigation and secondly, to see if the court transcripts were ready. He often marveled at how easy it was to get information if the questions were handled effectively . . . sometimes, pushing the truth a bit.

Still standing in the middle of the room and thinking

about interrupting one of the groups, a lady looked in his direction and asked, "Sir, can I help you?"

"Yes, I'm looking for Carly. Sorry, I don't know her last name."

"Who can I say is here to see her?" she asked professionally.

"My name is James Allen."

"Can I tell her what this is about?" she inquired firmly . . . yet in a questioning manner.

"Well, it's a personal matter," he answered.

She didn't move, seemingly waiting for more before James added, "Regarding the disappearance of a little girl named Jennifer Walker."

"I'll be right back," she responded, before briskly walking away and out of sight.

Good news, he'd not only found the right Boys and Girls Club, but Carly still worked there. While looking around for a chair, the lady returned. "I'll take you to Carly's office. Please follow me," she stated in a professional manner.

Wanting to hurry after wasting at least ten minutes, James quickly followed her down a short hallway. She stopped at a door with an attached placard "Activity Director." After a prompt but brief knock, James followed her inside.

The lady leading the way didn't leave the office but rather moved to the side, leaving James standing awkwardly in front of the Director's desk. The young woman behind the desk neither stood nor acknowledged his presence.

Oddly uncomfortable, remembrances of teachers taking him to the principal's office came to mind. As James looked down at the top of her head—while she seemed to be concentrating on paperwork—he spoke first. "I hope I'm not intruding. I'd like to ask you a few questions about the disappearance of Jennifer Walker."

Looking up but not necessarily in his direction, she appeared apprehensive when asking, "Are you with the police department?"

James glanced toward the other lady before asking, "Can we talk privately?"

The lady behind the desk—who he assumed was Carly—answered, "No," followed by complete silence.

"Okay, let me start again. My name is James Allen. I'm a private investigator. I'm helping the Walker family find out what happened to her."

"Do you have credentials attesting to that fact?" she asked, seemingly looking more in his direction but still not making eye contact.

"Yes," James answered, fumbling into his sport coat pocket.

Carly looked closely at his credentials before speaking to the lady still standing quietly against the wall, "It's okay. You can leave but please make sure the door stays open."

While thinking the lady behind the desk must be some kind of fruit-cake or hiding something, he waited until they were alone, asking, "May I sit?"

After receiving an affirmative nod, he slid a chair directly opposite her and sat down. Although he found her beautiful, this Carly person wasn't anything like he'd expected. Not only did she seem tentative, but his first impression of her was like an injured bird, damaged, afraid and vulnerable. His idea of an activity director was about being out-going, assertive, and confident. Go figure, he thought.

Fully aware of again wasting time, James cleared his throat and jumped right into his reason for being there. "First of all, I want you to feel comfortable about talking to me, so let me tell you how I came to be involved."

James began telling her how Jennifer's grandfather, Lukas Walker, was his dad's friend. How his dad would do anything to help Lukas, since Lukas saved his dad's life. How his dad asked if he'd check into what happened, because Lukas didn't believe the defendant should be free. He further told her that he came from Los Angeles—where he was an investigator—and would be in San Francisco for only a couple of weeks.

During this one-sided conversation, Carly didn't offer a single comment or ask any questions. In fact, she appeared uninterested, looking downward at paperwork on her desk the entire time.

Realizing he'd been rambling, James finally said, "Lukas doesn't want his son or daughter-in-law to know about my investigation, fearing it will open wounds for them that aren't necessary."

After pausing for a response, James decided to inquire

in a more direct manner, "Can we keep this conversation just between the two of us?"

At long last, Carly raised her head and answered in a direct manner, "I'll not lie if asked."

Sensing disinterest in what he was trying to accomplish, he replied, "I have no problem with that. I would not expect you to."

Interrupted by the same lady who'd shown him in, she announced, "Your 11:30 is waiting. Also, you wanted me to remind you about joining the children at lunchtime."

Turning toward James, Carly said, "I'm sorry, but we need to end our discussion."

"I'm sorry too," James replied. "I should have called to set up an appointment. Since we didn't have much time to discuss Jennifer's disappearance, can we talk again when it's more convenient?"

Handing James a business card, she offered, "You can call me. That should work."

"Since you seem to be busy here at work, maybe we could meet for coffee?"

"Better to call," she answered matter-of-factly.

Having no clue why he'd suggested coffee and wishing he hadn't, he said, "Okay, I will. Thank you for your time and nice meeting you."

When James left, he was both perplexed and embarrassed. Not having a chance to delve into Jennifer's disappearance was a total bust. Setting the reason for seeking Carly's input aside, he'd acted inappropriately with his coffee remark. Again, why did he say that?

Perhaps, he'd hoped she'd be more out-going if away from where she worked.

Thinking about his remark at the end of the meeting, he hadn't actually met Carly, only learning of her last name from the just received business card. She was one hard person to read. While her stunning big brown eyes were alluring, she sent out mixed signals, seemingly young in some ways yet more mature in others. While finding her extremely attractive, she was vastly different in disposition from any other woman he'd come across. There was something withdrawn yet strong about her.

Good Lord, for the first time in years, he thought about his first two meetings with Margie. Think about a difference, it was like night and day. Even questioning the difference was flat-out weird. Why now? Since parting with Margie, he'd had many first time meetings with women, but none had affected him like this one. Feeling ridiculous on many levels, he started the car and headed for the police department.

Carly finished her meeting with the Executive Director. It was a quick conversation about the scheduling of activities left to accomplish during school break and plans after returning to regular after-school hours. The best part of today was having lunch with the children. In-between discussing the importance of eating fruits and vegetables, thoughts of the detective returned. Could he possibly find something new about Jennifer's disappearance? Would he believe she was telling the truth about that awful man taking her?

Whenever coming into contact with an unfamiliar man, she reverted back to thinking of the man who'd kept her locked away. Even knowing he was serving years in prison, she considered the possibility of him sending someone to harm her. Then, there was the man who heard her testify in court against him taking Jennifer. No telling what he'd do to get revenge. He may have fooled the jury, but she knew he was guilty.

Her thoughts bouncing back again to the investigator, why did it matter if . . . ah, James Allen believed her? She'd probably never talk to him again, anyway. Sighing, she wondered if she'd ever feel comfortable around a man again.

Ever since Jennifer went missing and testifying in court, she'd had returning bouts of insecurities . . . more on guard than ever. Perhaps it would be a good idea to talk to the counselor again. Since the counselor was complimentary about her progress when their sessions ended, would she be disappointed if she returned to seek help? She'd talk to Charlotte and ask what she thought.

Looking down at the business card caddy, she'd given Mr. Allen the last one. Adding cards, she couldn't help but smile when looking at her last name . . . STRONG. Charlotte had helped her through the name change process. Actually, in her particular case, it was acquiring a last name . . . not changing it. Not too far into her mending process, Charlotte explained how important it was to have a legal name before entering college. Also explaining how it was needed to acquire a social security card, receive pay from the day care center, and other purposes. She'd eventually chosen her full name but with Charlotte's help. She seldom mentioned or used her middle initial "B" which stood for Bea . . . the only short name they could find that started with a "B". No one would ever know, except the two of them, that her name, Carly Bea Strong, really stood for: Carly, be strong.

Chapter 14

"Hi, I'm James Allen. I called earlier today about a police report," he stated to the uniformed female officer behind the counter.

"Did you already request a report and here to pick it up?" she asked professionally.

"No, I think I'm supposed to fill out a form requesting it. That's my understanding."

"Sure, hang on," she answered before opening an adjacent drawer.

Handing him a single sheet of paper, she offered, "You'll need to fill this out—both sides—and turn it in with a picture ID . . . driver's license preferably."

"How long will it take to get it after that?" James asked.

"It all depends. The request is reviewed and then . . ."

Interrupting her in mid sentence, James asked, "What can I do to speed up the process?"

"Well, if you fill it out and submit it before you leave, it will be a lot faster than mailing it back to us."

"I'm not trying to be pushy, but how long does it normally take all together? Like . . . if I leave the request today, when can I expect to receive the report?"

"Again, it depends . . . maybe five to six weeks."

"You're kidding . . . right?" James remarked in disbelief before adding, "Can I pay more to have it expedited?"

"Paying extra won't help. You can fill it out right now. Maybe we can rush it along," she answered pleasantly.

James told himself to remain calm. After all, she was just doing her job. Looking around for a place to write but finding none, he smiled and said, "Okay, I'll fill it out at the end of the counter . . . if that's okay with you."

"Sure, not a problem," she answered with a shrug.

Taking out a pen from his shirt pocket, he zipped through the form before moving back to the middle of the counter. When the officer didn't look up from the desk, he cleared his throat to get her attention.

"Wow, that was fast," she said with genuine surprise.

"Well, this isn't my first rodeo, James replied.

Glancing over both sides of the sheet, she then asked, "Can I have your driver's license, so I can make a copy? Oh, and I'll also need to copy your PI card."

Stepping away while continuing to look at the form, she paused before turning her head back and giving him a quizzical look. "So, you're investigating the missing child, Jennifer Walker?"

While answering, "Yes," he was already thinking of how to get on her good side in order to get the report sooner.

Walking back toward the counter, she asked, "Have you talked to Carly Strong yet?"

"I have. As a matter of fact, I talked to her this

morning."

"Poor thing, she hasn't been the same since it happened."

"I don't mean to pry, but it sounds like you know her. I mean . . . beyond the investigation of where she works and her statement?"

Carefully glancing around the lobby, the officer lowered her voice to just above a whisper. "I've known Carly for a long time. She lived with my Aunt Charlotte for quite a few years."

"Really," James responded with similar surprise. "How coincidental is this. Can I be totally candid with you?" he asked . . . lowering his head, as if ready to let her in on a big secret.

Receiving a nod, James continued, his voice somewhat muted, "I've taken off work in Los Angeles to help the family get answers to what happened. I only have two weeks and really pressed for time. If you could help me out with the report, I'd be forever grateful. Even more, the Walker family and Carly would also be appreciative."

"I understand. I feel badly for the Walkers, but since I know Carly personally, I've been more involved in the outcome . . . probably more than I should be in my position. Most likely, I'm saying too much already, but Carly has had such a terrible life and then this on top of it. Well, it's been devastating for her . . . and everyone involved."

"I mean no disrespect, but are you one hundred percent certain Carly had nothing to do with the disappearance?"

James asked with a quizzical look.

"God no! Why would you even ask that?"

Before James could reply, the officer looked down at her watch and quickly said, "I'm going to be relieved at any moment. Since my replacement will be here soon, call me tomorrow. My name's Janet . . . Janet Bigalow. Just tell the person who answers—if not me—that you want to talk to Officer Bigalow. If necessary, tell them it's about private business. I'll do my best to speed up the report for you. Off the record and on a personal note, I'd like nothing better than to get that creep under lock and key. He's a real piece of work. Carly can tell you all about him."

Abruptly looking to the side, Janet smiled broadly before saying, "Hi, Jack . . . right on time." Turning back to James, she addressed him professionally, "Thank you Mr. Allen for coming in."

James replied in-kind, "Thank you officer for your help."

Walking back to his car, he felt somewhat uplifted. Finally, some progress . . . well, maybe progress if he'd get the police report sooner than later. Now, off to the County Clerk's Office to see what county department or division would have the blueprints of Lehmann's building?

Once on the correct freeway and traveling in the right direction, he felt relaxed but hungry. It had been several hours since eating a stale breakfast roll and gulping down a cold cup of coffee in the hotel's office. It was definitely past time to put something substantial into his stomach. Surely, he could find an inexpensive spot to eat—someplace with a table—where he could jot down some ideas and reminders.

Knowing he needed to remain organized to minimize wasting time, it felt different than working from his own desk in Los Angeles. Not only a dissimilar work environment, but he wasn't familiar with the area. Although the traffic was hectic and typical in many ways to L A, he didn't know the ins and outs of short-cuts. Also, not having a working relationship with others—people who could give assistance in fact gathering—was definitely problematic.

Easy exit from the freeway, James pulled into the parking lot of a familiar chain restaurant. Ordering quickly, he began listing questions to ask various people, places to check out, and a reminder in capital letters to look at his original game plan. Barely filling out half a page, his investigation wasn't moving along as he'd hoped. While aware of being only into day two, he still didn't like his progress. Perhaps the feeling came from not having anything concrete to sink his teeth into. No pun intended, he thought with a grin, as he sank his teeth into a satisfying cheeseburger, followed by picking up a couple of fries and swirled them in ketchup. So, what exactly had he learned so far? Very little . . . except Carly Strong had had a terrible life.

After taking the last bite of pie and finishing off the soda, he stood, slipped the small notepad in his back pocket, and took a final look around, making sure he'd not left anything behind. As he placed a twenty dollar bill on top of the food check, he felt stuffed, noting the meal was excellent and satisfying but not cheap.

He would call Lukas tonight to tell him about talking to Carly. While knowing the call would make Lukas happy, he also knew he couldn't share what they'd talked about. Not because he didn't want to tell him what was discussed, but because nothing was actually said pertaining to Jennifer.

While he should be fixated on Jennifer's disappearance, his thoughts kept returning to Carly Strong. The police officer had definitely gotten his curiosity working over-time when mentioning her terrible life. What exactly did that mean . . . he wondered? Grinning, it had been a long time since he'd had two women to call on the same day . . . Carly Strong and Janet Bigalow. Tomorrow should prove interesting. Best to call Janet first, then he'd have something to discuss with Carly.

It was late in the evening when James returned to the hotel. It had been a long day of running around . . . nothing like his regular routine of waiting and watching. Although he'd spent a lot of time at several county offices, he'd eventually prevailed . . . receiving the blueprints and other requested information about Lehmann's property.

He set a container holding a half of sandwich and bag of chips on a small round table located in front of the room's only window. Although not really hungry, he'd still grabbed a couple of snacks when stopping for gas.

The last thing he felt like doing was going out again to find a place to eat.

Kicking off his shoes before hanging his sport coat over the back of a nearby chair, he turned on the television, thinking there should be a paper guide nearby. Not finding one, he flipped through the channels, eventually finding the menu, then locating a familiar sports program. Knowing how the rest of the night would go if he stretched out on the bed and got comfortable, he should call Lukas fairly soon.

What happened to the days when fun started as the sun went down? After getting his life sorted out, his nerdy personality had not only been suppressed but transformed into a late bloomer, catching on fast to having fun. Guess those days had disappeared, and that was okay. Not that he was old but didn't consider himself young anymore either.

Opening his lap top to key in today's notes, James noticed the last file entered was labeled "Mother." Damn, he'd temporarily forgotten what he'd found out right before leaving L A. He hadn't told his dad yet, because he wasn't quite sure how to approach the subject. He had been curious for some time about his mother's whereabouts. Never completely sure why he cared to discover what happened with her, but it did eat at him from time to time. He'd worked on it separately from his company's duties, so it took him several months . . . mainly because he had slim facts to work with. Eventually tracking her down under a different name, it had been a challenge.

If nothing else, he'd found closure to her existence and his occasional curiosity. She'd been married twice more, had no additional children, and died of alcoholism many years ago. The obit in the paper was brief . . . only mentioning the year of her birth and death. It should have made him sad, but it didn't. He treated it like any other investigation . . . permanently closing the file.

Not only had he not mentioned it to his father but hadn't told Jeremy either. Should he bother to tell them? What purpose would it serve? In the back of his mind, he wondered if they too had questioned what happened to her. Like before, he was still undecided.

Without being fully aware of what his hands were busy doing, he'd been chopping on chips. After wiping off the orange stain, he'd finish inputting his notes, call Lukas, and lie down to watch the remainder of the sports program. Sighing, he could only hope tomorrow would be more productive.

Chapter 15

Lehmann motioned for Gordon to follow him. They left the warehouse together and walked in silence to a secluded area near the water.

Already knowing The Club would be the subject of their discussion, Gordon asked, "What's up, Boss?"

"Our German member contacted me and wants a repeat experience of his last San Francisco party. Actually, he wants to make it a yearly event."

"I don't think we have enough time to set that up. I'm not even sure we can depend on the same procurer or even if we want to use him again," Gordon replied thoughtfully.

"I also have doubts and my reasoning for this immediate discussion."

"Hmm, so what did you tell him?" Gordon inquired.

"As you can imagine, last year's fiasco flooded my thoughts . . . finally telling him I'd get back to him."

"What did he offer?" Gordon asked bluntly.

"Guaranteed one mil in advance," answered quickly.

"Damn . . . twice as much as last year. It's hard to turn that kind of money down."

"Yeah, I hear ya. The German was careful with his words—even with the safe phone—but extremely pleased with the results of his last encounter. Saying things like visiting San Francisco is his most pleasurable experience. How he enjoys the special objects I have available for purchase. Let's face it, he doesn't care who, how, or why objects become available; just wants to play out his fantasy of having them completely under his control to enjoy."

Gordon grimaced before saying, "Regardless of the money, if we can't do it right this time without a major hick-up, then perhaps we should pass. That's my opinion."

"I know where you're coming from and don't need to be reminded of the dire consequences. I was the one on trial. We've never discussed what the exact problem was . . . too long on the ship from Nigeria? Too much dope for her age? Not enough ventilation in the shipping crate? Have you pursued the reason?"

"No, I can't find the contractor. Believe me . . . I've tried. He's more or less dropped out of sight. Not wanting to raise eyebrows and being cautious with my rummaging around, I've more or less quit looking. I'm sure word got back to him on the state of the arrival's condition."

"Well, the German has no idea we substituted with a local replacement . . . just pleased with the outcome. He did mention that he'd like to try a younger one next time."

"Do you want me to put out feelers? I mean . . . are we going to proceed with this or not?" Gordon asked directly but with a quizzical look.

"Okay, let's do it but get back to me as soon as

possible with an update. I'll need to advise the German one way or the other. You remember the criteria: black girl, virgin, and medically checked out to be free of Aids & HIV. Shoot for four or five this time. And Gordon, you need to make sure she arrives alive. What do you think about bringing her in a day or so early . . . not the day of the party? That way, if it goes badly, we'll have some wiggle room."

"Sounds like a good idea, but where will we keep her in the interim?"

"I'm just throwing out options. It might be a mute point if you can't timely acquire the perfect candidate. Once that's accomplished, we'll work on the logistics."

They walked without additional conversation until near the warehouse doorway. Lehmann entered to inspect a recent delivery of antiques, while Gordon left to begin contacting procurers.

As Lehmann reflected on his own personal appetites and cravings for young children—both girls and boys— the satisfaction derived from watching a child die during the act of rape was too far out . . . even for his comprehension and proclivities. Lehmann shrugged, thinking . . . it's not my thing but to each his own and hey, the price was right.

Chapter 16

After a restless night's sleep, James woke without the aid of an alarm clock. Throwing his legs over the side of the bed and sitting up, he rubbed his eyes and looked around. Blinking, it all came back . . . where he was and what he was doing. At least he couldn't blame being there on drinking too much the night before and ending up in an unfamiliar hotel with a barely known female. Still somewhat disoriented, he wondered if yesterday's activities and phone calls had disturbed his slumber. He'd certainly gone to sleep with a lot on his mind.

Although last night's call to Lukas had gone as expected—nothing really to tell him—Lukas seemed disheartened and especially quiet; his voice occasionally slurred. The discussion was mostly one-sided, and sometimes Lukas used words that didn't quite make sense.

Concerned about their conversation, he'd promptly called his dad. Unable to talk with him personally, he'd left a lengthy message, wanting to know if Lukas had a drinking problem or aware of something else going on.

While waiting for his dad to call back, he'd spread the blueprints out on the small round table. Not liking the way the prints draped unevenly off the sides, he had to stand and awkwardly lift one corner at a time. Beginning to nod off—the small letters blurring together—he'd decided to look at them tomorrow when his mind was fresh and more alert. His last thought before going to sleep was wondering why his dad hadn't returned his call.

His agenda for today was to get breakfast, peruse the blueprints, call Officer Bigalow, call Carly Strong, and take another look at the warehouse. He wasn't exactly sure of the order yet, but would definitely save the warehouse for last. Although more awake, he still wasn't close to fresh or alert. A shower and breakfast would hopefully move him along in that direction.

Probably wishful thinking, but how great to get the police report within a week's time. Not sure when Janet Bigalow began her shift, he'd call a little earlier than when they'd met yesterday. She obviously hadn't wanted to discuss the case in front of anyone, especially another officer. He respected her desire to separate her personal feelings from her official duties. Thusly, he'd be careful not to place her in a compromising position when contacting her.

After cleaning up in the small but practical shower, he did feel much better. After shaving, splashing on aftershave, and getting dressed, he felt even better and well on his way to meeting whatever the day had in store for him.

Opening the curtains to let in as much natural light

as possible, James spread out the blueprints on the bed, looking for anything out of the ordinary. After his recent drive-by, he already knew the building had three stories, a loading dock, and two separate metal roll-up entries. Looking down at the blueprints, nothing jumped up at him or seemed odd. The building appeared to have normal elevations, floor plans of each story with wall placements, doors, and windows. All seemed ordinary for a building that matched others in that particular locale. He noted the building's original date of completion. He also had acquired a couple of remodeling permits. They too didn't seem abnormal, since buildings were often altered to meet different usages.

Placing several notebooks, the blueprints, and permits into an over-the-shoulder satchel, he checked around to see if he had everything, especially the room key. Placing the DO NOT DISTURB sign on the door knob and making sure the door was completed closed, he left. It wasn't as if he had anything inside worth taking, but there was something about having someone in the room unattended that he didn't like. He'd ask for clean towels when he returned.

After stopping for a big breakfast, James called Officer Bigalow. Luckily, she answered. Speaking again to him in a professional manner, she said, "Mr. Allen, I was able to follow up on your recent request."

Here we go . . . James thought. The runaround's in launch mode. Instead, she continued, "The information you requested is available for pick up today. Thank you for your patience in this matter."

While wanting to say holy shit, that's terrific; he had sense enough to know how inappropriate that would be. Instead, he took in a substantial but quiet breath. Afraid the conversation was recorded, he calmly replied, "Thank you officer for your assistance. I'll be there within the hour. Should I ask for you?"

"Yes, I should be at the front desk. If not, please ask to have me paged."

Hanging up the phone, he was flabbergasted. Did she really say what he thought he heard? It sounded as though the report was ready. What a nice lady. Some officers could be real pricks, and many female officers felt entitled and were such bitches. Still waiting for the transcripts, it would be slow going without the police report and more wasted time.

While thinking it might be too early for the Boys and Girls Club to be open, he'd call anyway. Worst case scenario, he could call later after his stop at the police station. The person answering his call—who didn't bother to identify herself—asked several questions before placing him on hold. Eventually, she said, "I'll put you through to Ms. Strong." Well, that's not a shocker, noting Carly Strong wasn't married. By her attitude, who'd want to marry someone like her anyway? He shouldn't be so snarky; he wasn't married either. But then, he wasn't married because of a bad attitude. That led him to wonder if she was divorced, deciding she probably was. Well, he too was divorced. But then, he wasn't divorced because of a bad attitude. Stop with this silly conjecture, he told himself. Why do you even care? Nothing about her marital status has any relevance to the investigation . . . or to you. Your interest in her is about learning the facts surrounding the disappearance of a little girl and nothing more.

Brought back from his mental wanderings, Ms. Strong answered with a soft, "Hello."

"This is James Allen. We talked yesterday."

"I recognized your name," she replied flatly, followed by silence.

"Could I make an appointment for sometime today to discuss Jennifer Walker's disappearance?" he asked politely.

After more silence, James wanted to ask if she had a problem with him, or didn't believe what he'd told her yesterday, or what did he do to offend her? Thinking better of asking anything along that line, he wondered what approach would get the best results. He finally said, "I can really use your assistance in finding out what happened to Jennifer."

Carly answered quickly, "I will be too busy to see you this morning, and lunchtime is hectic. I should be available this afternoon at four o'clock. Please be on time. I have an appointment at five."

"Thank you," he responded; then waited for something back from her . . . like, see you at four, or I look forward to seeing you, or kiss my butt . . . but nothing.

Receiving more silence, James said, "Goodbye," and

hung up. Damn, she didn't know him, so why the attitude? Maybe it wasn't personal. Maybe she had a problem with people in general. Maybe she was just socially stunted. Whatever her reason, she could fake being polite. He'd been in that position many times . . . it was easy to do. Ms. Strong was only important to him because of being the last person to see Jennifer. All he wanted was a simple discussion . . . nothing more, nothing less. How difficult could it be, unless she had something to hide? In spite of Officer Bigalow thinking differently, he'd hold off judgment until later. Oh well, off to his next stop.

When James approached the police department, he reminded himself to be optimistic and not negative about what could transpire inside. Bigalow would probably say she'd been able to rush the process forward . . . maybe two weeks instead of five or perhaps had teased him into coming back to discuss something incidental. But then, she'd definitely said she had the requested information ready. That could only mean the report was waiting. Give it a rest; you'll find out soon enough, he thought and took a deep breath.

Officer Bigalow smiled at him when he walked in. Even before he'd reached the counter, she'd already opened a desk drawer and removed a large thick envelope. Placing the envelope on the varnished wooden surface, she offered, "There is also a disk inside with the report . . . ah, along with my Aunt Charlotte's telephone number. She and Carly are real close, so maybe she knows something Carly may have told her and forgotten."

"How much do I owe you?" James asked.

"Nothing. This didn't go through normal channels, so please treat it as confidential . . . for your eyes only. Also, nothing of a personal manner has been blacked out like addresses, names, or telephone numbers. I'm trusting this with you . . . if you get my drift. Good luck."

Smiling and almost blathering, James said, "This is unreal. Thank you so much. I'm indebted to you. Thank you again."

Walking hastily to his car, James wanted to leave as quickly as possible. Get the hell out of Dodge came to mind. Expecting a shout to return with the loot at any moment, he felt like he'd gotten away with something top secret. Officer Janet Bigalow was uniquely a nice person . . . the kind of person who just wanted to help with no hidden agenda. She'd gone above and beyond his wishful expectations, and he'd never burn her down or divulge where or how he'd attained any of the information contained in the envelope. He'd worked with many agencies before, and none had ever done anything like this.

Driving for several blocks, he pulled into a parking lot and opened the envelope. Sure enough, he found a clean, non-redacted police report. There was also a disk marked with a sticky note that read: Copied from search warrant video of premises—address on report. He stared down at the envelope's contents in total amazement. How great is this . . . unbelievable.

Looking at his watch and depending on whether

traffic cooperated, he had an hour or so to kill. Once he carefully read through the report, he'd then have something concrete to discuss with Ms. Strong, but mainly his thrust would be to see if she has additional details to reveal. He wouldn't be able to see the disk until returning to the hotel this evening, realizing he's left his computer in the room. Disgusted with himself for leaving without it, he hoped it would still be there when he returned. As he further chastised his actions . . . good job on checking the room before leaving . . . dumb ass.

James began to read the report. It was pretty much as Lukas remembered hearing in court but offered a lot of information on the actual arrest of Kenneth Lehmann. And yes, the name of the witness was listed. That was a great bonus. He could focus on finding him and learning what he was all about. Lukas was very specific about the witness changing his story from first talking to the police to when testifying in court. It did not list an address for the witness, stating no permanent address and presumed homeless. Locating him would prove difficult, but he was determined somehow to find him. After all, that's what he did for a living and considered himself fairly successful at it too.

Setting the report aside, he should call his workplace in L A and talk to Sam. Not only an associate but also a close friend, Sam could access the company's data bases to locate a hard to find individual.

"Hi, Sam," James offered when his friend answered. Without pausing, James continued, "Let me give you the name of a man I'm trying to track down."

After hearing the spelling of a person's name, receiving a last known location without an actual address, and a birth date, Sam asked, "Who is this?"

"It's James . . . you know that."

"Sorry, the James I know is on vacation."

"Well, I am . . . sorta. I can't seem to cut off the curiosity no matter where I go. It must be in my blood . . . like a human Bloodhound."

"Just because you look like a Bloodhound, doesn't necessarily make you one. I thought you'd be riding the cable cars and meditating in Sausalito by now."

"Not yet but on my to-do list."

"Okay, if I learn anything on your guy, I'll give you a call."

"Thanks, Sam."

"No problem and James . . . keep sniffing. You never know what or who you might find," Sam replied with a chuckle. Then, "Ruff, ruff, ruff," was heard.

"Bye, Sam"

Another sticky note on the last page of the report read: Mr. Allen, please treat Carly kindly. If you think my Aunt Charlotte can be of assistance, feel free to contact her. I've already spoken to her about you. She wants only the best for Carly and if you can locate Jennifer—one way or the other—it would be doing a good thing for all concerned.

Was Officer Bigalow's note a subtle hint to contact her aunt? He found the message both interesting and food for thought. Not kidding himself—after so much time—she was most likely right with her code words: "one way or the other." Sad but probably true . . . Jennifer Walker was no longer alive. Since he had time for a telephone conversation but not enough time to go back to the hotel and retrieve his computer, why not give Janet's aunt a call.

"Hello," she answered on the third ring.

"My name is James Allen. I'm investigating Jennifer Walker's disappearance. I hope I'm not disturbing you."

"Not at all. My niece said you were here in San Francisco and helping the Walker family."

Thinking she sounded pleasant like her niece, James asked, "Would you mind to answer a few questions for me?"

"I'll be happy to, but I really don't know anything other than what Carly told me."

"Well, this is a tad embarrassing to say, but when I spoke to her, she wanted nothing to do with me. I have an appointment to see her again this afternoon and was hoping you could give me an idea on the best way to approach her. I understand she lived with you for some time."

"Let me think how best to answer you. I can tell you from the get-go Carly is extremely shy. She'd had an awful life until coming to live with me. She was barely coming into her own and beginning to feel good about herself when the little girl disappeared. I really can't say much, but she's a private person and keeps to herself. She hasn't been the same since it happened."

Being careful with his comments, James said, "She was very hesitant to speak to me and didn't want to be alone with me with her office door closed. I found it very odd. I'm only here for a short time . . . coming from Los Angeles. Actually, here for two weeks and have already lost a few days of research. I don't have the court transcripts yet, so any information—no matter how trivial—could be helpful. That can only happen if she feels secure enough to be open and honest with me about what happened."

"Well, I understand. I really do. I'm not at liberty to discuss Carly's personal life or why she seems hesitant, but I can give you a criminal case she was involved in. It's old but public knowledge. It was even in the newspaper. But then, you're a detective . . . right? You'll have no trouble learning about it."

Perplexed because he'd not received a direct answer on how best to approach Ms. Strong, James continued. "My appoint-ment is at four today, so I won't have time to delve into it before I see her."

As if not paying attention to his last statement, Charlotte volunteered the name of a man presently serving time in prison and his approximate incarceration date. "You'll have a better understanding of Carly once you look into her connection to that crime."

While jotting down the information, James didn't have the heart to explain there wasn't enough time to deal with another mystery. Although curious about Carly's story, he already had enough on his plate. He'd save it for another time—but probably not—needing to concentrate on his main purpose for being in San Francisco.

"Thank you for your time. You've been most kind," James offered . . . ready to finish the call and move on.

"You're welcome. Did you write down what I told you?"

"Yes, I did," James replied but didn't say he'd done so mainly out of habit and had no plans of following up on it.

"I pray you find the precious little child. Before I let you go, I want you to know Carly and I are meeting for an early dinner today at five. If you've come all this way from Los Angeles to help the Walkers, maybe your investigation can aid her in feeling safe again. Janet told me you were on the up-and-up, and I'll pass that on to Carly. Perhaps, she'll be less hesitant and more open with you. I can't promise, but I'll try my best."

"Thank you again," James offered, but thinking . . . how can Charlotte see Carly at five and help him with fact-gathering during his four o'clock appointment? The scenario didn't compute. All he wanted was to have a few questions answered. If Carly would be half as pleasant as Charlotte and half as helpful as Janet, he could finish and move on.

"Bye, Mr. Allen."

Because James didn't know Charlotte's last name, and thought it too familiar to call her by her first, he answered with a simple, "Bye."

*   *   *   *

"Hi, Charlotte," Carly said when picking up the phone. "Are we still on for dinner? I can't wait to see you. It seems like forever."

"Yes. I was just thinking about you and wondering how you are doing."

"I'm okay; I guess."

"Is there anything new going on?" Charlotte asked, not knowing how to disclose her telephone discussion with the detective.

"I've had a busy day. It'll be nice to relax and talk to you later."

Okay, here goes Charlotte decided. "I understand you're having a meeting with the Walker's detective today."

"And you know this because?" Carly asked with surprise.

"Well, you know we don't keep secrets from each other. He called me today. He seems like a nice person and feels like he's offended you somehow."

"You know how I am. I clam up around men. Remember how it was when Janet's husband first came over. Remember, I'd take off and stay in the bedroom."

"I know Dear, but Mr. Allen isn't here to harm you, and he has absolutely no connection to your past. I know you want to find Jennifer, and that's what he's trying to do. Janet told me she'd checked him out, and he's a legitimate investigator."

"Whoa, back up a minute. You and Janet have both talked to him? I don't understand."

Without commenting on Carly's question but wanting to be up-front—yet not wanting to talk about everything discussed—Charlotte replied, "I don't mean to frighten you, but he asked Janet if you might be involved."

"Involved in what . . . Jennifer's disappearance? How could he even ask such a thing?"

"I can't say for sure but maybe because you acted hesitant during your first meeting."

"He caught me by surprise. You know how I get."

"I understand where you're coming from, but he doesn't know you. Have you talked to your counselor yet?"

"No, not yet. I keep thinking I will but just haven't."

"You know I love you, but honestly you're slipping backward since . . . ."

"I'm trying to fight my insecurities . . . I really am. The only place I feel safe is at home or at work. I'm sorry if I've disappointed you," Carly said, sounding miserable.

"No, Honey . . . not at all. You could never disappoint me. I'm just worried about you. Maybe you need to fight your insecurities harder. Think of all you've accomplished since first arriving at my house. Remember, you're Carly Strong."

Beginning to feel sick at her stomach, Carly asked in a pleading manner, "Could you come by the office and be here when I talk to him? I'd feel a lot better if you were here. You've always helped me feel stronger."

"I have even a better idea. I'd like to meet this James Allen fellow. Why don't you invite him to have dinner with us? That way, I'll be there, and you'll feel more comfortable when talking to him. Remember what the counselor said when you finished your sessions. Something about you'd broken through on your road to recovery. Well, this can also be a new break-through for you . . . having dinner with a man."

Thinking she was on the verge of throwing up, Carly finally answered, "About dinner . . . I don't think so. We were going to catch-up . . . just the two of us."

"Carly?"

"What?"

"You can't hide from men forever."

"I don't. I talk to men . . . sometimes," Carly answered forcefully.

"Carly?"

"I'm just careful. Okay, you're right about seeing the counselor again. I'll do it for sure."

"What about dinner?" Charlotte asked.

"I'll think about it. So, five o'clock at Buster's."

"I'll see you there. It's been awhile, since we've actually talked in person."

Charlotte finished the call . . . certain she and Carly would be dining alone. Shaking her head from side to side, all she could think about was poor Carly. In spite of the counselor's positive feedback and all of Carly accomplishments, was it possible she'd been permanently damaged beyond repair?

Meanwhile, Carly hung up the phone, devastated by what she'd heard from Charlotte. How could anyone believe she could be involved in sweet Jennifer's disappearance? The detective was just like that awful man's attorney. Swallowing, she ran to the bathroom to throw up.

Chapter 17

Normally, her office was neat; her desk perfectly arranged, but that was not the case at the moment. It was covered with schedules, budget sheets, volunteer lists, and the year's holiday event calendar . . . all left behind following her meeting with the Executive Director. Not only was the office cluttered but disgusting, she thought.

In spite of the detective coming in at any moment . . . or not, she couldn't leave it like it was. She also couldn't scrunch everything together into one pile and shove it to the side. In between straightening up the mess, labeling file folders, and opening and closing file cabinets, she continued to look at the clock and door. Not only was it natural to want her office to be tidy, but she needed to organize the paperwork . . . important when referring to it later. Once the desk was orderly again, she began tapping her fingernails against the desk's polished top.

Although knowing nothing about the detective, he didn't like people who weren't prompt. Carly wasn't sure why she cared . . . other than expecting him to be on time and not foul up her dinner plans with Charlotte. Thinking of Charlotte, she would try her best to be strong and forceful when dealing with Mr. Allen, trying somehow to convince him she'd never put a child in harm's way. How could she accomplish this when feeling responsible for letting Jennifer out of her sight? It was now fifteen minutes after four, finding Mr. Allen's late behavior both annoying and rude.

There was no kidding herself or hiding from her reality, she knew exactly why the detective's tardiness bothered her. Everything in her life had become planned, keeping herself and her surroundings in control with no surprises. But her controlled daily existence suddenly changed when Jennifer went missing. Since then, each day was filled with apprehension and anxiety. The worst part . . . her days were never routine anymore. After the trial, her thoughts were impossible to control. Sometimes, she wondered if she was going crazy . . . suspicious of everything and everybody. Continually looking over her shoulder and fearing every shadow had become her new normal.

Carly looked around the office. In spite of the detective's sudden intrusion yesterday, she still considered it her safe place. It was like her home away from home. Knowing she could never have children of her own—often causing pangs to her heart—she loved what she did. The joys of laughing, singing, and playing games with the children—regardless of whom they belonged to—kept her ugly past at bay. Cringing, she'd let Jennifer down; hence, the reason for the detective coming in today. Repeating over and over, I will be strong. I will be strong. I will be strong and make Charlotte proud of me.

At exactly twenty minutes after four o'clock, James Allen lightly knocked and casually walked in. Although alerting the staff she was waiting for Mr. Allen and to allow him into her office immediately, she still found his actions presumptuous. He should have waited until she acknowledged his knock. But no matter what he said, how he acted, or what he did, she was determined to be strong . . . even assertive if necessary.

Previous to seeing Carly Strong at her office today, James had already decided to change the narrative between them. Having struck out yesterday, he made sure the door remained open before asking, "How are you today?"

Answering differently than James expected, Ms. Strong replied, "I'm fine. Thank you for asking."

Her reply was typical . . . one normally expected when making a polite response. How about that? She speaks multiple words, answers back quickly, and nicely. She must have taken a non-attitude pill today, he thought.

"Sorry I'm late, the traffic was . . . ."

Cutting him off in midsentence, Carly stood, placed her arms across her chest, and said curtly, "I told you four o'clock and to be prompt."

"No, you asked me to please be on time. There's a big difference," James answered calmly.

Carly shook her head; her dark hair cascading unevenly over her shoulders. Scrunching her face, she muttered something unintelligible and sat down. The silence settling in between them seemed unnerving and awkward, yet neither gave the impression of noticing.

Good Lord, James thought. This lady is so bi-polar. She's gone from timid—like a wounded bird—to assertive—like a shrew. Usually, he could size-up a person during a first meeting, but here he was at a second meeting with no clue what made her tick.

In that brief moment, Carly couldn't believe what she'd just said. It was like an out-of-body experience. All she could consider . . . blame it on her earlier conversation with Charlotte about being strong.

Breaking the silence, Carly offered, "You're right. I have no idea why I said that. I'm sorry."

"No problem. I'm just here to do my job. I'll make sure to finish in enough time for you to make your five o'clock appointment. I hope it's not off the freeway to the south. I was delayed due to a bad accident. I apologize for being late."

As if her mind abruptly jumped to another thought—unrelated to their recent dialogue—she said in a stammering manner, "It was my fault."

"Do you mind if I sit?" James asked while thinking . . . get prepared for what might come next. Is it possible I'm finally going to get somewhere?

"Yes, you can . . . sure," she answered, her eyes seemingly far away.

James placed the chair as close as possible to the front of her desk. After adjusting into the seat, he began calmly speaking. "I'm hoping you might remember something you didn't say to the police or in court. I haven't been able to read the transcripts yet, but have a pretty good idea of what transpired. I guess what I'm asking . . . ah, have you thought of something you wished you'd said to the authorities?"

"No, I don't think so," she answered, wondering why he didn't ask . . . why it was my fault?

"Let's talk about the man who you saw take her. Did you know him?"

"So, you believe me," she responded in a surprised manner.

Puzzled why Mr. Allen would believe her over another man—a very rich man—Carly took in a big breath. While breathing in deeply, she caught a whiff of his cologne. It was a reminder of her master's scent, just not as overwhelming. She fought the urge to back her chair up; her master's face flowing across her mind in waves. Along with the inability to escape the memories associated with her master, she found herself holding her breath, finding it difficult to breathe.

Then, it dawned on her; Charlotte was right. She'd deliberately filtered out any and all possible encounters with men in general and never placed herself close enough to a man to smell his cologne. Not dissatisfied with her personal self-imposed isolation, she'd been content to hide away in her secure work or home cocoons . . . more or less shielding herself from adult relationships.

"Of course, I believe you. Carly . . . ah, Ms. Strong, we are both after the same thing, getting to the bottom of Jennifer's disappearance. I'm not here to interrogate you;

I just need something helpful to go forward with. Do you understand what I'm saying?"

As James answered and followed up with a question of his own, he looked directly at her face . . . actually into her eyes. His stare was met with an almost blank demeanor. It was like her physical body was there, but she'd mentally wandered off to another place or time.

Carly could feel her face flush. Why had this man affected her in such a strange way? His gaze was penetrating when he looked at her. It was like he was searching inside of her. What was happening to her? Why was he interested in what she had to say? He must already know much more than she did anyway.

Uh oh, back to the silent treatment, James thought. Although short, it had gone well for a little while. She was peculiar . . . bordering on . . . he wasn't sure what. He'd asked two specific questions about the defendant, but she'd ignored both . . . why?

James continued in spite of no feedback from her. He'd try differently . . . from the beginning. "Let me put it this way. I'd like to hear about everything that happened that day from the beginning . . . every minute detail. Maybe you could add why you think Jennifer would get into his car and what relationship he had to the Boys and Girls Club. Keep in mind the time is moving along, and I don't want to hold you up for your five o'clock appointment."

"Okay, but you keep in mind; you were twenty minutes late," Carly replied matter-of-factly.

James couldn't help but wonder if she was intentionally

dragging this out. She was exasperating his patience. "You're right . . . my fault, but I did tell you sorry."

Carly started from the beginning of the day. He didn't mean from the actual day's beginning, only from the start of Jennifer's involvement. Not wanting to interrupt or rush her, he settled back and listened, occasionally jotting down information. However, he did ask her to stop while he changed notebooks. He wasn't interested in the games played during the day or why the ping pong paddles were hidden away by a mad little boy who thought his opponent was cheating. As she continued, he took more interest when she started talking about what was happening right before Jennifer left the building.

"Can you tell me what she was wearing . . . if you can remember?" James asked.

"I told the police, so it's written down on the statement I gave. I think about it all the time." When her eyes began to water, Carly opened a desk drawer and removed a tissue. Continuing, "She was so cute in her little pink outfit. Her pants were pink; her white tee shirt had the capitalized word: LOVE enclosed in a pink heart. I can't remember her shoes, but her socks were pink with white ruffled lace." Carly's tears began to run freely down her cheeks.

"I know this is difficult, and I'm sorry. Do you need a minute?" James asked.

"No, if going back over this will help . . . then, I need to do it." Continuing on, "Jennifer loved pink . . . anything pink."

Carly pretty much recapped what he already knew from the police report . . . except the report stated she was wearing all pink. Not important at this point, Carly was about to talk about the events right before Jennifer left the building. The problem was . . . it was closing in on fifteen minutes to five.

"I need to ask you how far away your five o'clock appointment is? I don't mean to be nosey, but I feel bad about showing up late. I don't think we'll be able to finish before you need to leave. I also don't want to drag this on for another time. I'm sure you don't either, especially since you appear not to like me."

James waited for a reaction but wasn't surprised when she remained quiet. Smiling widely and hoping to brighten the mood, he asked, "Do you have any suggestions on how to permanently get rid of me?"

Thinking about what Charlotte said, Carly's mind began to race. Would it be better to endure another meeting alone with Mr. Allen or include him at Buster's, where Charlotte would be present? She was not living with Charlotte when the Jennifer tragedy happened, but Charlotte had been her rock while recovering from surgery and that awful time in her life. Could Charlotte possibly help her understand these new strange feelings she was having about the investigator?

Okay, I give up; James thought, deciding he'd tried his best. Nothing was working. "Hello, did you hear my question?" James asked, more perplexed than ever and thinking . . . thankfully—one way or the other—today's meeting will soon be over with or without additional information.

I've got to answer him, Carly thought. Looking at the clock and even though Buster's was close, she could barely get there by five. Now that he believed her, if she talked to him at dinner, she could tell him why she felt it was her fault . . . an opportunity to get it out in the open. Besides, for some weird reason, she wanted to see him again. What to do? What to say?

"Yes, I heard your question and might have a solution," she finally answered. "Charlotte would like to meet you. We are having an early dinner at five. She was my five o'clock appointment. Perhaps we could conclude our discussion there. Then, you can continue on with the investigation or whatever you do."

"I guess that would work," James replied.

After giving him Buster's address, Carly watched Mr. Allen walk quickly out of the office, stopping long enough to close the door behind him. She sagged into her chair, realizing she'd been sitting at attention since spouting off. Feeling relief when the detective was out of the office, she needed to hurry and leave herself.

However, instead of preparing to leave, Carly placed her head on the desk and closed her eyes. She needed to get a grip on herself. She'd gotten through much worse than this before; she could do it again. She straightened in the chair, turned off the computer, grabbed her purse, and removed her keys. Scanning her office, she flipped off the lights. Well, here goes, she thought. How strange . . .

she was actually looking forward to seeing the detective again in a few minutes . . . even weirdly excited.

James easily saw through the dinner rouse. Charlotte didn't need to meet him—probably didn't even want to meet him. More to the point, why did Carly want or need her there? Maybe he'd flat-out ask Carly what was going on in front of Charlotte. Besides the fact that Charlotte was a much better communicator; she also seemed like a straight shooter.

Chapter 18

James would have preferred to be waiting for Charlotte and Carly instead of the other way around. However, short on time and unfamiliar with the area, he needed to find a gas station. Not happy about being late a second time on the same day—although an actual time had not been established—his GPS sent him twice around the strip mall where Buster's was located. Eventually, he found it, and luckily plenty of parking was available.

When James stepped inside Buster's Restaurant, a pleasant lady behind the cash register picked up a menu before saying, "Hello . . . one?"

Before answering, he scanned the room—occupied by a handful or so customers—before easily finding Ms. Strong at a table with another woman . . . assuming the person beside her was Janet's Aunt Charlotte. Briefly watching, he saw Carly Strong tap the lady on the shoulder before whispering into her ear.

Turning back to the cashier, James answered, "No, I'll be joining two others already here."

Carly's friend promptly looked in his direction and waved. How odd Carly didn't wave, yet a stranger did? Although strange, it seemed to fit, he thought.

Crossing the room, he was aware of eyes watching

from in front and the cashier following closely behind. Arriving at their table, he offered, "Hi, Ms. Strong." Then turning, "You must be Charlotte."

Charlotte answered, "Yes, and you must be James Allen? Please have a seat."

Having a choice of where to sit, his options were either his back to the door or sitting next to Carly. Even though learned during his police training days—he still didn't like his back to the door. Quickly choosing, James decided to sit next to Charlotte and across the table from Carly. James took the menu from the cashier at the same time she asked, "Can I get you something to drink?"

"I'll have a black coffee," James answered but thought . . . a beer sounded much better, realizing he'd not had a cold beer in over a week.

Looking from one to the other, James asked, "Do either of you have a favorite food you like to order here?"

Charlotte answered, "It's all good. We've eaten here a lot, mainly because it's close to Carly's work and usually quiet. It's easier for us to hear each other. Well, it's easier for me; I'm a tad hard of hearing."

"They certainly have an extensive menu for a small restaurant. This will be tough," he replied.

Surprisingly, Carly said, "They have yummy French fries here. All men like French fries, don't they?"

"I can't speak for other men, but I sure do," James replied with a smile.

Carly pretended to look at the menu, or at least James perceived it as pretended. More than likely, she'd already decided on what she planned to order, having been at Buster's in plenty of time to look through the menu—plus having been at the restaurant many times before . . . per Charlotte. Even though he'd already decided on what he wanted, he too continued to check out the menu, wanting to see who'd speak next.

It was Charlotte who broke the silence, just as the waitress brought over his coffee. "I'm so happy to meet you," Charlotte began. "Like I told you on the phone, I hope and pray your investigation is successful."

"Well, the odds are against it, but I'm trying my best," James answered sincerely.

The waitress stood quietly by the table, seemingly not wanting to interrupt their conversation. When a break occurred, she finally asked, "Are you ready to order?"

With nods all around, they each ordered. After giving her order to the waitress, Carly asked if she could have a refill of her hot chocolate and water. While the waitress took their menus, Carly added, "Would you also bring the gentleman a glass of water?"

James automatically said, "Thank you," while stunned at Carly's polite request. Yes, definitely bi-polar, he reasoned. Not by what she said, but her words and actions seemed foreign compared to her previous attitude and way of communicating. Perhaps she was acting differently because of being away from her office. He couldn't quite figure her out.

Charlotte asked, "James, why don't you tell us about your family back in Los Angeles?"

Although knowing Charlotte was making polite small-talk, he wanted to get back to the unfinished business with Carly, ending too soon at the Boys and Girls Club. He would be brief about himself and then return to where their previous discussion left off at the office. Feeling somewhat obligated to Charlotte—most likely, she was responsible for this meeting—he'd even seek out information on Carly's involvement with the imprisoned criminal. Since seemingly important to Charlotte, he'd try to bring up the subject if time permitted.

"Well, let's see. Usually, I'm the one asking questions, so this feels kinda odd to be talking about myself for a change. I have one brother named Jeremy. He's married with two boys. My father is named Joseph. We refer to ourselves as the three "Js." My dad is a close friend of Lukas Walker—Jennifer's grandfather—and the person getting me involved in this investigation in the first place. That's about it."

Before he could move the conversation back to Carly and ask about Jennifer's disappearance, Charlotte asked, "Did your mom pass?"

"Yes," he answered simply—not wanting to go there—but Charlotte seemed determined to obtain more facts about his personal life.

Not stopping, she inquired, "I'm sorry. Was she ill?"

How in the hell did this happen? This meeting wasn't about him; it was about getting information on a child's disappearance. Not wanting to talk about his past—having not done so since therapy—James weighed his options of avoiding the subject and appearing secretive or being open in a straightforward but brief way. He decided to answer just enough to satisfy Charlotte without going into details. He answered frankly, "My mother deserted us years before she died of complications of alcoholism."

James realized he'd had his eyes directed at his coffee cup during his last statement. When he looked up at Carly, she sat there frozen; clutching her cup of hot chocolate like it was going to fly away. Unlike Carly's usual one word remarks, he'd put the truth out there . . . in all its glory. It was what it was, he thought.

When Mr. Allen used the word "deserted," Carly immediately thought of Thailand, a memory not visited in some time. At least Mr. Allen knew who his mother was, wondering if he'd had similar feelings of abandonment. Probably not, he'd had his father and brother to rely on.

Charlotte chimed in after a noticeable pause, "I didn't mean to pry. I just like to know about the people who come into my life."

"No problem. As I've gotten older, I've learned to say how things really are. It's not always easy but being honest encourages others to reciprocate in kind."

Deciding to ask one of several questions she'd thought about on her way to the restaurant, Charlotte asked, "Do you have children, Mr. Allen?"

Before James could answer, the food arrived. Just in the nick of time, he thought. Along with the food, the waitress brought him a glass of water, another water and hot chocolate for Carly, and refilled the two coffees. She then asked, "Can I bring you folks anything else?"

"If you don't mind, could I have ketchup for my fries?" James asked.

While they concentrated on eating, James felt he'd dodged a bullet . . . not answering the children question would be easy but feared a question might follow about his marital status. His marriage was what it was, but ashamed of the reason it broke up. Again, he'd been on the wrong end of this questioning process. Deciding to be proactive and return the favor—so to speak—James asked Charlotte, "So what's your family all about?"

He listened politely as she mentioned being widowed for years, having one sister, and several nieces and nephews . . . all living in the San Francisco area. She volunteered maintaining a half-way house for young women going through rough times. "It's my mission in life. I consider everyone who's lived with me a part of my family."

"What a terrific thing to do," James responded with admiration. When Charlotte mentioned the half-way house, Carly noticeably looked off to the side. It was easy to put two and two together . . . obviously the reason for Carly living with her. Interesting . . . he thought.

Looking in Carly's direction, James asked, "Ms. Strong or Carly Strong, is it okay if I call you Carly?" After receiving an affirmative nod, he asked, "So . . . Carly, what's your family like?"

Her expression went stony; her face turning bright red. He couldn't remember ever seeing a person so flushed, so fast. Her reaction caught him off-guard. Whoops, what have I said now? From the first moment they'd interacted, he'd convinced himself he felt annoyance toward Carly and an irritation to his investigation. Now, he wasn't sure how he felt about her.

"Charlotte is my only family," she answered, lowering her head. Looking up, she stated almost in a warning manner, "Don't ask about my past."

"Sorry, I didn't mean to offend you, James replied. He felt his face warm, wondering if he too had blushed.

So, back to business, he thought. "Let's talk about where we left off at your office. Will that be all right with you?" he inquired, still perturbed with her remark. It wasn't so much what she said—although adding please would have been nice—but how she said it. Continuing, James added, "Also, you can tell me why you think it was your fault?" James looked over at Charlotte who rolled her eyes below raised eyebrows. Wondering what Charlotte's facial expressions were about, were they directed at him or Carly?

Carly began speaking like she'd rehearsed what she planned to say. "The girls were making dolls. The table was cluttered with lots of doll preparations. There were scissors, glue, cloth pieces, and paints . . . that kind of stuff. A few of the girls finished their dolls that day; Jennifer was one of them. She and I worked especially hard on her doll. Since being African-American, she wanted her doll to have a dark skin-like look. I had purchased several shades of material for her to choose from. Since time was almost up, I asked everyone not to leave until we cleaned up the table. When almost finished, Jennifer said she was going outside to wait for her mom. I should have told her to stay inside, but she was so excited about taking her doll home to show her parents. Since close to her mom's pick up time, I concentrated on telling the others goodbye—making sure the ones who'd finished their dolls had them—when I noticed Jennifer's pink purse on the counter. At first, I thought her mother had already picked her up; but then thought she might still be waiting outside on the bench. While knowing she wouldn't ordinarily leave her purse behind, but also aware of her excitement about the doll, she'd probably forgotten it. When I went outside to give it to her, she was gone. I looked across the street and saw her get into his car. See . . . it was my fault. I should have made her stay inside."

"Why were you sure it was his car?" James asked.

"He . . . ."

Charlotte intervened. "Carly tell him about how you felt about him. It's okay. He needs to know."

Carly started talking even faster . . . like she'd been waiting for a long time to tell someone besides Charlotte. "That man had a creepy look in his eyes. He was way too touchy-feely with the children when he came to visit. Sometimes, he was there as often as once a week. Sometimes, a month would go by. He always seemed to show up when the younger children were there."

"Creepy . . . how?" James asked.

Looking again at Charlotte and receiving an affirmative nod, Carly continued. "He was into touching and hugging the children too much . . . mostly the girls. It really wasn't obvious unless you were paying close attention to his actions. I watched him and felt he acted inappropriately. He would make weird comments about how cute their lips and fingers were, or how he'd like to squeeze them to pieces. Once I heard him tell a little girl—her name was Carol—how he'd like to eat her all up, and did she want to kiss him? He even wagged his tongue at her."

"Did you ever say anything to him about your concerns?" James asked.

"Not to him but after he tickled a little girl—Sally—I talked to the E. D. She told me he was just being friendly and making the children happy. The last time I brought it up, she said, 'Carly, Mr. Lehmann is the Boys and Girls biggest contributor.' I tried my best to keep the children out of his reach, but it was all but impossible. One time, I overheard him tell Carol if she'd sit on his lap and kiss him, he'd give her a present."

"Wow, what did you do?" James asked, feeling uncomfortable about what he was hearing.

"I told her I needed to show her something in the kitchen. He knew I didn't like him, and he was right. I felt like a mother hen protecting my little chicks from the big bad fox. He often had an ice cream truck show up. He seemed to take pleasure in personally pass out the ice cream bars to the children. He liked to show them how to lick on the different ice creams. One time, he licked ice cream off a little girl's fingers. Each time he touched them; it made me uneasy. When he'd bend down and whisper to them, they'd giggle, and he'd laugh. It wasn't something I could directly complain about; it was more about the feelings I had when he interacted with the children. I can't really describe it . . . just creepy."

"And, you're sure it was his car." James inquired.

"Yes, positive. I saw it many times. I'd be so relieved when he'd finally leave; I'd make sure he was gone. I watched him get into that same white car."

James concluded—without any doubt or reservations—Carly would never be a part of Jennifer's disappearance. More than that, she seemed tuned-in to his behavior . . . almost like an inherent insight into what Kenneth Lehmann was all about. As he listened to Carly describe Lehmann, he concluded her words said volumes into her own personality. On top of that, her refusal to discuss her past was an obvious clue into how terrible it must have been.

While Carly was talking, James was aware of Charlotte speaking quietly to the waitress. When Carly quit talking, Charlotte offered, "I've ordered dessert for us."

"Sounds good . . . whatever you ordered," Carly said, and seemed to really mean it. "Before it gets here, I need to visit the restroom."

Normally, James would have helped Carly with her chair, but she was already on her way before he could remove the napkin from his lap and stand. He looked at Charlotte . . . almost like he wanted directions on how to proceed. He couldn't help himself; his focus on Carly had moved beyond fact-finding for the investigation. His attraction for her had become more than curiosity, wanting to learn what happened to her before she arrived at Charlotte's house. He couldn't help himself.

Charlotte said quietly, "She's said more to you than she's ever shared with anyone . . . except maybe her counselor and me. I hope she was able to add something to your investigation; something you didn't already know."

"Well, she definitely has insight into Lehmann's behavior. That's a new aspect . . . for sure. I still don't understand her determination not to talk about her past? I sense there's a story there."

James waited a moment, hoping Charlotte would share something profound about Carly's past. When she didn't, he continued, "I guess I can understand her reluctance. I don't like to talk about my past either. My early years were dysfunctional in many ways, and then I went through a failed marriage. I was a basket case after that. Guess everyone has skeletons in their closet, along with an unwillingness to discuss them. But with Carly, I'm assuming her past must have been devastating." James waited . . . but again, nothing was offered.

"I know what you're saying," Charlotte replied . . . thinking James sure hit the nail on the head.

Smiling, James said, "Charlotte, you're easy to talk

to. Carly is lucky to have you for a friend. Go figure, here I am talking about my past, and we've only just met."

After a return smile, Charlotte responded, "I wish you lived here in San Francisco or could stay longer. Carly could sure use someone to talk to other than me. I know you're busy with the investigation and only here for a short time, but it would be nice if Carly could venture out of her self-imposed solitary existence. Without going into details, she feels in danger all of the time. She hides away either in her office or at home. She never goes anywhere after dark, and it's all I can do to get her to meet me for dinner. Carly needs to make friends . . . especially with men she's not afraid of. While in town, it would really be nice if you'd call her just to say hello, how's it going? You know what I'm saying . . . that kind of thing. I'm sorry for talking so much . . . just wanted to tell you how I feel."

Uncomfortable and unsure how to respond, James answered, "I can't promise, but I'll see how my time goes. I've never been around anyone like Carly, and that's the truth." He then asked, "How long have you known her?"

"Several years, but she's never told me anything about her life as a young person—although she wasn't very old when I first met her."

James said in almost a whisper, "Carly's coming back."

Feeling guilty for talking behind Carly's back, Charlotte said, "Glad you're back, so we can dig into dessert."

As James finished his cake and ice cream, he said,

"Thank you both for including me in dinner, and Carly, thank you for your assistance. When I leave, I'll take care of the bill."

"No you won't," Charlotte said. "I've left my credit card with the waitress. We invited you."

"Thank you both again. I'll let you know how things are going with the investigation."

Watching the detective leave, Carly asked Charlotte, "Why did I talk so much?"

"You didn't. You just told him what he needed to know, but you're remark about not wanting to talk about your past was a little . . . ."

"But I can't talk about it. He'd know right away what an awful person I am," Carley interrupted before Charlotte could finish.

"Why do you say that? You're not an awful person."

"I am. I've done awful things," she answered.

"Carly, you didn't choose to do awful things. You did what you had to do to survive."

"There are things I've done; things you don't even know about," Carly uttered, lowering her head.

"Nothing you've done would matter to me. If it matters to someone else, then you wouldn't want to be around them anyway."

"It took me some time, but I finally told my counselor. She told me it would help to talk about it. She said, 'Get it all out in the open, leave it behind, and move forward with your life.'"

"See . . . your counselor didn't think you were awful.

In fact she told me you were one of the bravest people she'd ever known."

"Really," Carly answered with surprise.

"I was proud of you today. You didn't shake or look frightened . . . not one time. Why don't you talk to James on your own . . . without me?" Charlotte asked.

"I couldn't."

"Why not? You should be able to speak to him without fear. Since he'll be gone soon, you can enjoy his company while feeling safe."

"I don't think so," Carly answered, feeling uncomfortable with the conversation's direction.

"You could bounce ideas and concerns off him . . . about the investigation. He could become a friend . . . like we're friends."

"I could never have another friend like you."

"Sure you could. You could have lots of friends, but you need to put yourself out there and make the effort."

"I don't know. I get this strange, warm feeling when I'm around him. I don't know what it means. Please tell me what it means."

"It means you have feelings for him . . . attracted to him."

"Oh," Carly said, seemingly confused and frowning. I don't know about such things, but he could never have feelings for me. I'm damaged goods from my past."

"That's only true if you think of yourself as damaged goods. You have the power to make those thoughts go away. You've proven it before."

"How do I start?" she asked pathetically."

Charlotte made a tsk-tsk sound. "I know you. I can tell you like him. It's scary for you, because you've never experienced these feeling before. Yes, you've had a terrible young life, but you're a survivor. Where has the girl gone that learned to laugh and embrace everything around her? You can have the life you're supposed to have. James could be your trial run," Charlotte finished with a giggle.

"I want to be fixed and do what normal people do . . . I really do."

"Well, Honey, that's a start. It sounds to me like you want your life to change. Nothing would make me happier than to see you happy. You have nothing to lose and maybe a lot to gain. I don't want you to be alone the rest of your life and don't think you do either.

"I feel foolish. I'm afraid but in a different way," Carly responded, looking helpless.

"Give yourself a break. If you find you don't enjoy his company and don't want to be friends, then you'll be back where you started . . . but wiser."

Pausing like in deep thought, Charlotte asked, "Before you came to America, were you ever friends or in a relationship with a man?"

"No, never. Before then . . . that's when . . . well, I've always been imprisoned—one way or another—even in Thailand."

"I had no idea. Why didn't you tell me?" Charlotte asked.

"I was too ashamed," Carly answered, looking away.

"So, you've never known what it's like to interact with another person in a relationship?" With no response, Charlotte offered, "Think of it this way . . . James could be the first man to take you out of the darkness of your fears. I know you've been confronting your fears until Jennifer, but now it seems worse."

"It's different now from before. What if Lehmann comes after me or some of his men . . . like the one's in court, and my master's people are still out there."

"How can you be afraid when you're with James? I have the feeling he could take care of anything or anybody who'd want to harm you."

"Tell me what to do," Carly pleaded.

"Take baby steps. Talk on the phone, go out to eat, and learn to have fun. Above all, quit hiding away."

Leaving Buster's together and according to their routine, Charlotte followed Carly home. As they hugged and said their final goodbyes, Charlotte clearly remembered what Janet told her about the detective. He'd been married one time and was now divorced with no children. Also, he'd once been a policeman and had a clean record . . . not even a parking ticket. Was she doing the right thing by playing matchmaker? If nothing else, James seemed like the right person—a nice and safe man—at the right time to help Carly fight her fears and move on with her life.

As James left the restaurant, he was appreciative of Charlotte paying. Unusual for him, he didn't even argue.

His funds were already getting low and there was still more than a week to go.

He didn't want to care about Carly, but strangely he did. He didn't want to understand her, but now knew she wasn't the cold, obnoxious, and annoying person he'd once thought she was. There was definitely a story hidden away about her past. It was beginning to add up . . . the feelings regarding Lehmann's behavior and the worries and fears about her safety . . . like being alone with him at first.

Each time he thought of Carly; her penetrating eyes overshadowed the previous negatives he'd directed her way. Above all, she was different in every way from Margie, and—no matter how terrible her past—the difference was a good thing.

Chapter 19

James woke the following morning wondering why his dad hadn't called last night. Returning a call as soon as possible when either was out of town kept the other from worrying. Not like his dad—this never happening before—so he was both worried and perplexed. As soon as showered and dressed, he'd call again.

Toweling off, it was hard to believe he'd been in San Francisco only four days. It seemed like longer. Then, he wondered why he'd not accomplished more. Arguing with himself, he'd personally talked to Lukas, gotten the police report sooner than expected, picked up the blueprints, and came to terms with Carly's bazaar attitude—not the reason for it—but removed her from his list of possible suspects.

Picking up the envelope containing the police report, it dawned on him . . . he'd not looked at the enclosed disk yet. Too late, the call to his dad was already ringing.

"Dad, did you get my message?" James asked, relieved when his dad answered on the first ring.

"Yes," was the direct reply.

"What's the deal? I worry when you don't return my calls. Have you talked to Lukas yet?"

Again, James received a single response of, "Yes."

"Dad, talk to me. What's going on?"

"Yes, I should have called you back . . . sorry. Yes, I talked to Lukas. I wasn't exactly sure what to tell you so didn't want to call. Lukas swore me to secrecy. I've been wrestling with what to say to you."

"About what?" James asked, before quickly realizing, and then saying, "That was a stupid question."

"First, Lukas doesn't want Gabriel or Michelle to know . . . ah, what I can't tell you. Secondly, he's paranoid about anything getting in the way of bringing Jennifer and her parents the justice they deserve. He would like to be a bigger part of the process and more involved but at present is dealing with other issues."

"Okay Dad, I get it. So far, you've done a good job of not telling me anything. What else aren't you telling me?"

James and Joseph had played this game of words through the years, so both knew how it would eventually end. This time, however, the conversation was different than most. For a change James was asking the questions; his dad answering. In past word games, both would have an understanding of what was apparent, yet not actually spoken.

"Let's be philosophical here," his father replied. "Let's say for discussion sake that we're all going to die . . . some have more time than others, some sooner than others."

"Dad, is Lukas dying?" James asked, realizing this was serious and shouldn't be part of any back and forth word game exercise.

Having anticipated his son's next question, Joseph answered, "I didn't say that."

"Okay, for clarity's sake . . . let's say if what I expect is true, why keep it from his love ones?"

"It's complicated. He's complicated. Can I have your word not to divulge something you don't know for sure but might suspect?"

"Dad, how can I divulge something I have no knowledge of . . . ah, for certain?"

"Good man. How's your investigation going?"

"Slow going but making some progress," James answered.

"James, if anyone can get a handle on it, you can. Sorry, I didn't call back, but I . . . ."

"I understand. Say no more. Can I do anything to help Lukas while I'm in San Francisco? Should I go to his house and see him?"

"No . . . God no. I threatened to go visit him. That's when he opened up about what I didn't tell you. It's just a guess, but probably his motivation behind not wanting you to stay with him."

"I never considered that a possibility. Dad, tell me you didn't ask Lukas to let me stay with him?"

"Not exactly but may have suggested it."

"Well, that's embarrassing."

Responding thoughtfully, "In my defense I was thinking it would be cheaper for you and a chance for the two of you to get to know each other. Lukas dodged the subject, and I didn't pursue it. When I first put it out there—suggested it or whatever—I got the impression he was set in his ways and didn't want the bother."

"While I'm here and regardless of what Lukas needs, I'd be happy to help with anything. Dad, please give Lukas my telephone number—just in case he doesn't have it—and tell him to call if he needs anything . . . no matter what and no questions asked."

"That's a good idea, but he's already thankful for your help in looking for his granddaughter. I'll call him and make it sound like he's doing me a favor by keeping tabs on you. Please don't go over to his house unless he invites you. It would make him uncomfortable, and he'd wonder if I told you what was going on—which I didn't—and you were there to spy on him.

"I understand. I'll talk to you soon. And Dad, thanks for not telling me anything."

"You're welcome. Bye, Son."

After ending the call, James turned his attention to his laptop, looking forward to seeing the search warrant video. He closed the window curtains to block out the direct sun, determined not to miss a single detail of the inside of Lehmann's building. From the video's beginning, he was impressed with the thoroughness of the search warrant operation. It started in the warehouse area and then progressed to a 2nd floor showroom—full of large and small expensive looking objects— all displayed with notes stating: DO NOT TOUCH-ASK FOR ASSISTANCE.

From the 2nd floor showroom, the team back-tracked to the first floor in order to reach the 3rd floor above . . . unable to access it via the same elevator used to reach the showroom. Watching them return to the first floor, it seemed odd the building was set up in such an odd manner. This left him wondering why the process was so complicated and what was the purpose?

Continuing to watch the video, the only way to reach the building's 3rd floor was through a separate elevator entered from inside the parking area. Again, how strange, he thought. According to the police report, the witness stated he saw a young black girl's face inside a white car—maybe a Cadillac—before the car passed through the metal door leading to the parking area. The witness didn't get a good look at the child, couldn't say how old she was, and couldn't say exactly when it was . . . other than saying it was getting dark outside.

Since no white car was found on the premises, he wondered if the defendant's records were looked into, checked for both personal and business owned or leased vehicles—especially for a white one—possibly a Cadillac. It was a no brainer . . . if such a car wasn't found; it couldn't be impounded and searched. More than likely, Lehmann took care of making the car disappear. There seemed to be a pattern here, James reasoned. Still curious, he'd do his own background search to see if such a car existed on paper.

Following the search team to the 3rd floor, it looked like they'd entered a maze of hallways and doors before emerging into a room resembling an office but full of ornate furniture . . . not surprising because of Lehmann's business. They systematically removed and labeled several items—the biggest one—his desk computer. They briefly videoed an adjacent bathroom and storage room . . . again taking and labeling a few more items.

Setting aside the plastic bags of gathered items into boxes and paper sacks, the search team moved on to a large room filled with furniture, T V screens, and an especially long bar area. He stopped the disk and backed it up. Why was there a large round piece of furniture in the center of the room? It seemed out of place, and why were there spotlights above it? What would be the purpose of such a piece of furniture while entertaining guests and clients? It reminded him of a big round bed advertized for a fancy hotel's honeymoon suite.

Moving on, there were several bedrooms with their own bathrooms. They too seemed extravagant and excessive but the explanations given by Lehmann's assistant seemed plausible. Each bedroom area was videoed, including closets, shelves of toys and games, and its adjoining bathroom. So far, each bedroom seemed identical in size and contents to the others. A few items were also labeled and placed in plastic bags. Sometimes, it was difficult to see the exact items placed in the bags, but all were carefully gathered under protocol rules of evidence.

As the last bedroom was videoed—scanning the room as before—the camera moved across a shelf of toys. James stopped the video, backed it up, and played it again . . . three times. Whoa, is that what I think it is? Could the little brown doll in the middle of the others be Jennifer's? If so, it must have been missed during clean-up operations. He couldn't help but wonder if the doll was still there. Backing up the disk, James looked carefully at the toy shelves in the other bedrooms . . . no such doll.

Following a moment's exhilaration, reality set in. Even if another search warrant was issued, or Carly identified the doll, or DNA proved it belonged to Jennifer, it wouldn't matter. Lehmann had already been charged with kidnapping and acquitted.

As his excitement was replaced with despair, James began to sweat. It had nothing to do with the room's temperature. Damn, double jeopardy would apply. While his mind told him to remain calm, his mouth said out loud to the empty room, "I'll get you somehow . . . you creepy son of a bitch."

While wiping the perspiration off his forehead and deciding how to proceed, his phone rang. He recognized the caller's number, so answered, "Hi Sam, got something for me?"

"Well, that depends. Do you want the good or bad news first?"

"It doesn't matter," James answered somberly, still fixated on the doll and the double jeopardy situation.

"Found your person, but he's deceased. Seems he was in Vegas gambling. The theory is . . . he left the casino and was killed for his money. The last time he was seen, he was getting into a black SUV. Security cameras failed to catch the license numbers but noted it was a California plate."

"That's interesting. How does a homeless guy get money to gamble in Vegas . . . even get there from San Francisco?" While responding out loud with a question to Sam—but not expecting an answer—James was thinking . . . none of what Sam said made logical sense.

"I hear what you're saying. I'll e-mail the particulars, dates, etc in an hour or so. The gambling was some time ago; the body found recently in a shallow grave in the desert."

"Thanks Sam. It sounds like cleaning up loose ends to me. I was mulling over talking to other homeless people in the area but won't now. Besides, I doubt they'd be cooperative anyway."

"No problem Bro. Are you okay? You sound down."

"I'm bummed. I've been helping my dad's friend with a missing kid situation . . . actually the friend's granddaughter. I just found evidence to do the perp in, but it's after the fact. He's already been acquitted of kidnapping."

"James, don't do anything rash. I know how you get when an assignment doesn't pan-out. Maybe you're getting too personally involved. James, listen to me, before you do something you'll regret, let's brainstorm."

With no comment from James, Sam continued, "On a lighter note, I'm working on a case you'd enjoy. A woman suspects her husband of infidelity. I'm getting some great shots of the guy misbehaving."

"Is that what you're calling it these days?"

"What can I say? It's voyeurism at its best, and I get paid for it too," Sam answered with a chuckle.

"Save some of those good shots for me," James uttered . . . trying to sound up-lifted but could care less at the moment. If he sounded down, it was because he was. Wanting to get off the phone, James said, "Thanks again for the information. I appreciate it."

"You got it. See you soon and perk up. I'm sure you'll figure it out."

Okay, he thought. The disk was good news—or maybe good news—if he could get the doll verified. At least he'd have proof that scumbag Lehmann was definitely involved in Jennifer's disappearance. The phone call was not good news, but he'd hang on to what Sam was sending. It might be useful or lead to something later.

What now? Off to check out the 3rd floor of Lehmann's building . . . but again only from the street. He'd try to come up with a plan to somehow enter the third floor . . . maybe even retrieve the doll. Most likely, his thoughts were only wishful thinking. Worse than the double jeopardy scenario, where was Jennifer? If dead, no way could Lehmann be charged with murder unless a body was found. Like the witness, Jennifer was most likely in a grave somewhere. But unlike the witness, the possibility of her ever being found seemed slim.

Could she have been taken and hidden away. The latter would be the lesser of two evils. It was all too horrible and depressing. It was like breadcrumbs leading him to nowhere, and there was nothing he could do about it. Each bit of new information was beginning to wear on his emotions. He could feel himself getting sucked in. While telling himself to quit with the personal involvement and get back on an objective level, he knew it would be difficult to shut down his feelings . . . if not impossible. Besides, he didn't want it to.

James glanced at the blueprints again. An elevator was located on each side of the building. The most interesting discovery, both went from the ground floor to the 3rd floor. He then looked at the permits and remodeling plans, nothing showed any change to the elevators. Without the video, he wouldn't have known differently. He wondered if an elevator could be programmed to advance in a certain way. It made sense it could, but he'd add finding out for sure to his to-do list.

Whether personal or not—and not caring—James thoughts returned to Lukas, wondering what his exact medical condition was all about. Was he dying soon? How long did he have? Gosh, he hated to know something Lukas's own family didn't know. That didn't seem right.

Whether personal or not—and still not caring—he thought about Carly but not in an investigative way. He couldn't remember the last time a woman had affected him this way—if ever—and in such a short time. He'd learned a lot about relationships during and after his time with Margie. Since then, he'd discovered how to be flirtatious and say the common come-ons, but no one had captured his attention like Carly had, yet he barely knew her. Each time he thought of her, he saw her dark discerning eyes, along with an uncharacteristic desire to protect her. He wanted to learn everything about her. He wanted to dig into her life . . . especially her past. While knowing he was there to find Jennifer or to at least discover something about her fate, he was more fixated on Carly. What was wrong with him? He needed to get his priorities straight. Besides, he'd be leaving for Los Angeles soon.

Okay self, what would it hurt to find a library where he could look up information on Carly. What the heck; just a quick stop on the way to Lehmann's property. But first things first, he was really hungry. Perhaps, he was the one who was bi-polar. He could feel his mind jumping back and forth from one subject to another, his moods moving up and down, and then back up again.

*   *   *   *

Before walking into the library, James checked his money clip, wondering how much they'd charge to access information. Probably a lot . . . everything in Frisco was expensive, he reasoned.

After asking the librarian where he could find the archive section and if microfilm was available, he inquired about how the charges were handled. "It's on the third floor, room 303. You can buy a library card or pay a onetime fee. It's up to you." Learning a library card was cheaper—although never using it again—he was off to look into Carly's involvement with a criminal serving time.

Referring to notes taken while speaking with Charlotte, he started with the San Francisco Chronicle. After keying in a name and an approximate time frame, a picture of a man popped up along with pictures of two women . . . but neither looked like Carly. Also, there was a picture of an unnamed woman being placed into an ambulance. It wasn't a stretch to believe Carly was the woman on the gurney surrounded by paramedics. Reading through the article, the word "alleged" must have been used at least five times. The heading read: Wealthy Businessman Keeps Slave Den.

Next article's caption: Local Businessman Jailed. Both articles were difficult to read . . . worse than awful, downright sickening. No wonder Carly was hesitant to discuss her past. Although constantly referred to as victim, he had no doubt it was Carly. It was impossible to imagine what it must have been like for her . . . locked away for years.

Next article: Conviction for Businessman. Pictures of a mansion on a manicured estate in an affluent neighborhood took up several columns. The newspaper gave few details about the victims but did say one victim was from Thailand. Nothing was written about how or when the Thailand victim arrived in America, or how she became a captive. The words torture and sexual abuse were used throughout the conviction story. None of the articles disclosed either a first or last name for any of the victims. He'd like to ask Carly if she'd testified in court against her captor as she had against Lehmann, but at this point he wouldn't reveal—maybe never—having any knowledge of what happened to her. Okay, he'd read enough.

On the drive to Lehmann's property, it was difficult to clear his mind of what he'd read and the pictures he'd seen, but approaching his destination, his thoughts quickly changed back to reality. Understandably, Lehmann and his building needed to be his focal point and deserved his full attention. He believed Carly and what the witness stated on the police report. After seeing the doll, he had a better understanding of what he thought transpired there. Fearing the worst, the appropriately named Creep had gotten away with whatever happened on the third floor of his building. Jennifer was there; now she wasn't. Where was she?

Observing the building, the only thing that stuck out was the lack of windows on the third floor . . . why? The obvious reason . . . Lehmann didn't want anyone to see what was going on inside. Why the secrecy and who'd want to look into the third floor of a warehouse building . . . even with binoculars? What was he hiding? Too many questions were running rampant through his mind . . . and more scattered breadcrumbs. Regardless of the rhetoric, why the large area unless many people were involved? Someone . . . somewhere knew the answers to what was being hidden there. The worst part of where the breadcrumbs were leading, doubts were surfacing about his ability to successfully find the answers.

He decided not to say anything to Carly about the witness being murdered. Whether or not her feelings were justified; she was clearly afraid for her safety. Before learning of the witness's fate, he'd considered her uneasiness unfounded. Now . . . it was definitely food for thought. However, he did need Carly to identify the doll, and that was really gonna be tough on her.

Chapter 20

"Hi Carly, how's it going?" James asked, using Charlotte's words.

"I'm fine. Did you forget to ask me something?"

"No, I was just thinking about you."

"Really? Did I talk too much when we were at Buster's?" she questioned but pleased—bordering on excited—to hear his voice again.

"Of course not. I was wondering if you'd mind looking at a video to see if you could possibly recognize anything on it.

"Like what? I don't understand," Carly replied in a questioning manner.

"Could I meet you at your office and show you, or do you still feel uncomfortable about meeting with me?"

Without commenting, she answered, "I'm free most of the day, so whenever it's convenient for you."

"Okay, I'll see you after lunch . . . like around two . . . give or take fifteen minutes. I'll try not to be late this time."

Five minutes after two o'clock, James knocked on Carly's office door and waited to be invited in. After receiving an almost instantaneous, "Come in," James entered, finding Carly standing behind her desk with a genuine smile on her face. Smiling back, he turned to make sure the door remained open. To his surprise she said, "It's okay to close the door."

James placed his laptop on the corner of her desk before asking, "Can I bring a chair over next to you, so we can watch the screen together?"

"Sure, whatever you think is best."

Having a pleasant back and forth with Carly and enjoying one surprise after another, James hated to get down to business. However, there was soon to be one more surprise, and it wouldn't be a pleasant one.

"Before I start the disk, let me kinda prepare you for what you'll see. James began giving Carly an over-view of the inside of Lehmann's building before saying, "If you recognize anything, tell me to stop . . . okay?"

Beginning to tremble, Carly quietly replied, "Okay."

While Carly watched intently, she clasped her hands tightly together on her lap. As her eyes remained riveted on the screen, she sometimes looked confused, even frowned but didn't ask any questions. When the search team entered the last bedroom, James watched both the computer screen and for Carly's reaction. He didn't need to wait long.

She immediately let out a gasp; her knees hitting beneath the desk, jarring his laptop. Already knowing the reason for her reaction, James asked anyway, "What's the matter?"

Shaking uncontrollably, Carly stammered, "Please stop it. It's Jennifer's doll."

"Are you sure?" James asked. Since her reaction was even more extreme than anticipated, he was trying to decide how best to handle the situation and calm her down. She looked like a captured animal searching for a place to hide in an empty cage.

Instead of answering, she began to cry. Feeling helpless and although he tried, James couldn't decipher a single word Carly was mumbling. He wanted somehow to comfort her. Should he offer to hold her? That's what he'd done with countless others—both men and women—when giving devastating news . . . life shattering news. Part of his hesitation was due to the recently read newspaper articles . . . afraid to reach out and touch her. Although the doll was important in the broad scheme of things, he felt responsible for placing Carly in this position in the first place. He also felt guilty for underestimating her reaction. Understandably, the doll was Carly's last connection to Jennifer.

"Carly, please calm down," James finally said.

Instead of answering, she clumsily stood and began to pace erratically around the room, circling near the walls. "What to do? What to do?" she kept repeating over and over in a chanting fashion.

Afraid others would burst in—thinking he was harming her—James stepped in front of her and held out his arms. Amazingly, she melted into him but continued to sob and repeat, "What to do?"

Gently patting her on the back, he wondered . . . what should I do? "Okay, let's sit down and talk about this,"

James said quietly into her ear.

Carly allowed him to gently direct her to the pushed back desk chair. James watched as she sat down, retrieved a tissue from a desk drawer, and began to wipe her eyes; her hands noticeably quivering. Relieved she'd somewhat settled down, he returned to the chair next to her.

Carly's throat tightened, making it difficult to speak. In a course voice, she said, "Shouldn't we call the police?"

"I'm afraid calling the police will do no good," he answered as definitely and as composed as he could.

"What do you mean? They should arrest him. I'll tell them it's Jennifer's doll. I'll swear to it."

"Carly, please calm down. You're worrying me. Lehmann can't be tried again for kidnapping. He's been acquitted of that crime."

"That's wrong . . . you must be wrong. There's proof now."

"I wish I was wrong, but that's the law."

"Then, the law's wrong," Carly stated with a mixture of disgust and helplessness. "Something's gotta be done, or he'll be free to take another child. God knows where she is. I lie in bed every night wondering how she is or where she is. I also pray for you to find her and bring her home."

James could almost read her mind. She was probably wondering why he was there to investigate if nothing could be done. The silence and tension was thick between them. While knowing the tension stemmed directly from Carly, he'd created the situation by finding the doll and showing it to her. A loss for words, James did what made the most sense; he sat quietly beside her.

Carly's brain was like a whirl-wind, swirling around and picking up events of atrocities from her past. James watched Carly's dark eyes narrow before she clearly said, "Will this nightmare ever end?"

"Carly, I'm trying to find her. I've been following Lehmann in-between doing other things, but he basically goes from his home to work and back. He's never been married and has no children, seemingly has no personal life. He does travel a lot for business purposes. Short of breaking and entering his house and business, I'm finding little to go on or making much progress. I'm sorry about surprising you with the video. I was fairly sure you'd recognize the doll. Maybe I should have just described it. That way, it would have been easier on you."

Carly took a deep breath. "It's not your fault. You're just doing your job."

James wanted to tell her about knowing what took place before she lived with Charlotte. His curiosity was full of questions to ask, knowing the newspaper articles were just tips of many icebergs. However, it was a no-brainer that now was not the time to bring it up. He'd done enough damage already. Perhaps another time . . . if ever, he considered.

Breaking the silence, James asked, "Carly, would you like to go to dinner with me tonight?"

"Why," she asked puzzled. "I've told you everything I know and everything that happened that day."

Shamefully reverting back to a "poor me" come-on, he said, "I'm pretty lonely away from home and really don't have anyone to talk to."

"I can't tonight. I have other plans," she answered but dropped her eyes.

That figures, he thought, almost mockingly . . . returning to a hidden nerdy place. She'd allowed him to be alone with her, so pretty sure she wasn't afraid of him any longer. Taking her remark as a personal put-down, his conclusion on her refusal was pretty evident . . . she just didn't like him.

When it came to his occupation, he knew what to do and what to say. But when it came to women, he was careful not to place himself in the position of being rejected. He'd learned not to be impulsive . . . weighing his options of not pursuing anyone considered out of his personal reach. However, in Carly's case and in spite of her remark, he didn't want to give up.

To cover up his uncomfortable feeling of rejection, James joked, "I can't believe your plans could be more important than having dinner with me." Pausing, he added flippantly, "I guess you just don't like me. That hurts."

Carly shifted, feeling exposed . . . chastising herself for being untruthful to James. Why had she said that? Worse yet, he probably knew she was being dishonest.

"That's not true," she answered flatly.

"What's not true?" James questioned, outwardly toying with her.

Carly's face went to a rosy pink before becoming a bright shade of red. Folding her arms across her chest—a known defensive pose—she offered, "Well, maybe another time."

James continued to press her. "I'll only be here in San Francisco for another week. Maybe we could go to dinner this weekend . . . unless you also have plans for the weekend too. Would that be a possibility?"

"I guess that would be okay," she answered hesitantly.

"Well, that's not a very enthusiastic reply, but I'll take it you don't totally dislike me."

Carly stared at the ceiling, trying to think of how to answer James. She realized when saying "other plans," the conversation would become strained. It had nothing to do with not liking him; rather it was all about not knowing how to act or converse outside the investigation. Not only regarding the investigation, but anywhere with anybody on a personal level. She'd managed to protect herself for years, keeping herself clear of stressful situations. Charlotte was right. She didn't need to be protected from James, so maybe it was more about placing herself in a position where she didn't need protection. It was such new territory, like . . . what to do, how to act, what to say, and what not to say. If not about the investigation, why would James want to have dinner with me? She needed to talk to Charlotte again but already knew what Charlotte would tell her.

"I'll give you my cell number. I keep my phone with me at all times. It's like my security blanket," she answered softly.

Handing James the number, Carly felt the gesture would show him she didn't dislike him. Looking directly into his eyes, she asked, "Will you promise to keep looking for Jennifer?"

Damn, she was hard to gauge. Had she offered to stay in contact in order to keep informed about Jennifer?

"Are you doing okay," James asked. Before receiving an answer, he added, "I need to leave to follow-up on a few things. Sorry again about the doll bombshell."

"It makes me so sad," Carly answered, tears welling in her eyes again.

James wanted to take her in his arms and tell her everything would be all right. Yet, all the while thinking—even knowing—it wouldn't. When he held her before, it wasn't a sexual feeling . . . more of a protective and comforting gesture. Whether imagined or not, he could still smell her perfume inhaled before helping her back to her desk. Although aware of Carly's emotional problems related to her horrible past, he had to acknowledge—just to himself—that he desired her. How mixed up was that?

Watching James leave, Carly picked up the phone to call Charlotte. She wanted to tell her about seeing the doll and ask for help if she went to dinner with James . . . not if, but when.

Chapter 21

After learning of Lukas's circumstances, James hesitated to tell him Carly recognized Jennifer's doll in Lehmann's building. It would be devastating news and like Carly, Lukas would want to do something about it. Hell, he wanted to do something about it but hadn't quite come to terms with exactly what. Usually, his involvement was more about gathering evidence in preparation for a trial, but since there had already been a trial, this investigation had become totally different. His original purpose for being there was to search previously discovered information for leads to hopefully locate Jennifer—new eyes on the case—so to speak. Now he was dealing with this double jeopardy situation and feeling more and more discouraged.

Without any doubts, James was certain Lehmann took Jennifer—evidenced by the doll in his possession, Carly's intuition into his behavior, and the witness's changed statement and suspicious death. He was determined to uncover Lehmann's specific motive and if he worked alone. Even better . . . if he could trap him before he did something terrible again. Carly was right—along with his own gut feeling—something like this was bound to happen again.

Thinking of his involvement in similar cases, the

word—pedophile—had yet to be openly used. His expertise told him Lehmann's 3rd floor space wasn't set up for a one-time occurrence. His problem, unless something came to light within the next week, he would be out of time and out of luck. He found himself repeating Carly's words, "What to do . . . what to do?"

Sitting in his car, James pulled out his notebook, combing through the lined out items before placing checkmarks next to the items he planned to pursue in the next couple of days. Realizing it was already late Thursday and many of the places he needed to visit were closed on the week-end, the remainder of today and tomorrow were left to follow through with them.

Would tonight be too soon to call Carly and make arrangements for dinner Saturday . . . two days away? Would he appear needy—which he was—when it came to seeing her again?

Not wanting to stay in the Boys and Girls parking lot and make calls, he moved a few blocks away and parked. As he made his first phone call, he lined through the check-marked item at the top of his list.

"Hi Janet, this is James Allen," he said when recognizing Janet's voice.

"Hi Mr. Allen, it's good to hear from you again."

"I have some personal questions to ask regarding your Aunt Charlotte. Would you mind calling me when you're not on official time?"

"Well, I'm about to take a break. Give me five minutes or so."

"Thanks Janet."

"Talk to you soon, Mr. Allen."

Within seven minutes, Janet called back. "So, what's up with my Aunt Charlotte?"

"Nothing . . . there's no problem. I just wanted to discuss a couple of things and didn't want to talk on a recorded line."

"Gotcha. What can I do for you?"

"First, let me thank you again for the report and video. They've been extremely helpful."

"Good to know."

"Do you know if the white car—possibly a Cadillac—was checked out for Lehmann or his company? Per the report, no such car was found at the location."

After an extended pause, James asked, "Are you still there?"

"Yes, I'm here. I'll try to find out. Hang on, I'm writing this down on a napkin. I'm sitting at an outside break table, and it's pretty breezy out here."

"Sorry to ask but DMV wasn't helpful. In Los Angeles I have connections but couldn't get anywhere here. Also, I don't know if you've heard, but Carly recognized Jennifer's doll on the search warrant video . . . the doll with her when she disappeared."

"Holy shit . . . ah, sorry for the language."

Ignoring her remark—he'd heard and used much worse—so continued, "I really felt sorry for Carly. She got pretty upset. Her reaction got even worse when I told her Lehmann couldn't be tried for the same crime again.

I'm not sure she believed me."

"That sucks . . . doesn't it?" Janet responded, seemingly aware of the double jeopardy status.

"Something else, your aunt mentioned a lady who called police and helped Carly. She also told me—as far as she knew—the lady was never personally thanked. Would you feel comfortable giving me the lady's name? I think it would make Carly happy to thank her. If the lady is still in the area, I'd be happy to take Carly to meet her. It just dawned on me; that might not work. What if Carly doesn't want to return to the neighborhood where her catastrophe occurred? Perhaps, Carly could just give her a call. The paper referred to the witness as a person living in the neighborhood . . . not necessarily a lady . . . possibly to protect her."

Answering, "Either way would be nice but solely up to Carly's preference. I don't know why I didn't think of initiating something like that before. I'll get back to you on that too."

"I haven't mentioned to Carly my knowledge of those events. What's your opinion? I can't very well know about the person who called the police, if I don't know about her imprisonment."

"I hear ya. I'll give it some thought. Maybe Aunt Charlotte can advise us."

"One last thing . . . has there been a fire safety inspection done on Lehmann's property? I find it interesting there is only one entrance and exit to and from the 3rd floor via an elevator. That seems out of code to me. There are fire escape stairs on the blueprints, but I didn't see any fire exit doors in the video."

"Hang on a moment, need to turn the napkin over," Janet said, sounding frustrated.

"Sorry to lay all this on you, but you've been so helpful. Since I'm pushed for time, I want to come up with something before I leave. Naturally, I want to find Jennifer but having doubts about that happening."

"I understand and appreciate your efforts . . . no matter how this turns out. By the way my aunt is thrilled Carly has taken a liking to you."

"I don't think so, but she's partly right. At least Carly isn't keeping her office door open like when I first talked to her. She also seems a tad more relaxed. By the way, your aunt is really easy to talk to. Carly is lucky to have her for a friend. In fact, I told Charlotte the same thing when we met."

"Okay, my break-time is over. It's back to work for me."

"Janet, thanks again for your assistance."

"Glad to do it. Again, this can't go any further, or I'll be in big trouble."

"As before, you have my word. Carly has no idea where the video came from. I don't think she'd even care . . . too absorbed in seeing the doll."

"I'll get back to you on your questions," Janet stated. Then, added, "It might be the first of next week. I gotta go."

"Oh, I almost forgot and one quick thing. The witness

who changed his story was found dead in a shallow grave in the desert close to Las Vegas."

"Are you f'ing kidding me? You can tell me more when we talk again."

While responding, "Thanks and later," James liked Janet's upfront attitude.

*   *   *   *

Back in his hotel room after a quick drive-through . . . his burger and fries eaten while driving, James tossed his jacket on a chair and turned on the T V. As he watched the news, his attention remained stuck on Carly . . . unable to get the memory of her sad face and accompanying tears out of his thoughts.

Looking around the room, it was definitely time for a major clean-up. Once he stretched out on the bed, he knew nothing would get done. After pushing trash in the already over-flowing small trash can and placing dirty clothes in a plastic bag, he sat down on the bed next to the partially folded blueprints. Deciding to take one last look at them before putting them away, he looked again at the stairwells in the back of the building, plainly visible on the original plans but not on the video. Unable to see the building from the back, this seemed more than suspicious. More breadcrumbs, he thought.

He glanced around the room again, hoping he'd made some improvement, but it still looked messy and out of sorts, deciding tomorrow not to put the sign out, letting housekeeping come in and do a basic clean job. And tomorrow before leaving, he'd be extra careful not to leave anything important behind . . . like his computer.

In the back of his mind, Carly's reaction to the doll kept returning. He wondered if she'd adjusted to the bad news and doing better. Okay self, you've got her number, so why not call and ask her. He looked at his watch . . . six o'clock. Would she be home from work yet? Only one way to find out, he nervously pressed in her number.

Listening to the phone ring, he concentrated on what he planned to say when she answered. Instead of her answering, it went to a phone company's voice mail. He found it interesting she hadn't recorded a personal message . . . letting the caller know they'd reached a particular number and to leave a message. But then, giving it more thought and Carly's reserved demeanor, it seemed typical.

After leaving a short message, James reasoned maybe she was not home, not close enough to hear the phone, or had it set on vibrate. Perhaps she was taking a shower, outside for some reason, or listening to loud music. These were only a few of the many reasons he'd not answered his phone, learning later of missed calls. Giving up on the possibilities of why she didn't pick up, James decided to give it a half-hour or so and try again.

In the back of his mind . . . what if she's actually in peril? Remembering Charlotte's remark about Carly never going anywhere after dark, and Carly saying she kept the phone with her at all times, it made him wonder . . . bordering on concerned. Deciding he was being over-dramatic, he'd pick up the room a little more before calling again . . . in exactly twenty-five minutes.

Chapter 22

After leaving five voice messages and nearly an hour's drive, James arrived in the vicinity of Carly's residence. By the time he reached her actual address, it was almost eight o'clock. His biggest concern wasn't Carly not answering but not receiving a single call back from her. At first, he considered she might be ignoring him on purpose, but if she'd not wanted him to call, why offer a number in the first place. It also crossed his mind—but quickly disregarded—she'd purposely given him a wrong number. Bottom line, what if she was in danger, and he'd not checked on her?

James recognized Carly's car, having noticed it before in a reserved parking spot for the Activity Director. As he drove slowly past her house a second time, he concentrated on the surroundings. It appeared quiet and secluded . . . the house set back from the road among tall pine trees.

There were no street lights and traffic was non-existent; the only visible light coming from Carly's front porch. He parked close-by in an inconspicuous place and felt his waistband to adjust his weapon. He quietly walked toward the front of the house, all the while listening for any uncommon sounds. Even though her curtains and blinds were closed, faint light from inside was noticeable. During normal surveillance operations, he would have walked the perimeter of the house, scouting for the best vantage point. But in this case, he decided to first see if Carly answered the door.

When he knocked, the sound of intense and aggressive barking commenced immediately. The barking was forceful and concentrated near the front door. He couldn't decide how many dogs were barking, but knew the barking came from at least two dogs and they were large.

James called out, "Carly, it's me . . . James."

Out of the corner of his eye, James saw a curtain pulled an inch or so away from a nearby window.

Even though clearly seeing James standing outside the front door, Carly hollered above the barking, "Who's there?"

"It's James Allen," he answered, knowing she'd already recognized him . . . plainly visible under the porch light.

The barking ceased, as soon as he heard Carly say, "Quiet." After a minute or so, James heard multiple locks—at least three—being unlocked. As the door partly opened, a metal chain held it from opening completely. Instead of saying how worthless the chain would be in protecting her from an intruder—one strong shoulder or kick would do it in—he asked, "Are you okay?"

Instead of answering his question, Carly asked, "Why are you here?"

As his facial features changed from nervous concern to a more composed expression, he got right to the point. "I was worried about you. Did you get any of my messages?" Waiting for her to respond, he had mixed emotions. He was glad she was okay but felt a tad foolish for driving all the way to her house to check on her. Falling back into a dramatic mode, was it possible she was still in danger with a gun to her back? Better to be completely sure all is well and be cool, he thought.

"I've been busy cleaning out a spare room. Guess I didn't hear the phone. Are you sure you called the right number?"

"I feel silly standing out here. Can I come in?" James asked.

"Just a minute and I'll put the dogs away."

When Carly finally opened the door, she stood in front of James; her heart racing. "What are you really doing here?" she asked in disbelief.

"I told you. I called several times. I was worried about you."

Frowning, Carly stepped aside so James could enter. A few steps into the house, Carly offered, "As you can see, I'm fine." While feeling awkward—if his reason for being there was really on the up-and-up—she was amazed by his concern. Another first, she'd never been alone with a man in her home sanctuary before. Now what, she wondered?

"Well, that's good news. I'm relieved," James responded promptly.

"How did you find me?" Carly questioned.

"Duh . . . I have my ways. Besides, that's what I do. It's the Sherlock Holmes part of my disposition," he answered before smiling widely.

"I'm sorry. Would you like to sit down?" she asked, feeling ill at ease and back to . . . now what? Since he mentioned Sherlock Holmes, she could ask if he liked books written by Sir Arthur Conan Doyle. Arguing with herself . . . no, he didn't drive out here to discuss his likes and dislikes in literature.

Carly studied James as he walked past her and across the room. He looked different out of his sport coat and open collared shirt. He was wearing faded jeans, a bulky grey sweatshirt, and tennis shoes. His blond hair had been tossed by the wind; his face relaxed without hints of a business mannerism.

Watching James take a seat on her small couch, a strange shiver ran down her spine. "You look different without your sport coat," Carly remarked.

"I feel different," James answered while thinking . . . I wish she wanted to reach out and touch me and see first-hand how I feel. As he continued to smile at Carly, he kept thinking . . . she has absolutely no idea what I just thought about or why I'm smiling. He and Carly were opposite in so many ways with nothing in common. Speculating . . . maybe that was the attraction. Remembering back to how different he and Margie were should have given him pause, but it didn't. Rationalizing, the attraction was different this time, because he was different this time.

Carly didn't want to stand in front of James and talk, nor did she want to sit next to him on the couch. Either option seemed weird. Never having a need before to sit and talk in the living room, she opened a folding chair and sat across from him on the opposite side of the room. Still intrigued by his caring enough to drive to her house, she'd never been in this position before, having no clue how to behave. Let's see . . . what would Charlotte do?

"Would you like something to drink?" she asked, while doing her best to pretend she did this—entertained as Charlotte would call it—often.

"Sure . . . what are my choices?" James asked with another big smile.

Nervously smiling back, Carly replied, "I'm not sure what I have to offer. Usually, I don't have a guest over at this late hour. Well, if I'm being totally honest, I've never had an almost stranger to my house ever . . . at any hour."

"So, I've moved up in status from stranger to almost stranger," he quizzed.

Feeling ill at ease, Carly squirmed in her chair before saying, "I'm going to see what I can find. I'll be right back."

James watched Carly leave the room. She seemed to drift out of the space like a willow branch in the breeze. Damn, did I really think that? Okay, and to my defense, maybe it had something to do with the flowing green top she was wearing and her graceful gait.

Carly could sense James's eyes on her but didn't feel afraid. She didn't think it possible not be in absolute control . . . not weighing each and every decision in advance . . . when to go, where to go, and what to do. But here she was, looking in the refrigerator and pantry for something to offer James to drink.

Returning to the living room, she said, "I have orange juice, an old bottle of wine, and water. Sorry for the few choices. Oh, I could make coffee or tea."

"Let's see. It's too late for coffee, and I'm not much of a tea drinker. Orange juice would be okay, but let's give the wine a try."

"I hope it'll taste all right. Charlotte gave it to me when I moved in . . . a long time ago."

"I usually drink beer, but I've heard wine gets better with age."

"I've heard that too. I'll be right back."

A few minutes later, Carly returned without the wine. "I have a confession to make," she quickly announced.

Uh . . . oh, he thought. She's probably going to talk about her captivity but why now . . . why at this moment? Couldn't they first have a nice glass or two of wine and get to know each other. However, his assumption of Carly coming clean about her past was way off-base when she stated, "I've never opened a wine bottle before. Would you come and help me?"

Relieved they weren't getting into something heavy, James replied, "Sure."

Once the bottle was opened and a small amount poured into two regular drinking glasses, Carly suggested, "Would you mind to taste it first?" Quickly followed with, "No use both of us getting sick," said with a chuckle.

"If you insist, I guess I can be the guinea pig," James uttered.

Not a wine person and not knowing what to expect, James cautiously took a sip. Obvious by his scrunched face, it tasted awful. With pursed lips and eyes wide open, James looked around for a place to spit it out. Aware of his dilemma, Carly pointed to the sink and laughed.

After empting his mouth, James grabbed a nearby paper towel, wiped his mouth, and shuddered. "Yuck, it tasted awful . . . like a mixture of rotten eggs and spoiled vinegar. It's not fair to laugh; I saved you from it."

"You're right. I'm sorry for laughing. I've got an idea. How about I fix some hot chocolate?"

"Great idea. Hot chocolate sounds perfect. Where can I rinse out my mouth?"

While handing James a clean glass, Carly answered, "Follow me and I'll show you where the bathroom is." Almost at the bathroom door, Carly added, "I'm sorry for asking you to taste it."

Surprised by Carly's personal attitude—going out of her way to make him feel comfortable—he rinsed his mouth and ran his fingers through his unruly hair, wondering if he could hold off on a hair cut until back home.

Returning to the kitchen, James asked, "Do you want me to stay here while you fix the hot chocolate, or should I go back to the living room?"

"Wherever's more comfortable," was Carly's quick response.

James would have preferred her to give her preference, but since she didn't, he sat down at the small kitchen table and watched her gather the hot chocolate ingredients before removing two cups from the cupboard.

While busy preparing their drinks, Carly more or less ignored James and thought of what Charlotte told her about going to dinner with him. James won't harm you. James won't rape you. You'll be safe with James, so enjoy the moment and embark on a new adventure.

"Is this okay . . . ah, staying here in the kitchen?" Carly asked, placing the cups down on the table.

"This is nice and easier for us to talk," James answered.

Silent for a moment while both sipped their hot chocolate, Carly finally said, "Thank you for coming to see if I was okay." While James seemed to be watching her intently as she spoke, she wished she could read his thoughts. Did he really understand how grateful she was to have him care enough to check on her safety? Each time she was with James, the numbness disappeared, and she felt alive as a person. And each kind gesture by James reminded her of how opposite her life was becoming from before. There was something almost magical about the way she felt in his presence. These were new feelings, and she wasn't quite sure how to process them. Was she just over-reacting to his kindness? It suddenly dawned on her . . . it wasn't right or fair to James, that he didn't know the truth about her.

"Why have you become so quiet?" James asked, worried she'd gone to a dark place. Afraid she might ask him to leave at any moment, he said, "Before I hit the road, will you go to dinner with me Saturday?"

Without hesitation, Carly stated, "Yes, I would like to." Then with hesitation, she added, "I must tell you about myself. When you find out about me, you probably won't want to take me anywhere. If you don't mind to wait a minute, I need to find my phone and make sure it's working. I'll be right back."

Certain Carly was about to divulge what he already knew, he wondered how best to receive the news . . . either candid about knowing or with surprise. From somewhere beyond the kitchen, Carly hollered, "James, my phone is gone. That's why I didn't hear it."

Standing, he met her at the kitchen doorway. "Are you sure? Where did you have it last?"

"I don't remember, but I always have it with me. I'm lost without it."

"Don't panic. Where do you normally keep it?" James asked calmly.

"In my purse, but I already dumped the contents out. It's gone."

"Maybe you left it at work. Could it be in your car?" James asked.

"I don't think so. That's never happened before, but I can't look for it until tomorrow morning."

"Why not?" James asked, looking confused.

"Because it's dark out. I know that sounds dumb, but I just can't."

"I don't understand. Are you afraid?" James asked, trying to be understanding.

Dropping her head, Carly mumbled, "Yes."

"Even with me here?" James responded with a tilted head and questioning look.

Without specifically addressing his remark, Carly asked, "Will you go out and look with me?"

"How about I go and look for the phone? You can wait inside. Is your car locked?"

Not answering his question, yet determined to face another fear, "No, I want to do this . . . with you,"

They walked outside together into the crisp night air with no moon; the only light coming from Carly's porch light. James considered taking Carly's hand but decided against it. Since venturing out after dark was already a new experience, he didn't want to further complicate the situation by making her more uncomfortable.

And there the phone was . . . resting in plain sight on the passenger seat. Hastily grabbing it—like a lost treasure—Carly offered, "I keep my purse on the passenger seat; it must have fallen out. I guess I was hurrying inside . . . concentrating on cleaning the spare bedroom, and all I needed to do. I tend to get absorbed in projects that keep me busy . . . especially ones I've put off for a long time."

Stepping up the porch stairs, James turned and looked directly at Carly. "I'm glad your phone was left in the car.

If not, I wouldn't be here having hot chocolate with you."

Carly smiled—a facial expression he was getting used to seeing—before saying, "I think I need to heat some more."

Settling into the kitchen again with fresh hot chocolates before them, Carly asked, "I should tell you about myself, or do you need to leave?"

"It's your call," James answered with a sigh. While knowing what she was about to say, he felt compelled to emphatically say, "Keep in mind . . . no matter what you say; it won't make a difference to me. I want to take you out to dinner . . . on a date."

"I doubt that's true . . . especially after what I'm about to tell you." And so she began. She did not look at him as she recalled her captivity and rescue. After spilling her inner most secrets—leaving some of the worst details out—she continued to keep her head down. Telling James and putting words to her disgusting previous life was more intense than talking to her counselor had been, but it was the right thing to do. She rambled at times but also gave examples. "If I behaved certain ways, I'd be rewarded. If I didn't, I'd be stripped naked and beaten. If I refused to cry, I'd be splashed with alcohol on the open wounds."

When finished, Carly felt drained yet strangely better. She'd spoken the words out loud and not fallen apart. Her world had not crashed down, and she'd not even cried. Feeling strong, Carly could hardly wait to tell Charlotte about everything she'd said and done tonight.

When she looked toward James, he was looking down at his cup . . . as if in a daze. She couldn't help but wonder if he'd been so disgusted by what he'd heard that he couldn't even look at her. His prolonged silence didn't help her figure out the answer. She wanted to know what he was thinking, yet frightened to learn his true thoughts at the same time.

James finally raised his head; his eyes looking at her with admiration before saying, "Thank you for trusting me enough to share what you went through. I can't put into words my reaction to the awful abuse you endured. Even though we've just met, and I hardly know you, I think you are a very courageous person. Let me make this perfectly clear; I would never want you to do or say anything you didn't feel comfortable about. If you don't want to go to dinner with me, it's totally your choice. Pausing briefly and waiting for a comment, James added, "It is getting late, and it's a workday for you tomorrow. Why don't you think about dinner and let me know tomorrow."

"Actually, I'm taking a vacation day tomorrow. The E D told me to use my vacation days or lose them. I would very much like to go to dinner with you, but I'm not finished with being honest about my past. You still might not want to have anything to do with me."

"I'm confused. Didn't I say nothing would matter?" James questioned.

Carly drummed her fingernails against the side of the cup. Her face tightened; her eyes narrowed. "You are a nice person and deserve to know everything about me. I've been empty inside for a long time . . . more or less hiding away, and lost what I'd gained when Jennifer went missing." Not wanting James to interrupt, she continued quickly. "It started in the jungle in Thailand . . . ."

While unable to grasp the enormity of an innocent child being placed in such terrible and uncompromising situations, James listened intently. Her words were far beyond his comprehension.

When Carly finally looked at him, she said, "Now you know about my entire disgusting life. If you never want to talk to me again, I'll understand."

"I not only want to take you to dinner, but want you have fun and the best time ever. So, can I pick you up about seven o'clock Saturday?

"Yes, I'd like that. I have never been on a date before, so I don't want to embarrass you. You're right. It's late, and I'm tired. I've never spoken this much at one time in my whole life. You have a drive back to where you're staying too."

Asking to use the restroom before leaving, James was full of mixed emotions about saying goodbye. Instead of doing what he wanted to do—grabbing her up into his arms, telling her he could hardly wait until Saturday, and kissing her goodbye—he politely thanked her for the hot chocolate. He hoped never to discuss what she'd told him . . . not later, not ever.

"See you at seven . . . it's a date" James said with a

big smile.

Carly's answer back . . . "Okay," followed by a similar big smile.

As James stepped outside onto Carly's front porch, he heard the door close quickly behind, then the clicking of numerous door locks.

Chapter 23

Friday morning and a lot to do, James thought when turning off the alarm. Unable to fall asleep after spending time with Carly, he'd carefully set the alarm clock. Continuing to dwell on what Carly told him, it was past midnight before his mind settled down. Usually an early riser, he didn't want to chance sleeping in, determined to get a head start on what he hoped to accomplish before the week-end.

Before leaving the hotel, he wanted to touch bases with Lukas . . . just to let him know he was still working on finding Jennifer. At this point he didn't plan to mention the doll or the witness's demise—more accurately murder—but would later if the timing seemed appropriate.

Almost ready to leave, he couldn't put the call off any longer. Taking a big breath and hoping his dad's friend would sound more together, he punched in Lukas's number.

"Hello," Lukas answered on the fifth ring.

Sounding okay so far, James said, "Hi Lukas, this is James Allen."

"Yes, did you call me?" Lukas asked slowly.

"I did. How are you today?" James asked, hoping Lukas didn't take his question as a reference to his medical problem but just being cordial. While it took some time for Lukas to respond, his asking if he'd called didn't make sense. Giving him the benefit of the doubt, perhaps Lukas thought he'd called earlier and was unable to get to the phone. Maybe he'd been awakened from a deep sleep. Maybe it was as simple as misunderstanding Lukas's question.

"I'm okay. What day is it?" Lukas inquired clearly.

"It's Friday . . . almost the week-end." James replied.

"Thanks for calling Gabriel. I'm going back to bed. It's late," Lukas said before the phone went silent.

"Okay . . . take care," James answered, fairly certain Lukas didn't hear him.

How perplexing their conversation had been. Lukas was more confused and worse than the last time they'd talked. Before calling Lukas, he'd been apprehensive about keeping information from him, but now knew there was no need for concern. Lukas asked no questions about the investigation, and the questions asked didn't relate to reality. To top it off, Lukas called him Gabriel. If Lukas was his father, no way would he be allowed to live alone. Why Gabriel wasn't told about his father's condition—a major problem of dying—was hard to believe and even harder to understand.

Without Lukas's or his dad's permission, would it be wrong to have a conversation with Gabriel? Did Dad realize how bad it was with Lukas? Considering different options and the right thing to do, he came to a decision. Screw it, if his dad wouldn't talk to Gabriel, he would.

There would be no word games; he'd be up-front and discuss what he knew . . . which wasn't much. It seemed better to go against Lukas's wishes and tell Gabriel than to hide it and be sorry later. Understandably, it was really none of his business; he'd leave it alone for now but call his dad later and have a heart-to-heart talk.

Looking around the room a final time, James picked up what he planned to take, put out the request sign for housekeeping, and locked the door. As he walked down the hall, he couldn't get Lukas off his mind. How sad for the poor guy. Maybe he was confused because of taking drugs, wondering what he was taking and for what reason. More to the point, what was he dying from? How could he hide something so awful from his son? When he talked to Dad, he'd bluff him into spilling everything. If he still refused to tell him exactly what was going on with his friend, his decision to talk to Gabriel would be easier to make.

On a whim James stopped at the hotel's office for a free coffee and breakfast roll. Glad he did; the coffee was hot and the filled do-nut was tasty, deciding the key to finding both fresh and enjoyable was getting there early. He left with a second do-nut, wanting to skip the cost of breakfast.

Once settled in the car, James unlocked the glove compartment. Carefully going through several business cards, he found the one he thought would work.

Passing the restaurant he was taking Carly to for dinner, he parked within a few blocks of Lehmann's building. Having taken extra care in dressing this morning, James thought he looked the part of a casual tourist. Depending on how the conversation went, he could readily fall back on wanting to purchase a gift for a family member back home.

Walking up concrete steps next to a loading dock, he entered the warehouse through a large door opening. "Hello," James said to a man unloading a wooden crate several feet into the huge room.

In broken English the worker asked, "Ju want see boss man?"

Already aware of its existence, James asked, "Is there a place to see objects . . . ah, things?"

Nodding, the worker pointed to the showroom sign and elevator.

After saying, "Thank you," James asked, "Is someone there?"

Receiving another nod, the worker turned back to his unloading duties. Standing inside the elevator but still watching the worker, James pushed the 2 button, noticing the 3 button had been removed. How interesting, he thought. Quickly glancing around, he wondered if he was being taped by security surveillance. Okay, get ready Jack Dutton.

When the elevator opened, nothing seemed changed from the search warrant video. Perhaps the individual objects were different but the set up seemed the same. He took a quick look around the room for an exit sign but didn't see one. As James stepped further into the room, a man—sitting at a desk in the far corner—rose and walked toward him.

After introducing himself as Kenneth Lehmann, he asked, "What can I do for you?"

"My name is Jack Dutton. Let me give you my card. I was recently at a business meeting and told you acquired unique objects from around the world? Since visiting friends in San Francisco for a few days, I thought I'd stop by to see what you have to offer."

"What exactly are you looking for? I see you're located in Los Angeles," Lehmann replied.

"My interest in looking has nothing to do with my Los Angeles business. I'm looking for a personal object . . . something special and difficult to find."

"As I asked before, what type of object are you looking for? Forgive me but who exactly said I have objects from around the world?"

"I didn't say," was James's short and definite answer.

"Perhaps, you would like to browse the exhibits to see if anything fits your fancy. Most of the objects I procure are displayed here."

"And the ones procured but not displayed here?" James asked, purposely looking around in a sinister manner. "While attending the business meeting, I was told many of your objects are displayed on the 3rd floor."

"Yes, but those unique items are displayed only once a year and for a very select group. They are extremely expensive."

"If money is no object, how does one go about

viewing these unique objects?"

Frowning, Lehmann answered, "Credentials, financial records, and other documentations are checked out. It's a time consuming process but well worth it, because these objects are so rare and wonderful."

"Can this process be completed before the next 3rd floor showing?" James asked, prepared to look disappointed.

"I'm afraid not. Our annual display is only three weeks or so away. I don't think vetting can be accomplished by then. I will keep in touch to let you know exactly what is needed."

"Mr. Lehmann, you should be discreet when contacting my personal secretary at the number I gave you."

Although James knew it was necessary, it was difficult to extend his hand to Lehmann. As they shook hands and even though he smiled, he felt disgusted touching him, all the while knowing what a creep and murderer he was.

James calmly left the building and casually walked out of sight. As soon as he turned the corner, he hurried to his car to call Sam.

"Hi Sam, how's it going?" James asked when his friend answered.

"Hi James, the better question, how are you? You sound better than the last time we talked."

"Somewhat better . . . I guess. I'm calling to let you know Jack Dutton is in play."

"Really, we haven't used him in a long time," Sam

replied, sounding excited.

After telling Sam what he'd been doing while in San Francisco—his so-called vacation—and what he'd learned so far in his search for Jennifer, he added, "No way will I get into the 3rd floor—don't want to—but know something will happen there within a few weeks. I'm open to suggestions on how to proceed. Give it some thought. And Sam, be prepared when you talk to Lehmann or whoever and try to get a date for me."

"I will but remember what happened to the witness. These guys aren't messing around, so you also need to watch your back. I'll call as soon as I hear from your new buddy Lehmann or his assistant, or whoever reaches out. I won't let you down. I love it when my acting classes come in handy. I'm stoked."

"You know the drill and what to do. Get as much information as you can while not giving any out. Call as soon as you hear something. And, like Columbo always said, 'Oh, and just one more thing,' don't mention this to our boss. There's no money coming in on this one."

"You got it Jack Dutton. Later."

James was glad Sam was approaching this in an unemotional way. He wished he could do the same but couldn't. Adding a reminder to his list, he wrote: check on the exact day of the week and date of Jennifer's disappearance. If not mistaken, it's closing in on a year's time.

While stopping to check out the restaurant for Saturday and have a cup of clam chowder for lunch, his phone rang. Thinking it was probably Sam calling back to ask a question, he didn't immediately recognize the number. When he answered, it was Janet.

"Hi James, I was able to get some information for you . . . quicker than expected."

"That's great . . . you're great. What did you find out? Something good, I hope."

"Okay, let me start with the car. Yes, he had a Cadillac, and it was white. However, it was stolen sometime during the same night Jennifer went missing. Supposedly, it disappeared from his residence, but the security camera wasn't working. The car hasn't been found yet."

"How convenient and not surprising," James replied. Using Carly's verbiage, "That creep has a way of making things and people disappear," but thinking, now he knew for sure there was at least one security camera at his house . . . probably more.

"Also, he has two black SUVs leased under his company's name. Looks like a silver Mercedes was recently registered . . . most likely to replace the so-called stolen Cadillac. Do you want the plate number?" Janet asked.

"No, I've already got it." James replied. Trying to remember what he'd told Janet earlier, he added, "Did I tell you the witness was picked up in Vegas by a black SUV?"

"More ammunition . . . right? It doesn't take a rocket scientist to put this all together, does it?" Janet answered. "It makes me angry. I'm in law enforcement and can't do a damn thing about it."

"But you are doing a lot. You've been a tremendous help. Trust me . . . somehow, he's going down."

After an uncomfortable pause, Janet continued. "Let's see, what else for you. The lady who called the police for Carly moved to Florida and lives with her daughter. I can give you the daughter's telephone number if you want it. She got tired of dealing with the lookie-loos driving by and the notoriety of the awful person living near her."

"Hang on to the number for me. Carly told me what happened, so I'll ask her if she'd like to contact her," James offered.

"That's wonderful. Aunt Charlotte was right; you've really won Carly over."

"I'm taking her out to dinner tomorrow. She's a real special person, and I want to show her a nice time."

"That's amazing and so nice of you and so great for Carly. Have fun," Janet said.

"Is that it?" James asked, not remembering what all he'd asked about.

"One more thing before I toss the napkin," she responded with a chuckle. "Fire safety records are available to the public. However, forms need to be filled out, red tape, and blah, blah, blah. The building was originally inspected for fire hazards but the building is old and current regulations don't necessarily apply. However, there are no records of annual inspections except for the last five or so years. Usually, the inspections are conducted by field inspectors or fire marshals and signed off by the fire chief. The last inspections were signed off by the big guy himself, the fire commander. I can't understand why . . . just weird. Oh and something else, the box—fire exit stairs clear—was checked off. The last box—all in compliance—was also checked off."

"I'm guessing the fire commander usually doesn't sign off on small three story buildings," James said sarcastically, before adding, "It sure sounds strange to me."

"I don't know how it works but agree; it does seem strange."

"I was actually in Lehmann's building today."

"Wow . . . that blows me away. Good for you but please be careful," Janet responded.

"I could only go to the 2nd floor but didn't notice fire exit stairs. There was a closed side door, maybe leading to stairs but was unmarked with an exit sign."

"What can I say? I'm impressed with your persistence."

"If you think of anything else, please don't hesitate to call, and Janet, thanks again for your help. I couldn't have made it this far without you, and I sincerely mean it."

"You're welcome, bye."

After disconnecting, James became introspective. Yes, he'd gotten this far with Janet's help but no closer to doing something about it.

Chapter 24

Carly woke Saturday morning but not where she was supposed to be. She was alone in a dark dungeon, naked on a dirt floor. She looked at the walls made of large stones and then at the rusty bars, realizing there was no gate to open and no way to escape. As she was hollering, "Please help me," the alarm went off. The dream lingered with her as she showered, but disappeared sometime while dressing. She put on jeans, a sweat shirt, and tennis shoes, knowing she would be busy cleaning the house.

When she took the dogs out to do their business, it was gray and foggy out. Even from the backyard, she could hear the front porch wind chimes clanking in the misty breeze. Although most mornings and evenings were similar, she liked it better when the sun was brightly shining. On a clear day, she could easily see the distant blue of the ocean over the tops of the pine trees.

Letting the dogs run around and play, she spent most of the morning cleaning, wanting the house to be perfect when James arrived. She loved where she lived. Her place was modest but filled with items that helped her relax after a stressful day at work. She liked to collect knickknacks she found interesting, starting when she lived with Charlotte.

Charlotte and Charlotte's family helped her find inexpensive furnishings for her house before giving her a housewarming party. At first she missed living with Charlotte but knew it was past time to branch out on her own. She remembered Charlotte saying, "It's time for my little chickadee to fly away and make her own life." Sometimes too afraid to go to bed, she'd pace around the house to wear herself out. When it became too overwhelming to bear, she'd call Charlotte, who would not only reassure her but somehow calm her down.

Carly heard footsteps on the steps leading to the wooden porch and quickly ran to the bedroom for a final look in the mirror. She and Charlotte had gone shopping yesterday, preparing for today's dinner date with James. It had been a long time since they'd shopped together; the last time was to buy work clothes. She remembered insisting on outfits that would make her blend in . . . definitely nothing revealing that would make her stand out. Looking in the mirror, it felt odd to wear something other than a grey, black, or dark blue pantsuit. Charlotte had pushed her into buying the royal blue v-neck dress. Also, Charlotte loaned her the necklace with a single pearl pendant in the middle and the smaller matching earrings.

Deciding she looked presentable—even pretty— she checked on the dogs a final time. They were resting quietly in their own beds in the newly organized spare bedroom. Carly told the dogs to stay and be quiet, blew them a kiss, and slowly closed the door.

As she walked toward the front door, she reflected on how much she loved her dogs, Maggie and Penny. They were sisters—Golden Retriever and German Shepherd mix—acquired from the local animal shelter. Before taken in by the shelter, they'd been tied up, starved, and abused. Since the shelter wanted to keep them together, they were having a difficult time adopting them out, telling her they quit eating when separated. Charlotte was leery of having two big dogs in a small house, telling her they would be unmanageable. In spite of Charlotte's apprehension, Carly wanted them. Charlotte eventually helped her get them home and settled . . . small house or not. While the dogs gave her a feeling of safety, they also became her family. She could hear Charlotte saying, "Carly, I think you identify with your dogs' past, so it was meant to be." She loved them, treated them with kindness, and gave them a feeling of belonging; they gave her the same emotions back.

After knocking, James waited at the front door, wondering why it was taking Carly so long to come to the door. Slowly rocking back and forth, he finally heard familiar unlocking sounds. Once the door was fully open, James almost fell over. Carly stood before him in a blue dress . . . looking like a model out of a beauty magazine. Not only did she look fantastic but had a big smile on her face.

When she saw James holding a bouquet of flowers, her smile got even bigger . . . if that was possible.

Taking the flowers from James, Carly offered, "How nice . . . thank you. I love stargazers."

As she beckoned for him to come inside, James stammered, "You look incredible . . . just beautiful."

Once in the living room, Carly motioned for him to sit while she headed for the kitchen to put the flowers in water. Placing the vase on the kitchen table, she picked up the prepared tray of snacks. After finding the perfect dress—according to Charlotte—they'd stopped to pick up cheese, crackers, and small sausages. Looking back at the flowers, she kept thinking how this was like romance in stories she'd read.

Placing the tray of snacks on the coffee table in front of James, she said, "I'll be right back."

Carly opened the refrigerator, removed a bottle of beer, and hurriedly grabbed a beer mug from the freezer. What would she have done without Charlotte's help, she wondered?

Delivering the beer, Carly uttered, "One more thing, then I'll be back for good."

"Wait a minute, can't I do something?" James asked.

"I want to bring the flowers in, so we can enjoy them before we leave. I love stargazers . . . did I say that already?"

Once Carly returned—sitting on the opposite end of the couch—James said, "I'm really excited about taking you to dinner."

"I'm excited about going but real nervous," Carly answered.

Having zeroed in on Carly since arriving, James took a moment to glance around the living room, noticing several glowing candles and soft music playing in the background. The best part of the room, a gorgeous woman was sitting a few feet away from him. What more could a guy want? He did have an additional desire . . . maybe sometime, someday . . . but probably not.

"This is nice. Should we stay here and not go to dinner?" James asked in a kidding manner.

"If you want," Carly answered but didn't mean it.

Looking baffled, James said quickly, "Carly, I was kidding. I want you to be honest about what you want . . . remember, what you want. I was just kidding about staying here. Tell me the truth. Would you rather stay or go?" Finishing his question, James stared directly at her.

"Okay, let me see if I can do this. Yes, I would rather go to dinner than stay here," she answered with conviction.

Smiling, James had the urge to high-five her. While tempted to ask for another beer, he looked at his watch before saying, "Are you ready to go?"

"Yes, I'm ready," she answered. "While I get my purse and car keys, would you blow out the candles? Oh, I need to turn off the music too."

When Carly flipped a wall switch, the music stopped. Puzzled, James asked, "Why do you need car keys?"

"I figured we'd each take our own car."

"Are you afraid to go with me in my car?" he asked, not only surprised but not expecting to drive to the restaurant separately. Beyond his understanding, he wasn't prepared to address this situation . . . especially since it was time to leave.

"I'm not afraid of going with you. I guess I'm used to being in control. This is all new to me," Carly answered barely above a whisper.

"It's okay if that's really what you want, but we didn't have a date to meet for dinner, rather I thought I'd be taking you to dinner."

Cringing, Carly said, "You are right; I just wasn't thinking. I guess old habits are hard to break."

"True enough. I don't think there's anything wrong with being in control. But sometimes, giving up a little control with the right person can give you a feeling of freedom. As in . . . it's your choice to give up the control. Do you trust me enough to move away—just a little— from your self-imposed boundaries and relinquish—just a little—some control to me?"

Without further discussion, Carly answered, "Yes, all of the above." Aware of allowing James to enter her world without reservation, she didn't feel afraid . . . at least with James. He was right; as long as she was able to make her own choices, she was still in control. Being alone with James in his car to an unknown place was not only her choice but another new beginning.

She set her keys down, turned, and said, "I'm ready."

"Could I make a suggestion before we leave?" James asked.

"Of course," Carly answered with a smile.

"The restaurant is down on the wharf, so it'll be on the cool side. I think you'll need some sort of wrap."

"Good idea," Carly replied.

Back from her bedroom, a cape hanging over one arm, Carly picked up her keys again. With raised eyebrows James asked, "Did you already change your mind?"

"No, I need them to lock up."

James smiled and answered, "Right."

When James opened the car door for Carly, he took her wrap and placed it in the back seat. Carly marveled at his attention to her needs . . . such a considerate person. No and even better, such a considerate man, she thought.

James felt the beginning of the drive seemed strained. They talked about their likes and dislikes in music and about the weather. Deciding it was up to him to change the tone of the drive; he elected to talk about his life, hoping to make Carly feel more at ease . . . as in, his life was far from perfect. Before launching into his past, he wondered if Charlotte had shared any of their conversation at Buster's with Carly.

"Would you prefer to talk or continue to listen to music?" James asked.

"Whatever you want," Carly answered.

"Nope, that won't work. I asked you first."

"Okay, let's talk. I like talking to you. It's like we're becoming friends."

"How about I tell you a little about my life? You came clean about yours, so I should do the same. It will help us get to know each other better."

"You don't need to do that," Carly offered.

"Yes I do," and so he began. He talked about being afraid to have friends over, because his mother was an alcoholic and constantly embarrassed him. He told her about his parents fighting all of the time, feeling helpless, and how his mother finally left. "My life changed after she left and for the better."

As James talked about his life, Carly listened with interest and didn't interrupt.

When he moved to the time of Margie entering his life, he hesitated.

"Are you all right?" Carly asked.

"I was wondering if I should tell you everything," he answered with a frown.

"Well, as my wise friend, Charlotte, once told me and not too long ago . . . if it matters to someone what you've done in the past, you shouldn't want to be around them anyway. I guess what I'm trying to say; you can tell me anything . . . like I told you. Isn't that what friends are all about?"

James started slowly, telling Carly about his excitement when becoming a police officer. Skipping over the reason for leaving, he progressed to marrying Margie with its ups and downs, and finally ended with the reason for their divorce.

"Sorry," Carly said when James became quiet.

"I know my past pales in comparison to yours, but I was miserable for a long time."

"Thank you for becoming my friend and talking to

me," Carly replied.

James turned into the parking lot across from the restaurant and turned off the car. "No . . . thank you for listening and becoming my friend."

Chapter 25

James held the restaurant door open and motioned for Carly to enter ahead of him. Once inside, she stood quietly beside James and waited while he stopped to talk to the approaching host. Smiling and gesturing for them to follow, James hesitated, allowing Carly to go first. After pulling a chair away from the table, the host smiled again and offered, "Madam." Carly sat down carefully . . . afraid of being clumsy and disturbing the tablecloth and the items resting on it. Above all, she didn't want to embarrass James. Reflecting on how someone her age should be accustomed to going on dates and having similar experiences, most of what she'd done lately were first time events.

Before James took his seat, he spoke briefly to the gentleman who'd shown them to their table. Carly couldn't hear what was being discussed but didn't care. She took the moment to look around the restaurant in amazement, especially looking out the window at the water below. The view was magical, the yellow lights shimmering across the water, the clanking of buoys mixing with occasion barks from sea lions, and the sounds of fog horns off in the distance. Interrupting her thoughts of wonder, she became aware of the host offering her a menu. Smiling, she said, "Thank you."

Once sitting across from her, James asked, "Is this okay?"

"Better than anything I could have imagined, she answered."

"It was difficult to get a table by the window any earlier, but it gave us time to visit at your house and become friends. Right?" James questioned.

"Yes, you're right. Everything is perfect . . . just perfect."

"That's what I was hoping for, because you're perfect," James answered.

"Am I blushing? I feel like my face is warm."

"I'm not sure. All I can see is a beautiful woman's face with the most intriguing and alluring eyes I've ever seen."

Knowing she must have turned red; her face now hot, Carly directed her eyes—intriguing and alluring according to James—to the menu. Leaning forward, Carly whispered, "Oh my gosh, these prices are outrageous."

Not having a chance to look at the menu yet— concentrating on saying all the right things—James responded, "Not to worry, you're worth it." Remembering what the clam chowder set him back on the lunch menu, he'd come prepared.

"I'll just have a small dinner salad; that won't be too bad," Carly offered, speaking in a hushed tone.

"Thank you, but I have this covered. Order whatever you'd like to have. This is a celebration of us becoming friends. On this special occasion, would you like to toast with a glass of wine?"

"I'd rather toast with a glass of iced tea . . . if that's all right," Carly answered tentatively.

"That's fine as long as that's what you really want. I'll order an iced tea for you and a beer for me."

Their conversation was light, the meal delicious, and the surroundings lovely. Here she was on her first real date with a man she'd only known for a week or so, and it was wonderful.

"I'm stuffed. How are you doing?" James asked.

Saying, "Me too," Carly wanted to rub her stomach but, of course, she didn't.

"I'm sorry. I forgot to ask. Would you like dessert?"

"I don't think I can eat another bite, but go ahead if you want something. I'll need to diet everyday for a month," Carly replied with a smile.

"How about we share a dessert?" James asked.

Turning and signaling to the host, James held up one finger. Almost immediately, the waitress brought over a single piece of cake with a flickering candle on top. She placed the cake between them with clean forks to each side of the plate.

"What's this for and why a candle on top?" Carly questioned.

"For whatever you want it to be. How about this? Let's share the dessert for becoming friends. You can make a wish and blow out the candle."

"I can't tell what I'm wishing for. Charlotte says if I

do, my wish won't come true."

With a grin on his face, James quipped, "I've been told that too," but thinking . . . it never worked out for me. He briefly tried to remember the last time he'd blown out candles but couldn't. You can take the first bite and tell me what you think. I promise; it won't be like tasting the first sip of wine."

"I already apologized for that," Carly said with a pout to her lips.

"I know . . . I'm teasing. This is the restaurant's signature dessert . . . filled with banana custard and topped with warm caramel sauce." Although supposedly sharing the piece of cake, James took two bites to each one of Carly's. When the cake disappeared, James watched Carly take a paper napkin from under her iced tea glass, carefully wipe off the candle, and then place it in her purse.

Acting as if he'd not noticed and having no clue why she'd save a used candle, he said, "I have an idea; would you like to go outside and walk above the water."

"I'd like that, but I left my cape in the car."

"No problem. If you'll be okay to wait here, I'll go get it."

"I'm fine. In fact while you're gone, I'll use the restroom."

As Carly watched James leave, she again marveled at his kind ways. Were his actions like this to everyone, or did it stand out because she'd been hiding away for so long. Any attention—special or otherwise—was bound to stand out to her, she reasoned. She decided to enjoy each and every moment and worry about the reasons behind his actions later.

They walked down the damp wooden steps to the platform below. James thought about reaching out to hold Carly's hand and help her but didn't want to push his luck. Walking side-by-side to the railing overlooking the water below, the evening had gone better than he'd expected.

Even with her cape on, Carly thought it seemed much cooler out than when they'd first entered the restaurant. Maybe she'd been more concerned about what to do and how to act. She was very appreciative of James's suggestion to bring a wrap along. In order to show off the borrowed earrings, she'd worn her raven hair up and away from her face. However, because her neck was exposed to the cold breeze, she began to shiver.

Noticed by James, he asked, "Would you like to go to the car?"

"I'm cold, but it's so beautiful here. I hate to leave."

"Anywhere you are is beautiful," James answered. Even though using similar comments throughout the evening—comments sounding like come-ons—they were not. They were heart-felt and sincere. After having such a wonderful evening with Carly, he was already scheming how to see her again.

Off to the side and fairly close by, a loud splash was heard. Carly jumped, asking, "What was that?"

Admitting he had no idea, James offered, "Let's go

see."

Together they crept in the direction of the splashing noise and peeked over the railing to the calm water below. Within seconds, a sea lion broke quietly through the water, slapping a flipper against the ripple made when surfacing.

"Maybe it wants something to eat. Can we get something from the restaurant to feed it?" Carly suggested.

"No, it's not allowed to feed them. If we were here in the daytime, they'd be begging fulltime. I've heard they can be a real nuisance to the businesses close to the water.

"I think it's gone anyway. It looked big but cute. Maybe it realized we weren't going to give it anything and left. Okay, I'm ready to leave. I'm cold."

On the drive back to Carly's house, they again talked about a little of everything, but neither talked about their unhappy past or the on-going investigation. James found it difficult to discuss some subjects with Carly because of her limited exposure to normal situations. While talking about several of his cases in Los Angeles—staying away from the more disturbing ones—he tried to keep the conversation fun and upbeat, telling jokes and making faces.

Carly talked about attending college, about Charlotte, and her time helping at a daycare center. When she started to talk about getting her job at the Boys and Girls Club, she quickly changed the subject.

Arriving at Carly's, James offered to go inside to make sure all was secure.

Responding quickly to his offer, "That would be nice. Maybe you could also stay while I let the dogs go out into the backyard. Would you mind? I guess I don't need to hide my fear of going outside alone after dark, but I've been working on it."

"I don't mind, but they won't attack me . . . will they?"

"Even though protective, as long as I'm okay, you'll be fine. They're my friends too," Carly replied with a grin.

Once inside the house, Carly picked up two leashes and said, "I'll be right back."

James didn't want to admit to Carly how uncomfortable he was around dogs. If they didn't like him, he'd most likely be considered off-limits by Carly too. He'd heard that animals could sense fear. He'd also heard that dogs were a good judge of character. While thinking he might be screwed on both counts, the dogs appeared. Was it good they weren't barking? Was it good they weren't snarling? They were sitting on each side of Carly and obviously sizing him up. He took their inaction toward him as good news.

Continuing to look at them, he asked, "Carly, now what?"

"After I let them out, you can offer them their favorite treat. They'll love you forever and won't forget if they see you again."

"Speaking of seeing you again, what are you doing

tomorrow?" James asked. When Carly hesitated, James asked, "Is it too soon to put up with me again? I'm leaving next Sunday."

"I was wondering if we'd see each other again before you left," Carly stated matter-of-factly.

"I'd like to, but it's totally up to you," James answered.

"Just a minute . . . the dogs need to go out. Would you mind to get the treats? They're on the counter in the kitchen. I'll see you outside."

When James joined Carly in the backyard, he shouldn't have been concerned about the dogs. They were excited and running around free, sniffing, and doing their business. While watching the dogs enjoy themselves, Carly told James their names, how she'd acquired them, and how they'd do anything for a treat— considered a cookie by the dogs.

After hesitating, James gave each dog a cookie and said to Carly, "I've got to admit I was worried, even considered the possibility of one or both biting me. When Jeremy and I were growing up, we were never allowed to have pets."

"Okay, Maggie and Penney, time for bed," Carly told the dogs. She didn't put a leash back on them, but rather let them rush through the back door with wagging tails.

Once inside, the dogs wandered around the house quietly. Deciding it was time to leave, James again asked, "Can I see you tomorrow?"

"Yes, I enjoy spending time with you. It would be fun to see you tomorrow."

Taking note of Carly's answers becoming wordier since first meeting her, James replied with a one word answer, "Great."

"I've always wanted to go on a picnic. Would a picnic be okay with you?" Carly asked.

"Sure, what can I bring," James replied with surprise . . . never considering a picnic to be a possibility.

"Nothing after what it must have cost you tonight. It won't be as fancy, but I'll try to make it nice."

"What time?"

"How about eleven; we'll have a picnic for lunch?"

"Sounds good. Actually, I've never been on a picnic before either."

"Really," Carly responded before adding, "Then, it can be a first for both of us."

Before leaving, James wanted to take her into his arms and kiss her goodbye. Instead, he uttered, "I'll see you tomorrow. Thanks for a wonderful time."

"Thank you more," Carly quipped. "See you tomorrow."

After locking up, double-checking the backdoor to make sure it was also locked, and closing the curtains, Carly looked at the clock, realizing it was too late to call Charlotte. She already knew where she wanted to go tomorrow but didn't know how to prepare a picnic lunch. Thinking of where she wanted to have the picnic, she thought of picnics in the stories she'd read.

James drove away wondering if the moment would ever be right to get physically close to Carly. His past on-and-off relationships hadn't gone anywhere, which was usually his fault. He'd dated many women since leaving Margie, but none had affected him like Carly. He'd also been celibate for the last three months . . . maybe four. His main reason for abstaining . . . tired of game playing for occasional and meaningless sex. He wanted to have a lasting relationship and fall deeply in love.

If he shared his feeling about Carly with his dad, Jeremy, or even Sam, they'd tell him he was nuts. He could hear Jeremy say, "Get real . . . you've only know this girl for a week." He couldn't argue with that line of thinking and being pragmatic, what were his chances of a future with Carly? Thinking about it on a realistic level, Carly lives in San Francisco, and he lives in Los Angeles. Oh well, he'd concentrate on the here and now and seeing Carly tomorrow, he'd worry about the future later.

Chapter 26

Peeking through the blinds, Carly saw James's car in front of the house and hurried to unlock the door, telling the dogs, "Okay girls, don't bark and behave yourselves."

While Carly was inside anticipating his arrival, James took his time walking to the front door. Since his first time to be there during daylight hours, he was curious about the outside of the house and the immediate surrounding area.

His initial impression . . . the house had the appearance of a weathered mountain cabin—like a get-away cottage—where a person could escape the ordinary hustles of busy life. The wooden exterior looked basic with no frills and seemingly built to last. The nearby large pine trees appeared old and added to the rustic scenery, giving cover to hidden bird tweets occasionally escaping the canopy of branches. On his previous visits, he hadn't noticed the cushioned swing on one side of the porch or the small table and two chairs on the other side.

Raising his hand to knock, Carly slowly opened the door but not quite all the way. Glancing down at the dogs to see their reaction, Carly watched their tails begin to wag. "Hi, come on in," she said, trying to keep her excitement under control.

Stepping inside, James patted the dogs before saying, "I was admiring your big front porch. I live in a second floor apartment with a small balcony . . . barely big enough for two small chairs."

"I felt really lucky to find this place. It was owned by a co-worker's relative and used less and less as a vacation home. It's farther from work than I'd like, but it's worked out. I love it here."

Shifting away from talking about the house—which she could go on and on about—Carly asked, "Would you like to sit and have a beer?"

"No, I'm good. I'm curious about where we're going for the picnic?"

"It's a surprise. I sorta know where it is, so I'll drive if that's okay with you," Carly replied in a questioning manner.

"That's fine," James responded, even more curious than ever about their destination.

While busy loading the car, James could understand the picnic basket and blanket, but was intrigued by the jam-packed tote bag and small cooler. When Carly closed the trunk lid, James asked, "Are we camping out?"

"No, but I wanted to be prepared," she answered seriously.

Driving away and without mentioning the ending point of the trip, Carly offered, "I used to regularly pass the road leading to where we're going. It was between Charlotte's house and college. Each time I saw the sign,

I thought about veering off, wishing I was brave enough to see what was there. Of course, I never did, just kept going to where I was supposed to be. That was my way of life back then. Well, my way of life didn't change until you walked into my office."

"That's meant as a good thing . . . right?" he quipped with a grin.

Carly's answer was a serious, "Of course."

James marveled at Carly's ability to be upfront and open. She was able to say what she was thinking without reservation. If anyone deserves happiness, she certainly does, James reasoned.

As they exited the main road to the west, James noticed a sign that read: SEADRIFT BEACH. While thinking they were still miles from the ocean, he hoped they weren't on a wild goose chase, and Carly wouldn't end up disappointed. Worst case scenario . . . they'd find it, but it would be closed to the public. If he'd known of their destination earlier, he could have looked it up, wondering if Carly already had.

After following several winding roads—bordered on each side by pine trees—they found themselves driving along the side of a bluff. Looking ahead, James was able to get a clear view of the ocean through intermittent breaks in the thick vegetation. Since Carly was concentrating on her driving, he didn't think she'd noticed the ocean yet.

James offered, "I see another sign on your left. It's faded, but I think it says: BEACH ACCESS."

"Thank goodness," Carly quickly responded. "I was

wondering if we were lost and beginning to look for places to turn around. In retrospect I should have asked you to drive. I'm sorry; I didn't think it would be this far."

"No worries . . . by the weight of this picnic basket, we'll have enough food to last for quite some time," James joked but was half serious.

"I just hope we have enough gas to get us back home," Carly said and frowned.

"You're kidding . . . I hope," James answered quickly.

"I am," she replied with a chuckle.

"How about that . . . you made a joke. Good for you."

Turning onto the road leading downward toward the ocean, they eventually came to a small deserted parking lot. "It looks like we have the whole place to ourselves. Maybe it would be better to park next to the stairs . . . what do you think?" James asked.

"Good idea. If it's too much trouble to carry everything to the beach below, we can eat up here," Carly suggested.

"Let's see how it goes. I can make two trips if necessary. I know you want to have a beach picnic, so let's do it."

Opening the trunk, Carly asked, "Are you sure?"

Receiving a nod, Carly draped the blanket halfway around her neck and partly over her shoulders, before picking up the cooler by the handle and saying, "I've got my half."

"Yes, but I've got the bigger and heavier half. That

doesn't seem fair."

"Okay, I'll take the tote bag too. If the basket is too heavy for you, I can carry it."

"Carly . . . did you really think I was serious?"

"No . . . did you really think I was?"

"Wow, I think we're beginning to understand each other," James replied with a big smile.

While locking the car, Carly smiled back before responding, "I agree. Isn't that what friends do?"

Yes, he wanted to be friends but also wanted to be more than friends. What if Carly was so jaded from her past that all she could ever want from the opposite sex was a friendly relationship? He thought of his counseling talks and how being friends was important to any relationship. Perhaps he was pushing too hard to want her to like him.

James hooked the tote bag over one shoulder and picked up the picnic basket. They walked down the stairs fairly quickly but stopped halfway down for a short break on the landing.

Taking a deep breath, James said, "You know going back up will be more difficult, and since you volunteered earlier, you can take everything back on the return trip."

"Like . . . that will happen . . . not. All kidding aside, I didn't know there would be stairs. I'm sorry. I know this is a lot of trouble for you, but it's a dream come true for me."

"No need to apologize; I'm having a great time."

Once on the beach—halfway between the water

and the bluff—Carly spread the blanket over the sand and placed the cooler down. Watching James place his items down on the blanket with an obvious sigh of relief, she shifted her attention to the ocean. Giddy with anticipation, Carly asked, "Do you want to go with me to touch the water?"

"We'll need to take off our shoes and socks. Maybe roll up our pants too," he answered.

Carly hurriedly sat on the blanket, removed her tennis shoes, socks, and rolled up her pant legs, before James had a chance to sit down. When stepping off the blanket and onto the sand, she lost her balance. Falling sideways, James caught her in his arms.

When she felt his touch, she didn't understand what was happening to her. Her knees felt wobbly; her mind spinning. It was like a gust of hot wind surrounded her, melting away the hurts bottled-up inside.

"Are you okay? Did you get dizzy?" James asked.

"No, I'm fine. I just got off-balanced," she finally answered. "When I stepped off the blanket, I didn't realize the sand would be soft, and I'd sink in."

"The sand is harder near the water's edge where the waves come in," James offered, reluctantly releasing her.

Dropping quickly to the blanket, he removed his shoes, socks, and folded up his pants, before thinking . . . if at home on the beach, I'd be wearing cut-offs and flip flops. Finishing, he jumped up and said, "Take my hand for balance, and we'll go touch the water."

Without uttering another word, Carly extended her

hand and James held it firmly in his. "Are you ready?" he asked.

Watching Carly joyously romp beside the ocean, running from the waves spilling onto the beach, and stopping occasionally to reach down to touch the water, was a sight to see. Every so often, she let out a blissful squeal . . . like a child discovering a new toy. How anyone could harm a child or person and change their entire future was beyond his comprehension. Finally running back to James's side, Carly said, "I'm hungry; let's eat."

Carly methodically pulled food items from the basket and systematically placed linen napkins, regular plates, and silverware in front of each of them. It was like she was determined to follow an imaginary check list. After opening the containers of fried chicken, potato salad, and fruit, she asked, "Do you want me to serve your plate or would you prefer to do it?"

"No, I will. Now I understand why the basket was so heavy. This is a real feast," he said with amazement.

"Oh, we also have dessert. Wait, something's missing . . . our drinks." Opening the cooler, she handed James a beer and took out a raspberry iced tea for herself.

Not having breakfast—not even a freebie at the hotel—James realized how hungry he was. Digging into his plate with gusto, he said, "I didn't expect anything like this. It must have been a lot of work."

"Yes and no. Charlotte helped me," Carly answered but looked pensive.

Watching James chow down on the food, Carly

wanted to tell him something she'd been thinking about for some time. "You know how I said I had no life and my past was so awful. Well, every word was true, but when able to experience a new way of life, I still kept most everyone and everything at a distance. You've showed me I don't want to live like that anymore. I'm through with hiding from others and even from myself. I can't put into words all you've done for me. I know you'll be leaving soon, but I wanted you to know exactly how I feel before you leave. I will never forget how you've helped me, and no matter what happens in my life, I'll never go back to the way I was. You've make me feel accepted, rather than judged. Thank you."

James's first thought was to lean forward and kiss her. Thinking better of it, he didn't want to take a chance on ruining the moment, perhaps squelching what he'd daydreamed about soon after meeting her. Almost speechless, he answered, "You don't need to thank me; I just want you to be happy. If I've contributed to you feeling better about yourself and your life, then that's thanks enough for me."

They ate and laughed, then ate and laughed some more. As Carly cleaned up the area, she said, "I almost forgot . . . would you like a chocolate chip cookie? I made plenty."

"I can't eat another bite. Maybe you can send some with me when I leave for the hotel."

"Would you hold my hand and walk with me by the ocean before we go? I don't need help with my balance;

I just want you to."

When James helped her up with both hands, he again thought about kissing her—wanting desperately to kiss her—but didn't, deciding it was up to her to make the first physical move. After all, she'd been the one abused. He had no clue what made her tick. Maybe kissing was repugnant to her. Since holding hands was her idea—a move in the right direction—it was definitely a good start, he reasoned.

As they walked along the ocean's edge, Carly knew she'd changed from the inside out. She also knew it would never have happened without James. She was happy.

James drove on the return trip to Carly's house. When they reached the main road and turned in the right direction, Carly helped navigate the easiest way back to her house.

Once the car was unloaded and the sandy blanket placed on the porch, Carly asked, "Would you like to come in?"

"Yes, but do you need me to or want me to? It's still light out, so you can be out with the dogs without being afraid."

"When I'm alone, I'm not sure I'll ever feel completely safe in my lifetime," she answered.

"That's a little extreme, don't you think. Didn't you tell me you weren't hiding anymore?" James replied.

"You're right . . . sometimes I think one thing, say another, and do another. Being with you and having a good time makes me realize how lonely I've been. I'd like you to come in because I want you to, not because I need you to." Smiling, she added, "Besides, you can't leave without your cookies."

Carly took the dogs out to the backyard while James stayed behind to visit the restroom and get cookies for Maggie and Penny. While watching the dogs frolic about, Carly heard the backdoor quietly open and close. Knowing James was standing closely behind her, she pretended to watch the dogs and not notice. She considered turning and kissing him goodbye. Would James consider her actions whore like? She'd kissed many men in her lifetime but felt nothing. It was part of the job, part of surviving, but she'd never wanted to like this. No man had ever left her feeling like this whenever they parted. If what she was feeling was normal, then she never wanted them to change.

James was surprised when Carly knew he was behind her. Without acknowledging his presence, she reached out behind herself, touching him on the outside of both his arms. Almost in slow motion, he pulled her in against him, his chest pressed against her back. He was elated by her action, wondering where it might lead. It wasn't as significant as a kiss but definitely a move in the right direction. Carly took a hold of his arms and crossed them in front of her before placing her own arms tightly on top of his. He could feel her body trembling. James stood there with his arms wrapped around her and stayed quiet . . . afraid to move, afraid to speak, and especially afraid to disrupt the moment.

Feeling almost welded to James, Carly patted the tops of his arms before saying, "Thank you for a wonderful day. I'll go gather up some cookies for you."

"But this feels so good," James replied in a joking manner but was dead serious.

After James gently uncrossed his arms and lifted them away, Carly offered, "It did for me too."

James waited for more—wanted more—but the moment passed. He left with a bag of cookies, feeling unsatisfied and disappointed. He knew his thoughts bordered on bizarre. He wanted the whole pie . . . not just nibbles from around the outside. He wanted all of her. Yes, his thoughts were crazy. Maybe he was too, again reminding himself of the short time they'd known each other. Arguing with himself, maybe his feelings for Carly were almost love at first sight. His track record wasn't that great. He'd originally thought Margie was too until learning it was more like lust at first sex.

Carly watched James leave, feeling new emotions never felt before. Again, she didn't understand what was happening to her. The possibility of having sex with James surfaced . . . a new territory to consider. Not because she was made to, not because she was told to, and not because she had to, but because she thought she wanted to. Would she be able to discuss these feelings with Charlotte or would it be too embarrassing?

Chapter 27

Stepping out of his car, Steve saw his next door neighbor, Lukas, staggering down the walkway leading away from his house. Noticing his difficulty in walking forward, he couldn't help but wonder if Lukas was flat-out drunk.

As Steve continued to watch Lukas approach the median between the sidewalk and street, fearing he might fall off the curb or step into traffic, he hollered, "Hey neighbor, what's happening?"

Lukas stopped, looked around in a confused manner, and said something Steve couldn't hear. Afraid for Lukas's safety, no way could he ignore him, so asked, "Can I help you with something? Are you all right?"

Again, not exactly hearing or perhaps not understanding Lukas's response, Steve said, "Hold on . . . I'll be right there." Grabbing a small sack off the passenger seat and quickly locking the car, Steve hurried to Lukas's side. "I'm sorry Lukas; I didn't quite hear what you said."

"It don't matter. Don't reckon what I say makes no sense anyhow."

Aware something wasn't right, Steve asked, "Can I help you?"

"I came out here to do something but can't remember what."

Trying to reassure Lukas, Steve smiled before saying, "No problem . . . that happens to me all the time. Should I call Gabriel?"

"God no . . . don't," Lukas uttered; his words said firmly but still slightly garbled.

Thinking Lukas must have really tied one on and didn't want Gabriel to know, Steve answered, "Okay . . . I won't. I bet you were thinking about putting out your trash. It's trash pick-up day tomorrow."

"Maybe so . . . maybe so," Lukas mumbled.

"How about this? I'll put out your trash can but only if you promise to stay in the house where you'll be safe. Is that a deal?" Steve asked in a friendly manner.

Not receiving a response, Steve gently turned Lukas around in the direction of his house and walked with him until reaching the front door. "Take care and don't worry about your trash," Steve offered as Lukas stepped inside.

After taking care of Lukas's trash and his own, Steve told his wife how worried he was about their neighbor. "Lukas was outside really plastered . . . could hardly walk. You know . . . he hasn't seemed right since his granddaughter went missing—maybe not since Thelma's passing. To be out of it like he is in the middle of the day, he must have a serious drinking problem. I've noticed little things before but nothing like this."

"Shouldn't we let Gabriel know about your concerns?" she asked.

"I suggested that, but Lukas was adamant against it. I'll check on him tomorrow before leaving for work. If he's still under the influence, I'll call Gabriel. I hope Gabriel won't rat me out to Lukas when Lukas sobers up. I'd hate for him to be mad at me."

Lukas entered his house; his head pounding something awful. He couldn't remember when he'd taken his last pain pill. In fact, he could barely remember anything of late. Knowing he was failing fast and should get help; he just couldn't bring himself to go there.

Looking around the kitchen for the pain pill bottle, he found it next to the kitchen sink. The bottle cap was off and only a few pills remained. Even with his glasses on, he was unable to read the small print . . . the letters blurring together.

He'd talked to his doctor yesterday—or thought it was yesterday—and the doctor increased his pain medication. Even though the doctor said he had six to eight months and telling him what symptoms to expect, he'd failed to mention how his quality of life could possibly stop so soon.

Taking two pills and hoping for relief, how could he go to the drugstore for more pills? Maybe Steve would be willing to go for him. No way could he ask Gabriel without telling him what the medicine was for and about the cancer. Refusing to be a burden on his family, his life sucked. Face it . . . you're barely aware of what's what anymore.

Lukas laid down carefully and slowly on the bed,

praying the headache would ease enough to enable him to fall asleep. Squashing the pillow against his face, he heard the faint plastic rustling sound of his pill stash inside. Which was worse . . . the excruciating pain or losing his mind? Since going down-hill quicker than the doctor warned and much sooner than he expected, how should he proceed? He wasn't exactly sure how long it had been since learning of his fate. One thing he was certain about, each day had become a struggle . . . like living in a nightmare. I'm a mess . . . just a sick old man. I have no purpose and should be gone. Lying there alone, he began to cry.

There was no way he wanted anyone to see him like this. What he wanted was to have Thelma tell him what he should do. What he wanted was to be playing with Jennifer; cuddling with her while she told him her doll's secrets. What he wanted was to be able to do something important like saving Joseph's life. Realizing everything he wanted was in the past, he felt worthless. Was his pride getting in the way of talking to Gabriel?

Perhaps his thoughts had turned into a dream. He must be dreaming because names, faces, and places were so vivid. Regardless of dreaming or not, he liked where he was. The headache had all but disappeared, and he was young and full of life again.

After sleeping for a few hours, Lukas woke feeling surprisingly better. His head was still hurting but reduced from a pounding thud to a dull ache. Also, his mind seemed sharper. However, knowing the memory loss and erratic movements could surface at any moment—even returning worse than before—he needed to have a heart-to-heart talk with Joseph before it was too late.

Hoping the clearer mindset would help him communicate better, he still jotted down a few items to discuss with his friend. Because the light made his pain worse . . . if that was possible, he kept the curtains closed. Not sure if it was light or dark out, Lukas glanced at the clock to make sure it was an appropriate time to call.

"Joseph, we need to talk," said when his friend picked up the phone.

"Okay, talk to me."

"I'm not going to be around much longer, so . . . ."

"I'm on my way," Joseph replied, trying to hold back tears.

"I don't want you to come; I want you to listen to me."

"I'm listening," Joseph replied, almost holding his breath.

"I had a long talk with my doctor. He started talking about hospice care, nursing homes, and on-and-on."

"But . . ." Joseph interjected.

"Let me finish," Lukas said firmly.

"I need to address this while I can. For some reason— God only knows why—I'm more alert and clear-headed at the moment."

As Joseph listened to Lukas, he was already making plans to head for San Francisco. It didn't matter whether Lukas wanted him to or not. He was glad Lukas didn't want him to interrupt; he knew his voice would be quivering. He was also glad his friend couldn't see the tears running down his face. Both knew grown men weren't supposed to cry.

After listening to Lukas state matter-of-factly his wishes after he died and his desire to be in a better place . . . sooner than later, he abruptly changed the subject, saying, "I haven't talked to your son lately. I'm guessing he hasn't learned anything to tell me. Would you ask him to call me as soon as possible? Is he still here in San Francisco?"

Clearing his throat and glad the conversation had moved on, Joseph answered, "As far as I know . . . he is."

"If you can get in touch with him, I'd be grateful . . . like right away."

"Maybe you're just having a bad day? Except for the subject matter, you're sounding better than you have in some time."

"Yeah . . . maybe. Don't forget to have James call me right away. And Joseph, thank you for being my friend, my brother."

"Always Buddy."

"Goodbye, Joseph."

"Goodbye, Lukas."

Joseph hung up the phone with a feeling of utter sadness. In his mind the goodbye seemed final . . . not just the ending of their telephone conversation. He sat there depressed but knew his feelings were nothing compared to what Lukas must be having. When he talked to Lukas face-to-face tomorrow, could he convince him to fight the inevitable? Would it be selfish to ask him to stay in his life a little longer?

Shame flowed through him for not seeing Lukas more, for not talking to him more, and for not being more in his friend's life. Like so many things put-off to later, time moves on leaving regrets behind.

True to his word, Joseph called James immediately. James answered the phone on the first ring, answering, "Hi, Dad. Guess my ears were burning. I just picked up my phone to call you."

"Do you have a minute?"

"Sure . . . you sound down. Is everything okay?"

"I'm fine but just got off the phone with Lukas."

"You know . . . I've been thinking about calling him but not sure what to say about what I've found out."

"He's not doing good and wants you to call him," Joseph answered.

"Do you know exactly what he wants to talk about?"

"Maybe I'm over-reacting, but I've got the feeling he won't be around much longer. He was making total sense over the phone . . . not mumbling and sounded clear-headed."

"Dad, I'm really sorry. I know you're hurting, cuz I hear the quivering in your voice. I'll call Lukas right after we end our conversation. Should I tell him everything?" Not waiting for his dad to respond, James asked, "Do you think he'll try and take matters into his own hands . . . like we discussed earlier?"

"No, I think that mind-set has passed. Tell him

everything you know and don't hold back. I'm planning to go to San Francisco to see him. He doesn't want me to but I'm going anyway. I'll touch bases with you sometime tomorrow. I'll give you my definite plans then."

Without delay, James called Lukas. After hearing a faint voice, James offered, "Lukas, this is James, Joseph's son. Can you hear me okay?"

"Yes, I can."

"I'm sorry for not calling you. I'm ashamed to say I've not made much progress on finding your granddaughter. I was hoping to be able to give you good news when we talked again."

"Have you found out anything?" Lukas asked.

"Well, I can tell you that your hunch was right-on. Lehmann was definitely involved. Carly recognized the doll Jennifer had with her when she went missing."

"I don't understand. Of course, Carly would recognize it."

"My bad for not explaining better. Carly saw it in his warehouse."

"Carly went into that creep's building?"

"No, she saw it on the video taken during the search warrant."

"Good God, let's get him. Would you help me kidnap that sick S.O.B. and make him talk?"

Shocked by Lukas's request, James stammered, "That's against the law."

"Do I give a crap about the law?"

"Sir, with all due respect, I would be willing to do so

if I thought I could, but his building is very secure . . . like a fortress."

"Can we get him somewhere else?" Not receiving an answer, Lukas followed with, "I don't know why I'm saying we; I can't even drive to get my own medicine."

"Let me come over and get it for you," James offered, relieved the kidnap subject had changed.

"That's beside the point. This is what I need from you."

Afraid of what Lukas might ask him to do, James answered, "Anything you need . . . just name it."

"I want your solemn word—a promise . . . man to man—you'll find a way to get him and won't give up until you do."

"I promise to do my best to get him. You have my word on that."

"Okay . . . then."

"Sir, I have a question for you before I go. Shouldn't I tell Gabriel what's going on and why I'm here? I've kept this under wraps because of your wishes."

"Not until you make sure that piece of shit can't harm another child. Your word . . . remember?"

After disconnecting the call, James was left confused. He should have asked Lukas to be more specific about the timing but didn't. Wouldn't that be after the fact? Maybe he was wrong but wouldn't Gabriel want to know someone was still out there diligently looking for his daughter, or at least wanting to know what might have happened to her.

Chapter 28

Joseph woke James at 7:00 o'clock Monday morning. Sleepily, James answered, "Hi Dad, why the early call?"

"Sorry so early, but it's about Lukas."

"Do you want me to check on him?" James asked with concern.

"No, he's in the hospital. Gabriel called saying he'd found my number by his dad's telephone. He said the note—written in capital letters—said, "IMPORTANT—CALL IF A PROBLEM.""

"What should I do? Should I go to the hospital?"

"I'm not sure. Gabriel said he had a seizure in his front yard last night, and the neighbor called the paramedics. I don't think Gabriel knows the extent of his father's condition yet. When we talked, Gabriel was waiting to speak to the doctor and get test results. Gabriel's got to wonder why my phone number was there instead of his."

"Should I go to the hospital and say you called, asking if I'd check on Lukas on your behalf. I can be vague about my reason for being in San Francisco. What do you think?"

Receiving the name and address of the hospital, James asked, "Do you know if Lukas is awake?"

"I'm not sure. He's in the emergency room . . . I think, but may have been moved by now. Call me as soon as you know what's going on."

"I will . . . bye."

It had been some time since being in a hospital, but the smell of disinfectant returned like it was yesterday. His memories were mainly remembered from his police days. Since then, he'd been lucky enough to avoid hospitals, thinking the last time must have been when Jeremy's youngest son was born.

After first checking with the emergency room personnel, James walked into the small waiting room adjacent to the Intensive Care Unit . . . not sure if he'd find anyone there. Seeing a couple waiting, James walked over to them and asked, "Are you Michelle and Gabriel Walker?"

Looking up and before answering, Gabriel asked, "Do we know you?"

"No, I'm James Allen. You called my father, Joseph, in Los Angeles this morning. How is Lukas doing?"

"We don't know. The doctors are still with him . . . even his primary doctor—who is unknown to me—was called in," Gabriel answered with an air of frustration. "I didn't even know my dad was sick. He's been very secretive lately. We've been gone for awhile so haven't exactly been hands on with dad the last couple of weeks," Gabriel added in an apologetic manner. "I'm rambling. Sorry . . . glad to meet you."

"Is he awake? My dad said he'd had a seizure," James

volunteered.

"He must be because they're saying unless he wants us to know what's going on; they need to be careful about giving out his medical information."

"I think that's determined on a case-by-case basis. That's been my understanding," James answered. While already knowing but asking anyway, James inquired, "When did this happen?"

"It must have been sometime in the middle of the night. His neighbor heard a loud crash, finding him in front of the house close to the curb. It seems as though the neighbor put out Dad's trash can. No one can figure out why Dad was out there . . . especially during the night. His neighbor thought he fell against the trash can and hit his head, causing the seizure. I just don't get it. He seemed okay . . . maybe a little forgetful when we last talked."

"If you don't mind, I'd like to stay and wait," James remarked politely.

Even though Michelle and Gabriel both nodded in the affirmative, James suddenly felt uncomfortable— like an outsider . . . which he was—and quietly took a seat. Apprehensive to engage in small talk for obvious reasons, he scanned through his phone for any unread text messages.

Sitting in the same spot since arriving, Michelle felt like her rear had adhered to the hospital's molded plastic chair. The minutes had turned into hours, but no way could she feel sorry for herself while Lukas was there with a serious problem. Not wanting to stress Gabriel out with more questions—anymore than he already was—she couldn't understand why they hadn't been told what was going on. Her nature was to march up to the desk and demand answers, because not knowing—frustrated and in the dark—was the worst part of waiting. When they'd arrived at the hospital, Lukas had already been moved from the emergency room to intensive care. Gabriel had asked a couple of times and was told the same thing, "As soon as the doctors finish their evaluations, someone will come talk to you."

Michelle looked over at Gabriel, noting he also appeared uncomfortable. He had been shifting in his chair, leaning forward, stretching his back, twisting from side to side, and sighing loudly. While knowing there was nothing she could do or say to reassure him, she continued to reach out and pat his leg or shoulder.

Finally, a doctor appeared, asking to talk to Gabriel privately in the hall. Michelle watched Gabriel leave before leaning forward and saying to James, "You're Lukas's friend's son. Did I hear that correctly?"

"Yes," James answered, worried more questions would follow . . . and they did.

"So, do you live in the San Francisco area?" she asked quietly.

Not wanting to open a can of worms without Lukas's approval—unless absolutely necessary—he responded, "No, I live in Los Angeles. My dad, who also lives in L A, asked while I was in San Francisco to stop by and visit with Lukas."

"I'm confused. You've already met Lukas," Michelle replied in a surprised manner.

"Yes, we had coffee not too long ago."

"I've got to admit that surprises me. He's been so reclusive of late since . . . . "

"I'm sorry," James interjected. "Lukas told me about your daughter's disappearance."

Without further comment, Michelle looked away and again at the hallway. This time, however, she was unable to see Gabriel, wondering if he'd gone to see Lukas or perhaps to another area to continue talking with the doctor? Either way, she hoped Gabriel learned what was going on.

Almost to the point of bolting out of the room to look for Gabriel, the doors to the intensive care unit opened. Gabriel appeared alone and walked out slowly; his eyes full of tears. Michelle jumped out of her seat and ran to meet him.

James stood from his chair but hung back, wondering if he should even be there. It was understandably a private and difficult personal moment. Continuing to stand quietly, the thought crossed his mind that Lukas may have already passed. Regardless of his reason for being in San Francisco, he needed to focus on what was happening with Lukas and leave as soon as possible to report back to his dad.

As James intently watched, Gabriel wiped his eyes with his fingers and mumbled something to Michelle.

After receiving a nod from Michelle, he stoically walked over to speak to James. Clearing his throat, he said, "My dad's in really bad shape. He can barely talk and is extremely agitated. When he first came in, they thought he was incoherent due to the seizure . . . perhaps caused by the fall. Michelle told me you recently had coffee with Dad. Did he say anything about being sick?"

"No, not a word," James answered honestly. Wanting to skirt any questions about what he and Lukas discussed, he asked, "Is Lukas going to be all right?"

Taking in a quacking breath, Gabriel answered, "No, my dad is dying."

"Oh my, I'm so sorry," was his heartfelt reply.

Seemingly more in control, Gabriel continued. "I talked to dad's specialist, who's been treating him for some time for a cancerous brain tumor. By what he told me, Dad's been dealing with the brain cancer way before Jennifer was taken." The tears beginning to show again, Gabriel shook his head from side to side before questioning, "Why didn't he tell me?"

Before a response could be offered—perhaps Gabriel wasn't expecting any—Michelle offered, "Let's sit down."

Barely seated, Gabriel continued speaking—almost like talking out loud to himself—as if trying to resolve in his own mind what had been happening. "The seizure was part of the tumor pressing on his brain and had nothing to do with the fall. Although the doctor did say the pressure could cause muscle weakness and coordination problems. He couldn't say exactly what my dad had presently experienced, thus the reason for a multitude of tests.

Michelle asked, "What about chemotherapy or radiation? Couldn't that help?"

"I asked, but it was too late when Dad finally sought help. Once discovered, treatment options were no longer possible. They're doing their best to keep him more or less sedated." Again, Gabriel asked, "Why didn't he tell me?"

Without divulging the reason they weren't told, James asked, "Is your dad aware you know the truth about his condition?"

"I can't say for sure. When I tried to talk to him, he just mumbled and shook his head. I could only understand a few words."

"Maybe he's sorry for not telling you and can't communicate his feelings," James offered. "What does the doctor say should happen now? I mean . . . will he stay in intensive care, be moved to a room, or what? I don't mean to pry but want to let my dad know his situation."

"The doctor didn't say other than keeping him for observation before recommending the next step. I'm sure he'll never go back home," Gabriel answered flatly.

Michelle interjected, "I want to go see Lukas."

"I'll go back with you," Gabriel replied. Turning to James, Gabriel said, "Thank you for coming to the hospital."

"You're welcome. I'll let my father know what I've

learned. By the way did you know Lukas saved my dad's life?"

"Yes, he told us about it years ago. I'd forgotten until seeing your dad's name and phone number on the note."

"Would it be okay if my dad contacted you?" James asked.

Michelle responded by handing James a card with their home telephone number on it; then said, "Thank you again for coming."

*   *   *   *

Before entering Lukas's small room, Michelle hesitated, momentarily taking her husband's hand and squeezing it tightly. Separating, they each stood on opposite sides of the bed and looked down at Lukas's face. In spite of the surrounding equipment producing noisy beeping sounds, Lukas appeared to be sleeping peacefully.

"This is much better than before," Gabriel said barely above a whisper.

Sighing deeply, Gabriel leaned over and gave his dad a kiss on the forehead, saying, "I love you, Dad. I'll be back later and bring your pillow."

Looking questionably at her husband and doubting Lukas heard his son; Michelle looked carefully at her father-in-law's closed eyes and stated, "I'll come back too."

Leaving the hospital, Michelle quizzed, "What were

you saying about a pillow?"

"I couldn't understand Dad, but the nurse told me he wants his pillow from home. He wouldn't calm down until she restated his request to me. After I understood he wanted his pillow, he clearly and forcefully uttered the word, 'Promise.' Once I promised to bring it, he was somewhat better and settled down. Maybe it was the pillow mother slept on. I have no idea, but a promise is a promise. You don't need to come back with me if you don't want to."

After a silent moment, Michelle asked, "Did the doctor say how long?"

"No, and I couldn't bring myself to ask. The plan is to keep him as comfortable as possible. I think that means giving him heavy drugs. I tried to keep up, but the doctor talked fast . . . throwing in a lot of technical stuff. He gave me the impression; he'd know more tomorrow on the best way to proceed."

As Michelle stepped into the car, she said, "I want to come back to the hospital when you deliver the pillow." She didn't add what she was really thinking . . . it might be the last time she'd see Lukas alive.

Gabriel started the car but left it in park. "I still can't believe Dad didn't tell me what was going on. That really hurts."

Offering the only explanation that made sense, Michelle replied, "I think James was right about your dad being sorry for not telling you. I'm thinking he didn't want to add more stress on you after Jennifer went missing and didn't want to burden you with something you couldn't control anymore than he could."

Michelle turned away as Gabriel put the car in gear to back out. She could feel the tears running down her cheeks . . . tears for Lukas, tears for Gabriel, tears for Jennifer, and tears for herself.

*   *   *   *

When James walked out of the hospital and into the cool morning mist, he began to fixate on how unfair life could be. Watching Gabriel and Michelle walk through the intensive care doors to see Lukas was a good example. Was there anyone in this whole wide world spared from some sort of pain? Thinking more along those lines, maybe suffering was a normal part of life. If people existed who'd not suffered, they were extremely lucky. Some would say blessed. Feeling reflective and philosophical, life seemed to ebb and flow for most—if not all—of us, he thought.

Looking around the parking lot, he'd been in such a rush to get inside; he'd forgotten exactly where he parked his car, finally locating it after a couple of trips through one section of parking lanes. Knowing his father would be nervously waiting to hear about Lukas, he needed to call him immediately.

Answering on the first ring, Joseph heard his son say, "Dad, the secret's out about Lukas dying." After relaying the conversation he'd had with Gabriel, James followed up with, "I'll give you Gabriel's telephone number. He said it would be okay for you to call him."

"Hang on while I get something to write on." Returning to the phone, Joseph asked, "Does Gabriel know the reason you're in San Francisco?"

"No, it wasn't discussed."

While talking with his father, James saw Gabriel and Michelle walking toward the parking area, seemingly engaged in deep conversation. Since in San Francisco because of Lukas, should he continue his search? Guess that would depend on whether Lukas was aware enough to tell him his wishes. If not aware, should he talk to Gabriel and Michelle anyway?

He wished he could get answers for them about their daughter's where-abouts within the next week but realistically didn't consider it a possibility. Not wanting to admit it—but needing to face facts—answers may never come.

Instead of organizing his plans for the week, he'd rushed to the hospital to check on how Lukas was doing. He needed to return to the hotel to begin his Monday all over again. He fought off the urge to contact Carly, hoping she'd make the next move. The last thing he wanted to do was to put pressure on her and scare her away.

Chapter 29

Sitting at his dad's kitchen table and realizing Dad would never return home, Gabriel cried like a baby. Since no one was there to witness his lack of control, he allowed his emotions to run free without worry of being judged. Never discussed when growing up—just assumed through the years—men who cried were considered unmanly or sissy-like. Men were supposed to be tough, while women were allowed to cry without judgment.

Looking at the multitude of prescription containers, his tears were mixed with anger. There were notes everywhere—some impossible to decipher—and the house was in total disarray. How could he have been so self-absorbed in his own misery not to see what was going on with his father? He had taken his dad's words at face-value when told all was fine, no need to visit, or wouldn't be home due to other plans. While thinking of Jennifer with every waking moment and wanting to find her, his dad was dealing with the same mind-set plus a brain tumor that was killing him. Jennifer's kidnapping was a family crisis, while Dad had been facing his predicament alone. It was beyond his understanding why Dad had shut him out.

Taking the lone pillow off his father's bed, he continued to wonder why the pillow was important. But then, since Jennifer went missing, everything in his life had become beyond his understanding. There was no use guessing why Dad wanted the pillow . . . just take it to him. What did it really matter . . . a promise was a promise, he reasoned.

Looking more carefully at the pillow, it appeared yellow and dingy . . . far from the white color it was supposed to be. He considered looking for a clean pillow case, but perhaps his dad liked it the way it was. Knowing Michelle would be embarrassed by its shoddy appearance, he decided not to worry about it. As he would tell Michelle—knowing she'd complain—if Dad didn't care, then they shouldn't either.

Tucking the pillow under his arm, Gabriel looked around his childhood home a final time. It seemed wrong his dad wouldn't be returning, but then, everything seemed wrong right now. He knew the day would eventually come when he'd need to say goodbye, but naturally thought they'd have more time together . . . expecting years. Turning off the lights and locking up, Gabriel sighed. His family was shrinking, and there was nothing he could do about it. His mom was gone, Jennifer was gone, and his dad would soon be gone.

Gabriel remembered asking his mother why the other kids had brothers and sisters, and he didn't. Her answer was always the same, "God blessed us with you, and you filled us with all the love and happiness we needed." Walking down the steps, he wanted to kick something, put his fist through a wall, scream, or rant. While knowing there was nothing he could do to change the past, make anything better, or make his sadness go away, he would try to be strong and handle what would come to pass like his dad would . . . facing it with dignity and strength.

*   *   *   *

When Gabriel and Michelle returned to the hospital, his dad was still resting quietly. Looking again at his father's closed eyes and not expecting a reply, Gabriel said, "I brought the pillow. I'll see you tomorrow."

Before leaving, they stopped at the nurse's station, so Gabriel could ask, "Is my dad in a coma?"

"No, I don't believe so, but I'm not sure. Usually after a seizure, a person will sleep for quite some time. But in your father's case—because of the brain tumor— this might be a different situation. Probably, you should discuss it with the doctor."

"About that," Gabriel inquired, "Who exactly is my father's doctor?"

Receiving the attending physician's name, Gabriel followed with another question. "Do you know when I can talk to the doctor tomorrow . . . like how early will he be in? I have a lot of questions not asked when here this morning."

Answering with an approximate time, the nurse

pleasantly said, "You can always call the nurse's station to receive updates on how your father is doing."

Gabriel's final question after thanking her for the information, "Could you make sure my dad gets the pillow he wanted? I put it on the chair next to his bed. It seems very important to him. Please don't forget."

*   *   *   *

Gabriel found it difficult to fall asleep. When he closed his eyes, his dad's face appeared . . . intermittently with Jennifer's . . . remembering how his dad laughed and Jennifer giggled when they were together. Maybe, when they saw Dad tomorrow, they'd be able to discuss his wishes for care going forward. Giving it more thought, it would be better to talk to the doctor first. The last time he looked at the clock; it was closing in on one o'clock.

At almost three, the telephone rang. Since the phone was on Michelle's side of the bed, she answered. In a fog Gabriel heard her say, "Just a minute."

Not fully awake—even wondering if he'd gone to sleep—Gabriel answered, "Yes," and then, "I will."

"Gabriel, what's going on?" Michelle questioned.

Momentarily unable to respond, Gabriel handed the phone back. Wanting to be brave but finding it impossible, he finally answered; his voice quaking, "My dad has taken a turn for the worse. They want me to return to the hospital as soon as convenient. She said there was no immediate hurry. I think that's code for my dad has died.

Why else would she say that?"

Before responding, Michelle walked around to his side of the bed. Sitting next to him and taking his hand, she quietly said, "I'm so sorry. Maybe they're preparing you for the end. Maybe he's lapsed into a coma. Wouldn't she say he'd passed if he had?"

"It was just a feeling I got when talking to her. If you're not up to it, I can go and call you."

"Don't be foolish, we'll get through this together," Michelle answered.

Expecting the worst, they arrived at the hospital within an hour. Not sure who to ask for, they were met by an intensive care nurse, asking them to have a seat in the waiting area. After a minute or so, an unknown doctor walked toward them. "Mr. and Mrs. Walker . . . I've been attending to ah . . . your father, Lukas Walker. I'm sorry to inform you of his passing quietly in his sleep."

Dropping their heads and looking downward at the floor tiles, neither Gabriel nor Michelle gave an immediate response.

Following an extended silence—giving the couple time for his statement to settle in—the doctor asked, "Can I do anything for you? Do you have any questions?"

Gabriel was determined not to cry when asking, "Where is my father? Can I go see him?"

"I just came on duty. I think he's already been moved awaiting placement instructions."

"Would you check for us?" Gabriel asked, confused about where they'd move him.

Leaving the Walkers, the doctor returned inside the almost full intensive care area. Not seeing a staff member available to ask, and those he could see were busy attending to other patients; the doctor decided to look into the room where Lukas Walker had been cared for. The body had been removed; the room empty except for housekeeping personnel already diligently cleaning the area. Nodding to them, the doctor returned to tell the Walkers their father had been moved to the hospital's morgue.

When the doctor left the patient's room, a member of the cleaning crew—ready to mop the floor—bent down beside the bed and picked up a small plastic bag with flakes of white powder inside. Told to hurry and clean the last available intensive care room, he quickly discarded it into a full trash receptacle—already brimming over with a dirty pillow—and began mopping.

Chapter 30

"I don't know where to begin," Gabriel said to Michelle. "Dad handled Mom's funeral. I basically went along with what Dad said she wanted."

"Could I make a suggestion?" Michelle asked.

"Of course," answered like a given.

"I've been thinking . . . well, about your dad's friend's number by his phone. I know your feelings are hurt because your father didn't confide in you, but why not call Joseph, letting him know of your dad's passing. Knowing your dad, he had his reasons. Maybe see what Joseph has to say. Feel him out. He might be able to share something about your dad's illness or about his plans . . . ah, afterwards. It's just a thought. If you don't want to call him, I've kept the funeral book from your mom's funeral."

Without much deliberation and reminding himself to be strong, Gabriel entered his office and sat in front of the phone. He inhaled slowly before picking up his dad's note—now resting beside his phone—and calling Joseph.

"Is this Joseph Allen?" Gabriel asked when the phone was answered.

"Yes, Gabriel . . . this is Joseph. I was just about to

call to see how Lukas was doing this morning."

Determined not to fall apart, Gabriel answered straight-forwardly, "My dad died early today."

"Dear God, I'm so sorry; I have no words." After a brief silence and with a husky voice, Joseph continued. "Regardless of the passing years, he is, was, and always will be my best friend. Gabriel, I'm here to assist you in any way I can."

"I'm still in shock . . . ah, hoping you can help me understand what's been happening with my father. Maybe you can help me with suggestions or ideas on Dad's wishes . . . even funeral wise, since he confided in you," said in a somewhat sarcastic manner.

Ignoring the edge in Gabriel's voice—finding it understandable and time to let it all out—Joseph responded, "I'll try to answer as best as I can."

"Did you and Dad talk about his illness?" Gabriel asked, wanting to get right to the point.

Joseph began as gently and thoughtfully as he could. "Once your father knew there was no hope, he didn't want to burden his illness with anyone . . . especially wanting to protect you and your wife from it. To my knowledge he told no one except me. He wanted all of the attention directed toward finding your daughter. He did plan to tell you in due time but wanted to find Jennifer first, using any means possible without regard to his own safety. He was angry after the trial, wanting to take out anyone involved in her disappearance or involved in freeing the man responsible for abducting her. Because of his illness, he felt he had nothing to lose."

"What do you mean take out anyone?" Gabriel asked hesitantly. Waiting for an answer but receiving none, Gabriel continued, "That's unbelievable but so much like Dad."

"I was sworn to secrecy. I hope you understand my first obligation was to my friend's wishes. I could never betray the trust he gave me."

"I sorta understand. That's not to say I like it."

"Lukas also gave me his thoughts . . . well, in case something happened to him . . . either while getting revenge or when the cancer took him. I don't think I'm doing anything now against his trust. No matter what you may feel, he loved you with all his heart. If you can grasp any of this, you need to hold on to that." After an uncomfortable silence, Joseph asked, "Gabriel, are you still there?"

"Yes, I hear what you're saying, but I feel cheated. I should have spent more time with him. It's just a lot to take in."

Understanding Gabriel's bewilderment, Joseph said, "Believe me, if I had any idea it would be this soon, I would have been with him too. You didn't know he was sick, but I did; so I'm full of a lot of guilt.

"We briefly discussed his thoughts on his funeral wishes. I didn't want to talk about it, but your dad insisted. He just wanted a simple graveside service with a military color guard. He said he wanted you to contact the same funeral home that took care of your mom. The grave plot next to your mom is already paid for. He told me all of this because he was afraid if he told you, you'd get suspicious and start asking questions. He didn't want to lie to you. I'll not fault you on whatever you decide to do. I'm just passing on what Lukas told me."

"Thank you for your honesty." Gabriel offered. "I'll call and let you know when the funeral service . . . ah, graveside service will be."

"I'll be there. You know . . . I just read something you might find interesting . . . food for thought so to speak. When a person dies, they're not entirely gone . . . we just can't see them. Then, when they're buried or cremated, they're still not entirely gone. It's not until their name is no longer mentioned or they're no longer remembered by those left behind, that they'll finally be gone forever. I'm sure we'll both think of him and say his name and remember him for as long as we are living. Take care and call me anytime."

"Thank you for your help. Again, I'll call you with final plans and times." Somehow coming more to terms with his loss, Gabriel asked, "Before I let you go, is there anyone close to Dad that might want to attend the service?" As he waited for an answer, he was feeling less angry, realizing it did no good to find fault with his dad or his dad's friend.

"You might let Selma know. Do you know her?"

"No, I don't think so."

"She owns the Coffee and More Diner not far from your dad's house. She and your mom were really close . . .

best friends. I can't think of anyone else right now, but Selma will know of others. I'll call if someone else comes to mind. Take care and call me anytime."

Finishing the conversation with Gabriel, Joseph called James.

"Have you heard the sad news?" Joseph asked when James answered.

"Not a word, but I'm guessing Lukas passed."

"Yes, early this morning. I just got off the phone with Gabriel. Maybe it's better than a long drawn-out suffering battle with terrible pain. I should have gone to San Francisco with you."

"I think it was more sudden than any of us thought. I can only imagine how Gabriel feels . . . in the dark and all. I wish I could have found Jennifer for Lukas. What should I do now?"

"What do you mean?" Joseph questioned.

"Should I stay through the two week period and keep delving into her disappearance? As far as I know, neither Gabriel nor his wife knows why I'm here. Did you say anything to them?"

"I told him nothing about you. I told him that Lukas didn't tell anyone about his illness except me . . . which is true. I tried to help him understand why I knew about his dad's illness, and he didn't."

"How did he take it?" James asked.

"I'm not sure. I also told him about Lukas wanting only a graveside funeral."

"I hope Gabriel can wrap his feelings around how

special you were to each other."

"I hope so too," Joseph replied before sighing.

"What do you think? Should I talk to Gabriel?

"Let me think about it. Gabriel is going to call with the service particulars. When I hear, I'll call you."

"Dad, I'm really sorry for your loss. Promise me if you find yourself in a similar situation, you'll tell me the truth."

While not imagining ever being in a similar situation, Joseph answered, "Of course" but couldn't promise he wouldn't have done exactly as Lukas did."

Chapter 31

When Carly opened her front door, James found a new woman staring back at him. After inviting him in and acting mysteriously, she said, "I'll get you a beer, leaving him standing in the living room playing with the dogs. He watched her leave, zeroing in on the blond wig cascading down the back of her short black dress and swaying back and forth with each step. Almost to the kitchen door, she said loudly over her shoulder, "I bought some wine too." She sounded different—bordering on giddy—when she disappeared into the kitchen. Soon, she hollered, "This is fresh wine. Well, not exactly fresh but not spoiled." Baffled, James wondered if she'd already had a couple of glasses. She not only looked different but sounded different. What was going on?

Instead of waiting for Carly to return with his beer, James decided to follow her. Walking quietly into the kitchen and almost behind her, he put into words what he'd been thinking, "Where did Carly go?"

As James awkwardly waited for an answer, Carly turned to face him but didn't speak right away. Looking downward, she stammered, "I've transformed myself into another person . . . the kind of person I'd thought you'd like."

Hoping his true feelings weren't showing, James took a closer look at her face. Since he'd been captivated by her amazing natural look, he couldn't remember ever seeing her with bright red lipstick or intense blush on her cheeks. Giving her the benefit of doubt, maybe she was blushing. No, it was definitely makeup. Thank goodness, her beautiful dark eyes were still unchanged. Since liking the before Carly, he became tongue-tied . . . not knowing how to reply, or exactly what to say.

James skirted her remark by saying, "You look so different. What brought this on?"

"I had a long talk with Charlotte. I told her I wanted to be "pretty" for you. She told me to go for it. So, what do you think?"

Still stunned and again not sure how to answer, he took the cowardly way out . . . answering her question with a question. "What do I think?"

"About my new look," Carly responded with raised eyebrows.

"I liked how you looked before. I like everything about you. You are beautiful just the way you are without changing."

Her answer was a simple, "Thank you."

Not sure how to interpret Carly's reply, James offered, "If changing your look makes you happy; then you should . . . but not for me. Feeling uncomfortable, he gazed into her eyes before saying, "I think I need that beer."

James wanted to tell her about Lukas's passing but

didn't think the timing was right. Not sure there was ever a good time to discuss someone's dying; he'd tell her later. Still thinking of Lukas and his reason for being in San Francisco, James took the beer and watched Carly pick up her wine glass, noting the wine bottle was already half empty.

As Carly placed her wine glass on the coffee table, he couldn't remember her drinking alcohol before on any of their earlier encounters . . . even at dinner by the wharf.

Breaking the silence, he said, "This is the first time I've seen you drink."

"I know. In my past it was a way of escaping. It helped me be numb to what was happening around me and to me. It's different now with you. I can relax and be myself with no need to be afraid or wanting to hide away."

While Carly talked about her feelings of vulnerability and exposed more of her past, James asked if he could get another beer from the kitchen. "No, I'll get it," she quickly responded.

When he reached for her hand, almost automatically to help her up, her body jerked back . . . a little like she'd touched something dangerous. Standing and confused, James apologized before stating, "You don't need to wait on me."

"No, I apologize," Carly said quickly.

"Carly, what should I do? Should I not reach out to you? You are sending out a lot of mixed signals. I thought we'd made a connection after our beach outing. I waited for you to call but gave up and finally called you."

He started to tell her about Lukas but again didn't. He could have told her over the phone when asking if he could come to her house but used the information as a reason to see her again. He was the one messed up. She obviously thought of him as a friend. She'd already said as much . . . using comments like he was easy to talk to and feeling safe with him.

Not receiving a response, James swigged the last remaining drop of beer, saying, "When it comes to your own personal space, you can always be in total control with me. I wanted a relationship with you but either you're not ready or you don't feel the same way about me. That's on me for reading something into it that wasn't there."

"You are mistaken. You are the first man I've wanted to like me, and the first man I thought wanted to be with me for who I am. The first man I felt didn't see me as damaged goods. I never considered it possible to be with a man who cared about my happiness." Pausing and taking a big breath, Carly continued. "James, I never thought I could know what desire feels like. It's not a feeling I've hidden away, because I've never felt it before. I'm not afraid for myself; I'm afraid of disappointing you. I'm afraid of making you unhappy." Thinking of her hysterectomy scar, Carly added, "I'm afraid of you running away in disgust."

"Carly, none of that would happen because none of that is true."

Carly lifted her shaking hands and placed them

against the sides of his face. What James did next seemed a natural reaction, wrapping his arms around her and pulling her in for a kiss. It was now or never, he thought. Win or lose, it seemed like the only response that made sense. James felt her body against him from head to toe, but regardless of how much he wanted her, he would not make the first move.

"Tell me what you want?" he asked in a raspy voice.

Feeling the closeness between them and finding it difficult to speak, Carly felt the kiss deep inside, sparking a previously unknown yearning. She would no longer fight the unknowns and was about to embark on another new experience. She grinned to herself when thinking the moment had arrived to be bold, similar to the female protagonists in many of the books she'd read. Backing away, she raised her eyebrows in a come-hither look and said, "Shhhh, follow me."

As they parted, James said, "I'll follow you anywhere." Walking closely behind Carly, he was taken aback by her eagerness to take him to the bedroom. Was this really going to happen?

When they reached the bedroom door, Carly stopped, threw off the wig, and took James's hand.

For a sliver of time—just a moment of uncertainty—he stared at her. However, before stepping through the bedroom doorway, he was already kicking off his shoes.

*   *   *   *

Their first night together was full of intimate abandonment. For James it was more meaningful on an emotional level than ever experienced before. It was not just the excitement or attraction for Carly but a more mature and wiser connection and tenderness for another person.

For Carly it was a time of trust and healing, and believing she had fallen in love. She had never dreamed of what loving someone would feel like. Of all of the new feelings, the one that astonished her the most was the utter contentment.

James had forgotten how good it felt to wake in the morning feeling close to the person beside him. He tried to sneak to the bathroom without disturbing Carly, but she raised her head and gave him an electric smile before saying, "Hurry back."

Finishing another blissful time together, Carly said, "I'm famished." After both equally devoured a box of frozen waffles—eaten as quickly as they popped up from the toaster—Carly offered, "I'm going to take a shower and then come back and clean up the breakfast dishes while you take one. I mean, if you want to take a shower."

"Bossy already," James said with a grin.

"No, I want to learn everything about what you like and don't like," she answered with a faint frown.

"I thought you already had."

"Already had what?" Carly quizzed.

"Learned what I like and don't like," James replied with a wink.

Blushing, Carly asked seriously, "Was it okay?"

"It was better than okay; it was wonderful. More importantly, was it okay for you?"

Before she could answer, they heard the dogs barking from their closed dog's room. "Oh my gosh, I've forgotten about the girls. They must really need to go outside. You've ruined my entire schedule."

"I'm sorry," James replied seriously.

Grinning, Carly said, "I can tease too. I already told work I was taking a vacation day today. In fact I'm taking the rest of the week off."

"When did you do that?" James asked with curiosity.

"After you called and asked to come see me," she answered coyly. "Would you take Maggie and Penny out while I take a shower?"

"Yes, but only if you'll kiss me first," he replied and puckered up.

By the time they'd both showered and straightened the kitchen, the early morning mist had disappeared, leaving behind a beautiful warm day. Carly and James sat on the porch swing, talking about a little of everything. Although James did not delve into his investigation, he did finally tell her about Lukas's passing.

"Would you go to the graveside service with me Friday?" James asked.

"Of course I will. I only met him a couple of times but it was easy to see how much he loved Jennifer."

"Something else I'd like your opinion about. Do you think I should tell Gabriel and Michelle Walker my reason for being here in San Francisco? They don't know."

"Do you plan to continue with your investigation regardless of their reaction?" Carly quizzed.

"I'm not sure. Wouldn't they want me to . . . like do whatever I can to find her?"

"I think they would. I want you to. How much were you charging Lukas?"

"Nothing, because of my dad's friendship with Lukas; I just wanted to help."

"Wow, you are a good son and a good person," Carly said with a big smile.

"So are you. I wish I was rich enough to give you all that you deserve."

"Being safe with you and no longer afraid is something money can't buy."

For a split second, James thought of Margie and how her mind-set was so opposite from Carly's. Margie had always gotten her way while Carly was just beginning to find her way. Carly seemed appreciative and content with the simpler things of life, while Margie could never have enough material things.

Okay self . . . listen up. In the future you will never again compare Carly to Margie. In fact how can anyone be compared to Carly? She is such a unique and special person. While contemplating on how different Margie and Carly were, James realized how much he too had changed into a different person. Like Carly, he was ready and willing to embark on a new way of life.

Chapter 32

Not sure how long it would take to pick up Carly and find the cemetery, James thought he'd planned on plenty of time. However, due to road repair and a detour near Carly's, he was running late.

Rushing Carly into the car, he said, "You look nice. Sorry, for hurrying you along but the service starts at 10:00, and we'll barely make it."

"Are you sure I'm dressed appropriately?" Carly asked for the second time.

Smiling when saying, "Yes, you look real nice," but briefly thinking of the blond wig and hoping it never surfaced again.

"This is a first for me, and I'm kinda nervous. I've never been to a funeral before," Carly confessed. "Charlotte said to wear something dark and conservative."

Fibbing a little but for a good cause, James squeezed her hand before saying, "I think you always look great."

Locating the cemetery quicker than expected, James looked for a place to park, passing his dad's car while searching. Surprised by the large turn-out and number of cars, they hurried to join the group of mourners already sitting or standing in the direction of the casket.

Relieved the service hadn't started yet, James looked

for his father, spotting him standing in front of two empty chairs. That told him two things . . . Dad came early enough to save a place for the two of them and was standing in order to watch for him. Since his father was a stickler for promptness, James knew he would be anxiously waiting for his arrival and had probably already noticed him. It suddenly dawned on him that he'd not mentioned Carly's name during any of their conversations and especially that he'd be bringing her.

"Carly, I see my dad," James offered before waving.

Following James's gaze, Carly saw a gentleman wave in their direction.

Leaning over to whisper in Carly's ear, James said, "Let's go over and say hello before the ceremony begins."

After James introduced Carly, he explained how Carly worked at the Boys and Girls Club where Jennifer went missing. Wishing he'd phrased the introduction differently, he noticed Carly take a deep breath before extending her hand and saying, "Nice to meet you." James wanted to tell his father they were more than acquaintances but in due time, he thought.

Joseph offered Carly the empty seat beside him. Realizing the seat was intended for James, Carly looked quickly at James. He whispered, "Your choice," and smiled.

After thanking Joseph for his offer, she added, "I'm fine standing."

Thinking James and Carly might be closer than mere acquaintances, Joseph shrugged before saying, "Well,

I'm going to sit my old bones down. If you change your mind . . . little lady, help yourself."

Noticing the minister was walking toward the group, James took a moment to scan the mourners, beginning with Michelle and Gabriel sitting in the front row and directly across from the flag draped casket. Uniformed servicemen were showing their respect for an honorable veteran by standing at attention beside each end of the coffin.

Thinking about his dad's and Lukas's special relationship, it seemed fitting for Lukas to have a funeral service with the American flag draped respectfully over his casket. Although seldom discussed—his father clammed-up about specific details of those awful war days—James knew his father appreciated the respect his friend had earned and deserved. He also noticed the large bouquet of white flowers with red, white, and blue ribbons. It crossed his mind he'd never talked about funeral arrangements with his father, making a mental note to do so in the near future.

Continuing to look through the crowd, it was not surprising the mourners were comprised of mostly older people. He'd attended quite a few funerals while doing investigative work so scanning through the mourners seemed natural . . . almost routine. Although attending this service was personal, James couldn't keep from looking at the different faces . . . wondering if the neighbor who found Lukas was there.

After glimpsing through the ones standing, he began

scanning the faces of those sitting, immediately doing a double-take when noticing the two people sitting at the end of the last row opposite where he was standing. He recognized the lady from the coffee shop where he'd met Lukas . . . remembering her name was Selma. He'd easily recalled her name because it was similar to Lukas's deceased wife's name.

At first glance—noticing the man sitting beside Selma—he assumed Gabriel had moved back to talk to Selma. However, looking back again at the front row, Gabriel was still sitting there. What the heck? The man next to Selma was the splitting image of Gabriel. Looking closer—outright staring—the man was obviously dressed differently but both were wearing dark glasses with wire frames. It was difficult to tell if they were the same height . . . thinking maybe Gabriel was a little heavier. The similarity was uncanny.

Leaning over to his dad's ear, James asked, "What's with the guy sitting in the last row next to Lukas's friend . . . ah, Selma from the restaurant?"

Without turning—why should he . . . he'd already seen them—Joseph replied, "Later, the minister's about to speak."

Throughout the service, James continued to sneak quick looks in their direction, while Joseph pretended not to notice and stared straight ahead.

As he watched the color guard fold the flag and hand it to Gabriel, Joseph knew the ceremony would soon be concluding. Motioning to James to come closer, Joseph asked, "Do you and Carly want to go with me to offer our condolences to Michelle and Gabriel?"

Neither answered but both nodded in the affirmative. Once the ceremony was officially over, they walked toward the front and waited while others before them stopped to briefly visit.

Joseph was the first to speak. After introducing himself, he said, "I think you've already met my son, James, and ah . . . Carly. I'm sorry, I don't know Carly's last name."

"It's Carly Strong, and yes, we already know each other," Carly said without hesitation.

Once their condolences were offered, James suggested the three of them go somewhere to have lunch and chat. James looked around for the mysterious man, but he and Selma were nowhere to be seen.

Sitting comfortably in a booth and after ordering, James asked, "So, what's the deal with the guy who looks identical to Gabriel?"

"That's because he is," Joseph replied calmly.

"I'm confused. Say that again."

Looking in Carly's direction, Joseph said, "First, this conversation should remain strictly between the three of us. It's very personal so please don't let it go any further."

Receiving a nod from Carly, followed by, "Of course," Joseph continued. "He's Gabriel's identical twin."

"No way," James responded. "I mean . . . I believe what you're saying, but it's hard to believe. I researched Gabriel, and there was no mention of a sibling."

Understanding James's confusion, Joseph resumed. "I was surprised to see him at the funeral. It's been a big secret all these years. I'm thinking Gabriel has no idea he's a twin . . . much less an identical twin. If he did, they'd most likely be sitting together. Maybe the brother—sitting by Selma—does, but I have no idea so can't comment on that."

"Dad, could you start from the beginning? This is fascinating," James uttered.

"Okay, I'll tell you what happened. Wait . . . before I do, Selma might be the only person alive—other than me— who knows the truth. I'm not even sure she knows I know."

Joseph's eyes, slightly watery and appearing far-away, began again. "Lukas and I . . . well, as far as I know, never had a single secret between us. He certainly knew all about my dirty laundry. Let's see, where was I? Oh yes . . . Thelma and Lukas couldn't have children. Well, Thelma couldn't. Thelma and Selma were like sisters, so it was agreed Selma would carry a child for them. So the story goes—and I have no reason to doubt it— there were different techniques suggested by the doctor used to get Selma pregnant. I won't go into the details of what Lukas told me was tried, but official fertilization procedures were too expensive. When nothing happened with what the girls tried, Thelma asked them to do it the old fashioned way. It took . . . after just one time . . . supposedly."

"Meaning . . . Lukas and Selma slept together?"

James asked.

"Way to go detective on figuring that out," Joseph responded with a chuckle. "Yes, Lukas told me Thelma insisted on watching, so there was "no hanky-panky" going on. Thelma was something else, willing to do anything to have a child."

"Unbelievable," was all James could say.

Obviously relieved to get the more personal part behind, Joseph began telling them what happened next. "When Selma got pregnant, the sonogram showed she was pregnant with twins. After a lengthy heart to heart conversation, Lukas said the only decision that made sense to all of them . . . Selma would keep one and Lukas and Thelma would keep the other."

"Was Selma married then?" James asked.

"No, but eventually married and her husband adopted her child when he was two years old."

"So, where's the husband? I didn't see him at the funeral," James inquired.

"I'm not really sure. Early on, all I ever heard was he was a good person and father. Later on, it was never discussed. I didn't ask and Lukas never volunteered. You can't imagine the memories that flooded back today when I saw them at the funeral."

Following up on the bazaar story, James couldn't help but ask, "Why do you think Selma brought him to the funeral. Wouldn't she be afraid of Gabriel seeing him or maybe you recognizing the connection?"

"Good question and one I can't answer," Joseph

replied with a shrug. Almost like thinking out loud, Joseph added, "I should probably touch bases with Selma before leaving but . . . probably won't."

Thinking how awkward such a meeting would be, it dawned on James that in reality, Jennifer was actually Selma's biological granddaughter. There were so many questions wandering around in his head like: Did Gabriel's twin know he was adopted? Did the twin know Lukas was his biological father? Would Selma ever spill the beans to Gabriel and Michelle? Did Selma's twin have children? If Gabriel looked at his birth certificate, would he think his mother's first name had a typo error? What about the last name? Surely, he'd know his mother's maiden name. The big question . . . why did Selma publically flaunt her son at the graveside service knowing there could be consequences if recognized? He could understand Gabriel being distracted by grief but wouldn't his twin notice how similar in appearance they were. Even though his curiosity was running wild, he doubted he'd ever know the answers . . . and probably shouldn't. After all . . . it was a personal matter and really none of his business. Let it go, he told himself. Let it go.

Carly had been sitting quietly, listening intently but not wanting to interrupt with questions or comments. After Joseph's last remark and a short lull in the discussion, Carly said, "How fortunate for both boys to have families who loved them and wanted them.

Before anyone could respond, James's phone went off. Glancing at the screen, he saw the call was from Sam.

Saying, "Sorry," to no one in particular, James answered with a guarded, "Hello."

"Can you talk?" Sam asked.

"Sorta . . . hang on."

Excusing himself from the table, James asked, "What's up?"

"I was . . . I mean Jack Dutton's assistant was contacted. The conversation was really strange from the get-go."

"That's interesting. Who did the contacting?" James quizzed.

"An actual name by the caller was never offered. The conversation was a weird give and take of innuendos from the beginning. No names were used but a prospective attendee to an annual antique gathering was alluded to. Seems this person—not named—was inquiring about an annual event and the production of needed paperwork. I played it cool, mentioning the necessity on our end to be cautious, asking exactly what was needed. I told him I was sure he understood my meaning."

"How did the conversation end?" James asked.

"I said I would pass on the information to the un-named prospective attendee. I also asked what the timeframe was like for getting the information sent back. Was time of the essence?"

"Good," James commented.

"He said the next annual San Francisco event was only two weeks away and better to plan on attending a future event, giving both parties time to vet each other. I tried to narrow the date down without sounding suspicious, saying the prospective attendee would be disappointed and couldn't the paperwork be hurried along. I tell you, it was like talking to the CIA, regarding a clandestine operation."

"Good job, Sam. I've checked the day and date when the girl went missing. It was on a Friday, and it's been about a year. I have no doubt the creep is going to strike again in two weeks. Sam, thank you. I should be back at work next Monday. I have some ideas, and we'll talk then."

"James, no need to thank me; it was fun. See you Monday."

Quickly joining the others, who seemed to be having a nice discussion, they both looked up questioningly, before Joseph asked, "Everything okay?"

"Yeah, just talking to a guy I work with. He wanted to know if I'd be back at work soon. I told him I'd see him Monday."

As they continued with lunch, even ordering dessert, James noticed Carly becoming less and less talkative. Something was obviously bothering her. Had his dad said something to offend her? As soon as they were alone, he'd find out.

Chapter 33

Placing his luggage by the front door, James took Carly's hand before saying, "Thank you for letting me stay the last couple of days."

"My house isn't fancy but the company must have been better than at the hotel," she replied with a grin.

"Slightly better, but the best part was being with Maggie and Penny," James quipped.

Looking closely at Carly, he realized tears were beginning to trickle down her cheeks. He pulled her to him, cradling her securely against him. Carly placed her arms tightly around him and laid her head on his chest . . . never wanting to let go.

"Hey, I thought we had this all worked out. Remember . . . I'll be back soon, and we can talk every day on the phone."

"What if you don't?" she asked without releasing him.

"What if I don't what?" James asked calmly.

"What if I never see you again? What if you forget about me when you return to your friends in Los Angeles?"

"Carly, I want to be with you as much as you want to be with me. I need to check in at work and then come back to finish up loose ends here in San Francisco. Your job—while I'm away—is to decide what you want to do with your future. Like I told you; I'm open to anything. I can move to this area, or you can come to L A. Again, it will be your choice."

Listening again to James's words of reassurance, Carly felt somewhat better. He'd told her the same things earlier, but his leaving was now more real. She turned her head upward, wanting more than anything to believe him.

James looked deeply into her dark glistening eyes before gently kissing the tears on her cheeks. Smiling, he followed with an equally tender kiss on the lips.

"Carly, you've made a profound difference in my life. Even though we've only known each other for a short time . . . a very short time, I can't imagine being with anyone else. I'm not perfect and will make a lot of mistakes going forward, but I'll always want to be with you . . . always."

"Promise you won't forget me," she said pathetically.

"Never, never, never . . . I promise," James replied.

For a split second, Carly remembered Ayand's lies and promises before she came to America. Remembering the anticipation and excitement before leaving Thailand and the utter disbelief and disappointment that followed, she cringed. Scolding herself for having such thoughts, James was nothing like Ayand, and her old life was permanently in the past. Carly ducked her head against his shoulder and whispered, "I love you." She purposely didn't say the words loud enough for him to hear. While she hoped he'd say those exact words to her some day, she didn't want James to ever feel obligated.

As she watched him drive away, she wondered whether there would ever come a time in her lifetime when she wouldn't thank James for saving her from her life of self-imprisonment. Even if he went home and never saw her again, her heart would have a connection to him forever. By his actions he had taught her what true kindness was all about. He had showed her that enjoying sex was possible. He had helped her understand how a man and a woman could be together and have a normal relationship . . . full of fun and trust.

Carly continued to watch his car until it disappeared completely. She missed him already. She had disclosed her real self . . . unprotected by lies or cover-ups, and he still wanted to be with her. How amazing was that? He had seen the sick and damaged person she once was and accepted her for what she yearned to be. She would cling to the words he told her last night until they were together again. "Carly, I will hold you in my arms forever, keeping you safe and loving you always."

Chapter 34

Walking into his office, James was met at the door by Sam. Seeing a big smile on his friend's face, James remarked, "You're here early. Guess you missed me."

"I wanted to hear if you had more news or ideas on what you planned to do. A meeting is scheduled for 9:00 o'clock in the conference room, so I wanted to talk to you early. I even made coffee in the break room."

"Damn, you did miss me," James answered with an equally big smile. "I have some ideas but need your help and input. Let's get some coffee. I'm bushed . . . had a long drive home last night."

"You got it . . . Bro."

After pouring their coffee and noticing the break room was still empty, James got right to the point. "Do you remember

the smoke bomb we made for the Ferguson job?"

"Yeah, the one used for diversion," Sam replied.

"Would you help me make another one?" James asked.

"Help you? Get real . . . if I remember correctly, I made it; you used it. It didn't have explosives . . . right?" Sam quizzed.

"Right . . . no explosives. I don't want anyone to get hurt. On second thought, I'm thinking maybe at a minimum . . . two would be better."

"Okay . . . but what's your end result? One with explosives would be more fun."

"You have a sick mind . . . but no explosives."

Seeing the secretary walk in behind Sam, James let Sam know they were no longer alone by looking up before saying, "Good morning, Silvia."

Seeming not surprised to find James in the break room and probably already aware of his return, she replied, "Welcome back. How was your vacation?"

"It was great. Thanks for asking."

"Did Sam tell you about the meeting this morning?" she asked. Receiving a nod, she immediately said, "I smell coffee."

"You can thank Sam for that," James offered.

After taking a sip and looking in Sam's direction, she said, "Thank you Sam; it's good. Would you like a side job?"

"No, I think I'll pass."

Discussing nothing of consequence—San Francisco traffic and weather—they waited for the secretary to leave before Sam returned to their previous conversation. "Let me know amounts, distances, and etc, so I can gather materials for our project."

As James replied, "Will do and thanks again," the company's two other investigators entered the break room. Exchanging niceties about his vacation time away,

James left to check out his cubicle, finding it just as he'd left it . . . in total disarray.

While sorting through miscellaneous files and paperwork—trying to get a handle on what to do first—he came upon a file marked: San Francisco. Although curious to see what information Sam gathered on the creep, he set it aside. Seeing the file also made him think of calling Carly, but that also needed to wait. Besides, this was also her first day back at work, and she would be busy too.

Before leaving for San Francisco to help his father's friend, he'd been fixated on work and nothing else. Admittedly his job and the accompanied investigations had been his whole world.

As his mind continued to intermittently wander back to Carly and her girls, it was difficult to get back into a work related routine. He could never admit to Sam or anyone else how much he missed Carly and the dogs. Yes, his life had definitely changed. And, for all the naysayers involved in his life, understandably two weeks was a ridiculously short time to get to know someone . . . much less fall in love with them.

James attended the company meeting—thinking the rah-rah pep talk was a waste of time—before having a brief one-on-one meeting with his boss. After discussing his vacation, briefly describing what he'd done but not mentioning Carly or his personal detective work, his boss said, "Glad you're back. Get up to speed on your next assignment as quickly as possible; lots of bad people out there doing lots of bad things."

His reply, "So true, and looks like I'll be leaving for Las Vegas tomorrow on the Granger case."

"Don't gamble all your money away," his boss replied with a grin.

"What money? I just returned from two week's vacation in San Francisco," quipped with an equal grin.

Needing to organize his plans for the Granger investigation and knowing he wouldn't be in the office for a few days, James didn't take a lunch break.

It was early in the evening hours when James finally decided to call it quits. He stopped by Sam's cubicle to tell him good night, but found it vacant. Glancing at the items he was holding, it dawned on him he'd left the San Francisco file on his desk. As he returned to his spot and picked up the file, he realized he was both tired and hungry. Having no idea what was at his apartment to eat—probably a lot of rotten food in the refrigerator— he'd stop and grab a bite on the way home. No matter how exhausted, he'd not hit the hay before calling Carly.

The conversation went well with Carly, but he'd made the mistake of stretching out on the bed before calling her. Aware of her insecurities regarding them talking again—much less seeing each other again—he wasn't surprised by how excited she seemed to hear his voice. After talking almost an hour and listening to the different interactions with the children on her first day back to work, he'd felt himself beginning to doze off. Apologizing for needing to go, he'd told her about his business trip to

Las Vegas the following day. She sounded jealous when she mentioned, "Don't look at all those beautiful show girls . . . just think of me and how much I miss you." He'd grinned when answering, "Why would I do that when I know the prettiest girl in the whole world?"

Their discussion ended when he assured her he'd call the next day but wasn't exactly sure when. Not wanting her to think he was ignoring her, he also let her know— because of his line of work—he sometimes needed to turn off his phone. "Of course, if an emergency . . . you can always call me," he added quickly

*　　*　　*　　*

James woke the next morning still dressed in the same clothes he'd worn to work. Disoriented at first, he wasn't sure of his whereabouts. Realizing he was back in his Los Angeles apartment and not in the San Francisco hotel room or Carly's house, he jumped out of bed and headed for the shower. Mad at himself for not setting the alarm, he wasn't going to be on the road as early as planned.

Leaving L A's heavy traffic behind, James put on his favorite tape and let his mind wander. After his vacation time away, he was surprised to be given an assignment out of town. He wondered why Sam or one of the other investigators weren't offered the job, deciding his boss probably had a good reason. While caught up in the smoke bomb discussion, he'd forgotten to ask Sam what case he was presently working on. Since infidelity surveillance was Sam's favorite assignment, it was a given he would have already volunteered the graphic details even before being asked.

Thinking about his destination, he'd been to Las Vegas many times, but it was always work related. He made a mental note to visit Las Vegas with Carly. What a new experience it would be for her. How much fun it would be to watch her encounter the places so many others took for granted. He could take her to the zoo and what about Disneyland. The possibilities were endless. Maybe it would be better to let her make a list of the places she wanted to visit instead of making suggestions. Even if she was into the arts, which he wasn't, it would be fun to watch her experience new opportunities. He thought about her touching the ocean for the first time and smiled.

Pulling into the circular driveway of the hotel where he had a reservation and most likely where his person of interest was staying, James reminded himself to concentrate on his job and set aside any distracting thoughts . . . especially thoughts of Carly.

Once settled into his room, James laid out several phones. Separating the phone which took the clearest videos from the others, he made sure it was fully charged and ready to go. After familiarizing himself with the case facts a final time, he checked around the room to make sure he was ready, not wanting to forget anything when he went hunting. Knowing this could be the last opportunity and perhaps the only chance to get the projected results his company was after, he didn't want to mess up.

Per the paperwork, Granger was due in court in less than a month. Mr. George Granger stated he was unable to walk without assistance—either a wheelchair or walker was needed—could not lift anything over five pounds, and was in constant back pain. According to Granger and his attorney, his supposed accident occurred at a fast food restaurant due to employee negligence . . . not cleaning ice off the floor in front of the ice dispenser, causing him to slip and fall. The security camera showed him from a back view getting ice but could not verify—one way or the other—the existence of ice on the floor. Before appearing to fall to the left, his arm did drop oddly to his left side and briefly shake.

While doing everything possible to acquire incriminating information . . . short of trespassing, the chain's insurance investigators had been watching his home and his few public outings. Since trying to catch him doing something he said he was unable to do, the insurance broker finally hired his company to directly delve into areas they were afraid to venture into for obvious reasons.

During the meeting with his boss, he was told of recently acquired information through social media followers that Granger would be in Las Vegas for a class reunion. Supposedly most of the out of town attendees would be staying at the same hotel where the festivities would be held in one of the hotel's banquet rooms. If Granger was registered there, James planned to check him out today, tonight, and—if necessary—tomorrow in order to obtain incriminating information on video. If not register there, his job would become more difficult. Worst case scenario, he wouldn't show at all.

When James entered the hotel to register, the signs welcoming different events happening within the hotel were abundant, so he was going back downstairs for a closer look.

Walking up to the receptionist counter, James asked, "I'm here for the class reunion in the "Glory Room."

"Yes, do you want to check in?" she asked pleasantly.

"No ma'am, I've done that. I forgot my buddy's room number." Trying to appear not too bright, he asked, "I'm sorry to bother you . . . cuz you're so busy and pretty, but could you give it to me . . . like help me out?"

As if answering the same way hundreds of times before, she responded, "Sir, it's against our policy to give out room numbers."

Appealing to her kinder side and looking as disheartened as he could, James asked, "What should I do? He has my ticket for the get-together. I've come a long way and won't be able to go."

"Let's see what I can do. What is his name?" she asked.

"It's George Granger."

"And what is your name?" she asked, looking at the line gathering behind him.

"Just tell him it's . . . ah, Big Boots is here for the class reunion." James said seriously.

"I'll be right with you," she responded with a smile, again looking at the line forming behind him.

Returning, she offered, "It's okay. The room number is 1612."

"Thank you . . . you're the best," James replied, while thinking that went well . . . both easy and successful. If the name he'd used from social media hadn't worked, he would have used another follower with a different receptionist. He'd not only learned his person of interest was staying there and had already checked in but also knew his room number. How good am I, giving himself an imaginary pat on the back.

Off to phase two, he thought. As his time would be filled with a lot of watching and waiting, he needed to return to his room and make a pot of coffee. Noting Granger's floor was only one below his, he'd be getting out on the wrong floor many times. That happened a lot when drinking, but not when drinking coffee, he thought with a grin. He again glanced at Granger's recent picture—tucked away in his shirt pocket for easy access—and focused on his prominent features.

Hating the down time of meandering around, watching, and waiting, he'd not seen his mark all afternoon. After numerous cups of coffee, frequent trips down the hall by room 1612, and several trips to the bathroom, he decided to change into nicer attire, something more appropriate for the banquet. Not interested in eating—he'd already eaten two hamburgers from the casual diner downstairs—his main focus would be directed to the dancing afterwards.

Dressed in a dark suit, he had about an hour's lead time before the banquet began but knew there was a meet-and-greet social time beforehand. Grabbing the big screen phone beside his room key, he left for the 16th floor. As the elevator opened and he started down the hall—maybe for the tenth time today—who should he meet but Mr. Granger; his arm around a lady's waist who looked half his age. Not recognizing him at first, his brown hair dyed black and much longer, he seemed in no pain—no pun intended—and walking without assistance from either a walker or wheelchair.

Quickly taking his phone out—like he was answering a call—he held it to the side of his face and in their direction before asking, "Would this be the 15th or 16th floor?"

Granger answered, "The sixteenth," while his lady friend replied with a giggle, "I don't know."

Walking casually past them before eventually turning around, he got a great shot of them waiting for the elevator, and even a better shot of Granger lifting her up in a bear hug. James gave a quiet description of where he was and what he was recording. Unsaid but thinking . . . the guy's lady friend definitely weighs more than five pounds.

Arriving at the welcoming reception table adjacent to the room's entrance, he saw Granger and his companion already mingling inside with others and wearing large white nametags. If possible, he'd get close enough to get a shot of his name tag before the night was over. Although focused on Granger's actions, he was curious what her nametag would read. While knowing the guy was married, he had a hunch she wasn't his wife.

"Hi, is it possible to buy a ticket at this late time?" James asked to one of the three ladies sitting behind the table.

"Reserved seats need to be purchased in advance. If we sell you one now, it will cost an extra fifty dollars and your table seat will be way in the back."

"That works for me. I've been out of the country and didn't think I'd be back in time."

Taking his two hundred dollars, she offered, "You can sit anywhere in the back section that doesn't have a reserved card in front of it. Just let the waiter know whether you want chicken, steak, or salmon."

Saying, "Thank you," James turned to leave.

Wanting to catch him before he got too far, she said loudly, "Wait a minute, you need a nametag." Quickly handing him a tag and marker, he wrote down his real name . . . just in case he needed to verify he was a guest at the hotel and there for the reunion. As he slapped the tag on his suit jacket and turned to leave again, she asked, "Excuse me . . . for our records what year are you?"

Sorta waving her off, he replied, "Gotta go, I see friends waving for me to hurry."

The banquet part of the evening was uneventful

with lots of talk about how wonderful everyone's life was, how prosperous they'd become, and how great their children were. At best, he figured maybe half of what was said was true. Everyone was busy taking videos and pictures, so his video actions didn't stand out. He took several shots of Granger during the meal, but other than sometimes being loud and obnoxious, his behavior was nothing out of the ordinary. He did get a good shot of him pulling out his lady friend's chair with her in it, so she could exit the room for a short time . . . probably to go to the bathroom. She passed right by him . . . her tag reading only "Alice." Although his wife's name was not listed on the paperwork, if he was a betting man, he'd bet Alice's last name wasn't Granger. Just in case it would be useful later, he took a clear shot of her nametag. He also questioned whether the other attendees knew his wife, thought he'd divorced, or even cared, deciding to quit wondering.

After the completion of the meal, tables were moved back to reveal a dance floor area, and curtains were opened on a raised stage where musician were beginning their first song.

James concentrated on George Granger, hoping it was now or never. Disappointed, he seemed uninterested in dancing. However, on the third song, young Alice dragged him out on the dance floor, moving sexily to the music as she led the way. James zeroed in on every angle of his body. Not the best fast dancer but he tried to keep up with her gyrations of hip thrusting and twirling. Wanting to tie the dancing video together with his nametag, James entered the packed dance floor unattended, working his way toward the couple, wanting to get as close as possible. Unnoticed by Granger or other dancers, James finally got the perfect shot. As the song ended, while James continued to video them, Granger picked her up and twirled her around in a complete circle. All that went through his mind . . . busted.

Returning to his table, James wondered if he should stay until the bloody end. He was tired, his stomach beyond full, and he wanted to talk to Carly. He missed her. He could work tomorrow to see how Granger exited the hotel. He could see if he loaded his own luggage. Maybe the guy would stay longer. Regardless of Granger's plans, James felt his job was done. He was more than satisfied with the outcome and certain his boss would think so too.

After hurriedly returning to his room and getting undressed, James called Carly. Apologizing for the lateness of the call, he stated, "I wish you were here with me."

Answering, "I wish I was there with you too. I'm lonely without you."

Telling her what he'd done during the day and evening and hearing about her day, he ended with these words, "I love you. Have a nice sleep."

Stunned to hear the words she'd been wishing for, she answered, "I love you too."

Neither disconnected the call and after a long silence,

James said, "I'll talk to you tomorrow after I'm back in Los Angeles.

"Thank you," Carly replied.

"Thank you for what," James asked.

"Just thank you . . . goodnight."

Chapter 35

Closing in on a week before their annual event, Lehmann wanted the San Francisco party to be the best ever. No expense had been spared in obtaining the desired object for each attending member. The criteria ranged from gender, age, race, color of eyes, color of hair, body type, and one odd request . . . a mute male child.

Gordon had been instrumental in acquiring the German's request, placing her in an off-site warehouse and hiring around-the-clock handlers to watch over her. Promised to arrive healthy and on time, she'd been secreted in from Nigeria a few days earlier. Wanting to make sure their most expensive commodity was well taken care of; Gordon made a point to check on her daily. While walking by the wharf, Gordon reported to Lehmann, "She's ideal and said to be about four years old . . . give or take a couple of months. Our German member should find her picture perfect and unspoiled as requested."

After last year's fiasco, they decided not to take any chances on crating in a special item on the same day as the event, preferring to go in a different direction. Those coming from out of the country had already arrived, quietly removed from the vessel by their handlers and kept in a secluded apartment building. The few snatched from locations in America were kept locally in quiet unsuspecting neighborhoods. After dark, all would be blindfolded and transported into the building's parking area and personally met by Lehmann and Gordon before the party's commencement. The older ones would be blindfolded and their hands tied behind their backs—some even gagged to prevent speaking—if necessary. To keep them from running, the group would then be tied together. No infants had been procured for this particular event.

Once the handler's turned over their human commodities, they were not allowed to leave the parking garage until the event ended, even told to stay close to their transport vans until all members exited the premises. As in past events held at the San Francisco building, sometimes the handlers were told to wait until Lehmann and Gordon finished with their personal activities with one or more particular captives that might have caught their eye during the evening. Other than the predicted death of the Nigerian object at the hands of the German, all others would be returned to the handlers for whatever they planned to do with them later. A captive's physical condition after a party was of no concern to either Lehmann or Gordon. As far as they were concerned . . . they were just damaged objects.

While all of The Club's world-wide events provide a lucrative business for Lehmann, Gordon, and the others involved in the background work, the Club created a night full of unqualified fulfillment for the members attending . . . regardless of the cost.

For the select group of members, it was a time to do or play-out their wildest dreams in a safe environment without regard to legality, family reproach, or public recrimination. Some pretended to be married to their chosen victim, some played doctor and patient, some played king and maid servant . . . the options were endless. Since the party was a one night event, most wanted to come as early as possible in order to use every possible moment to create their own personal fantasy.

As an extra bonus this year, the attendees would be offered a personal video of their activities to take away with them. If so desired, the four bedrooms could be set up accordingly. The beds would be enclosed by white panels so that no description regarding room decor or furnishings could be traced back to Lehmann or his building. The member involved could control when the filming was turned on or off.

By the time the final attendee numbers were in and verified, the human objects—almost twice as many as needed—had already been ordered. In past events usually a few more were ordered than needed, but this year's abundance would allow for additional choices and a bigger variety for the members to enjoy. Afraid the small member response had something to do with last year's trial—even though no member mentioned it as a problem—they decided to try the filming on a one year trial basis. The possibility of the video being distributed to other venues was carefully discussed by Lehmann and Gordon, but they ultimately decided their members would not incriminate themselves for obvious reasons and releasing the tape would open them up to blackmail and perhaps being personally traced . . . no matter what they were offered in compensation.

One of the bedrooms was set up for the German's personal use, having received extra attention because of the predicted nature of his final activity. He would be able to lock the room and would not be disturbed until he was finished. Once the German's ultimate desires were fulfilled, after the party's completion, and after Lehmann and Gordon were alone; the girl's body would be disposed of in the same manner as the two were taken care of after last year's gathering.

Feeling confident—even relaxed—the preparations were ahead of schedule. Lehmann and Gordon planned to spend the remaining days concentrating on each and every minute detail associated with their premiere event happening Friday . . . only a few days away.

From the existence of The Club, Friday had been the day most voted on by the members as their attendance preference. Friday was quoted by the majority of the members, because it gave them the weekend to get back into a normal routine after traveling. Most local attendees used the excuse of leaving for a three day weekend.

Beginning to feel giddy, it would soon be their opportunity to cut loose and have fun in their own environment. Looking forward to the possibility, each was unable to hide his excitement, giving each other an unusual high-five before leaving the dock.

Chapter 36

Back to work after a successful Las Vegas trip, James was scheduled to meet with his boss early, prepared to turn over the Granger discovery information.

Barely settled into his cubicle, Sam showed up. Looking up, he found his co-worker with a big smile on his face and holding two cups of coffee. Returning Sam's smile, James quipped, "Did you make coffee again . . . just for me?"

"Well, Silvia and I made it together. It's a very important and difficult task . . . not to mention a two person job."

"Really, you and Silvia, huh?" James replied with a knowing look.

Leaning over and whispering, Sam said rather proudly, "She brought me coffee on my last stake-out too."

"None of my business but I hope no one was staking the two of you out . . . company rules and all. And she's single . . . right?"

"Of course, and I've personally checked her out," Sam answered with raised eyebrows.

"I bet you have . . . very personally," James responded with a robust head nod.

"How about we take a quick walk to my car?" Sam asked.

"Okay, but it's got to be quick. I need to turn-in my Las Vegas file in about half an hour."

"It won't take long. Here, take your coffee," Sam answered.

As they walked, Sam asked, "By the way, how did Vegas go?"

"Better than expected. The guy is so busted."

"Good job. I wanted to go but sorta got into trouble the last time I was in Vegas."

"Really . . . I didn't know that," James replied with honest surprise.

"Yeah, I lost my head and tackled the guy I was watching. I compromised the assignment and almost lost my job. Not an excuse but I'd dropped a lot of money and had too much to drink. In my defense he was man-handling the gal he was with. When she screamed, he took off running."

Opening the trunk of his car, Sam bent over and carefully removed a box before saying, "I made four. After you gave me the numbers, I decided a couple wouldn't quite do. They all work like the ones we used before, just a quick pull on the top cap. Remember, you'll only get maybe five minutes out of each one. If you think you'll need more, you can buy some to fill in. Just keep in mind the bought ones only give you a minute or so at best. Response time will definitely play into it."

"Thanks. Speaking of time, I'm going to ask the boss

for time off again. I hope he'll go along with it, cuz if not, I'm leaving anyway."

"It's that important to you?" Sam asked bewildered.

"I'm fairly sure it's going down next Friday. If I lose my chance, the creep will continue his sickening ways. If my plan doesn't work, then I'll be screwed. Either way, I want to give it a shot."

"If it'll help, I'll fill in for you. Wish I could go and see how it all plays out," Sam offered.

"Me too. Guess we should go back in . . . it's time for my meeting." Stopping in mid-stride, he quickly added, "I should put these in my car. Thanks again and I'll let you know how the meeting goes."

Giving the thumbs-up signal, Sam said, "Good luck and see you later."

Holding the Las Vegas file and other gathered materials, James knocked on the boss's door. Noticing his boss was on the telephone—seeing him through the glass on both side of the door—he hesitated to walk in without being acknowledged. Listening as the phone conversation terminated,, he heard, "James, come on in."

Unloading an arm-full of investigative bits and pieces on the boss's desk, James took a seat. While inhaling deeply, he was already contemplating the best way to address his time-off request.

Getting right to the point, his boss said, "From our earlier conversation, you had a successful Vegas trip."

"Yes, the guy is quite the scammer. I think the client will be very pleased with our results."

"No problems to share?"

"No, it was actually a piece of cake. I even cut my stay short."

"Good work. I already have a couple of other jobs lined up for you. They're both local and fairly straightforward.

"Actually, I would like to go out of town again . . . on a personal matter."

"Didn't you just come back from a two week's vacation?" asked in a serious manner.

"This wouldn't be a paid vacation situation. I need time off to help my dad with something personal."

"Would you like to elaborate on what the something personal is?"

"While I was on vacation, my dad's best friend's granddaughter was kidnapped. Before she was found—well, still hasn't been found—my dad's best friend died."

"All this happened while you were in San Francisco?" he asked.

"Let me back up. The man who died—his name was Lukas—was not only my dad's best friend but also saved my dad's life. The short story is: his granddaughter was seen getting into this guy's car. He was arrested, tried, and eventually acquitted due to lack of evidence. The grandfather's dying wish was to get justice for his granddaughter, hopefully finding her and making sure the guy got caught."

"Didn't you say he was acquitted?"

"That's true, but after looking through the facts, I'm certain he did it and think he'll do it again."

"So, bottom line, you pretty much had a working vacation."

Ducking his head a tad, James answered, "I just volunteered what little I could to get some information on him."

"Okay, let me see what I can do to move the schedule around. When do you want to leave and how long do you anticipate being gone?"

"I'd like to take off Thursday . . . back to work the following Monday."

"Are you talking about this coming Thursday . . . like next Thursday?"

"Yes, and I'm sorry it's so soon. It's been a year since the child was taken, and I have a feeling he's going to strike again real soon."

"Okay, I get it. Thank you for being upfront with me. I can see you're bound and determined to see this through. That's what makes you a good investigator. If I wasn't such a softy and didn't have grandchildren of my own, I'd say no way. Also, we'll be getting a nice bonus if your Vegas surveillance work comes through. In the meantime I've got a short job for you to do."

"Thank you. I really appreciate it," James answered with sincere relief.

As James opened the door to leave, he heard his boss say, "James, I don't know what you're planning and don't want to know . . . just stay out of harm's way."

Hurrying back to his desk, James pulled out his note pad. Thinking, he didn't want to leave anything to the last minute, he called Janet.

When the call was picked up, he asked, "Could I speak with Officer Bigalow?"

"In regards to what?" was the rather curt reply.

"It's regarding a personal matter . . . about a family member," he answered, hoping he didn't need to elaborate.

"What's your name?" the officer asked.

Giving his name, he wondered if Janet was still working in the office. Preferring not to but could call Charlotte if Janet didn't pick up.

"Hi James, what's happening with Aunt Charlotte?" Janet asked in a knowing manner.

"Because it's a personal matter, could you call me at home tonight . . . say around seven o'clock?"

"I take it; you're back in Los Angeles," Janet said matter-of-factly.

"I am and it's very important that I talk to you."

"Okay, no problem. Talk to you later."

The rest of his day was spent in the office making business calls on the latest project he'd received from his boss. Getting time off was a great relief, but his mind was still in major over-load with necessary things to accomplish before leaving. He was doing his best to concentrate on work, but thoughts of Lehmann and his connected upcoming plans were continually on his mind.

Pushing the unpleasant thoughts to the side, he couldn't wait to tell Carly he'd see her late Wednesday night after work. He'd try to leave work early and beat the traffic rush. He had a lot to do in the next few days to get ready. He still needed to do laundry from his San Francisco and Vegas trip. His car was past due for a service job, and he needed to pay some bills. No way could he pay the full amount due on the credit card used in San Francisco. He'd prided himself on paying his credit cards off each month, especially after the financial bind Margie left him in. Knowing his time in San Francisco had been unusual, he'd take care of the charges in a couple of months but hated paying interest fees.

Staying at Carly's house would avoid hotel expenses and a definite plus, but staying with Carly meant more than financial savings. Gosh, he missed her.

Chapter 37

After running various errands—especially stopping at the bank to deposit his payroll check—James finally arrived at his apartment. He wanted to call Carly right away but knew once on the phone, it would be hard to end the conversation by seven o'clock.

First things first, he was starving. Unable to locate a clean plate or even a paper plate, he used a tablespoon instead of the enclosed chopsticks to dig into the carton of Chinese food. Chopsticks were too slow, and he was too hungry. Wondering if Carly had a favorite Chinese dish, he stood behind the kitchen counter and shoveled in the rice and Kung Pao chicken.

While eating, he glanced around the kitchen and the adjoining living room. He didn't remember the apartment looking so awful before leaving for San Francisco or before the rushed Vegas trip. Reconsidering, he'd obviously ignored the kitchen sink piled high with dirty dishes. Finishing the last of his dinner—even scrapping the last morsels of rice off the carton's bottom—it must have been Carly's neat and clean house that made his messy apartment stand out even more.

Smashing the plastic bag together, he felt something inside. Feeling around, he pulled out a fortune cookie.

Dessert and a fortune, he thought, as he broke it apart and read: The choices we make show who we are...more than our abilities. He couldn't agree more . . . knowing he'd finally made the right choice in Carly.

He tried to fit the plastic bag, the empty carton, and a few close-by paper cups into the kitchen trashcan. Unable to do so—no matter how hard he shoved the trash down—he picked up an empty pizza box and the smelly bag of trash and headed downstairs to the dumpster. Opening the lid, a thought crossed his mind. Did Lehmann have a trash bin near his warehouse? If so, it would be a good spot to place a smoke bomb.

Still working on the kitchen, Janet called. After a few back and forth pleasantries, James said, "Since you trusted me with the video and helped me in other areas, I want to trust you with what I'm planning to do. While we're talking, I'm open to any suggestions you may have."

Janet's reply was a quick, "I'm listening."

After explaining what he thought was going to happen the following Friday and his reasoning—even explaining how he used his co-worker as a go-between—he told her how impenetrable the building was . . . especially the third floor. Not expecting her to comment, he asked anyway, "Are you following what I'm saying so far?"

"Yes, but I'm at a loss on how you'll pull this off."

"Well, keeping in mind how Lehmann's third floor is like a fortress, I'm hoping you can help me with that. Remember the witness—the one who showed up dead in the desert—he said a white car with a child inside entered the garage. Remember, Lehmann's white Cadillac just happened to be stolen. I'm assuming whatever takes place on the third floor, starts through the garage. For me . . . that's a given. Doesn't it make sense those perverts and their equally sick host will gather on the third floor via the garage elevator and leave the same way."

Again, not waiting for a response, James continued. "I've been unable to look at the back of the property but wonder if exit stairs exist. They're on the original plans but maybe closed off. There were no exit doors or windows visible on the search warrant's video. Using my binoculars, most of the building's backside is blocked by another building, so I can't see below the third floor. There are definitely no windows evident on all four sides of the third floor. To my knowledge, other than several large air vents, there's only one window located in a small office fairly close to the door's entrance to the warehouse section. Are you still with me?" James asked.

"Still listening," Janet answered.

"I'm sorry if I've repeated anything from our previous conversations. Okay, here goes. Do you have an idea on how to see the back of the building without raising any red flags? The last thing I want to do is alert Lehmann that we're on to him."

"Sounds like you're been busy doing extensive background work. I need to give this a lot of thought," she answered uncertainly.

"Please don't directly involve the fire department.

My gut feeling is someone high up is somehow involved. I'm not sure for what purpose or why the commander signed off on obvious code infractions. Hell, he could even be a member of the sick group."

Almost interrupting, Janet asked, "What if I find out the back has a working fire escape . . . then what? Sounds like you're planning on starting a fire. I won't be a part of that."

"No . . . no, I want to give the appearance of a fire. I need to know if anyone can safely escape from the back of the building without being seen. Knowing what I think will transpire there, I envision catching Lehmann, his associate, and the party goes with their pants down . . . no pun intended. Believe me; I've envisioned many different possibilities and scenarios. I've even considered calling several departments with anonymous tips but timing is so important. It would be a plus to have the media there." James didn't bring it up to Janet, but thought about the police being called when Carly was saved and the accompanying pictures in the paper.

"Janet, didn't you find it strange the computer taken from Lehmann's office was listed as brand new . . . not whipped clean of input. Who has a new computer installed—just in case it's looked into—unless they're hiding something? Going back to the importance of response time, I want to catch him in the act with no time to hide his actions. I'm sorry for going on and on, but it's been all I can think about."

"I hear what you're saying and know where you're

coming from. I'm just trying to figure out how best to help. Can I call you tomorrow?"

"Please do. Again, thanks for letting me be candid. I can't bounce this off anyone else. I'm afraid the window of opportunity won't show itself again for another year. Did I tell you this is an annual event?"

Not answering his question, Janet asked, "So, when will you be coming to San Francisco?"

"Wednesday night. That will give me all day Thursday and Friday to finalize my plans and get ready for what I think will go down Friday night."

"Will you be staying with Carly?" Janet asked, wanting James to know she knew about their relationship.

"I hope so. I'm going to call and ask after we hang up," James answered, feeling a tad embarrassed but not sure why.

"My Aunt Charlotte says you guys have gotten close. She wanted her to branch out but worried about her getting too attached and then getting hurt."

"There's no need for anyone to worry . . . placing the emphasis on anyone. I know how special Carly is and what she's gone through. I would never hurt her. Please pass that on to your aunt."

"I believe you. I'll call you after my shift tomorrow. Hopefully, we can get him somehow."

"Thanks. Talk to you tomorrow."

Having worked on the kitchen throughout the conversation with Janet, he was fairly pleased with the results. It wasn't perfect but definitely much better.

Opening a beer, James sat down to call Carly. Knowing Carly confided in Charlotte and Charlotte talked to Janet, would Janet discuss the conversation they'd just had? Should he tell Carly what he was planning to do? No, he wouldn't say anything until they were face to face . . . maybe not even then.

Their phone conversation was light and fun but turned serious when he asked, "Can I come see you Wednesday night after work?"

"Do you really want to come and see me?" she asked with slight disbelief in her voice.

"Didn't I tell you I'd be back?"

"I wasn't sure and so soon," she answered honestly.

"No matter how much you try; you can't get rid of me," James replied flatly. Waiting for a response, he added, "Carly, I'm kidding."

"When will you get here?" Carly asked.

"I'll try to get away from work early. I'd say around nine o'clock."

"Do you want me to fix dinner?"

"No, I'll grab something on the way but thanks. I think you'd be impressed with me. I've been doing major kitchen clean-up."

"I've been impressed with you from the very beginning," she replied seriously.

"That's a nice thing to say. I'm off to work on the living room. It'll be tough to find a dump truck at this time of the night."

"You're too funny," Carly said with a chuckle.

"Funny and impressive . . . I like it. Okay, I better go before I run out of gas. Sleep well and I'll call you tomorrow. Carly, I love you."

"I love you more," she answered quickly.

"That's debatable, but I really need to go. We'll debate that subject when we're together. Bye."

Clearing off the coffee table until it was bare, he placed an empty duffle bag in the center and systematically began placing items inside the black bag to take to San Francisco . . . items to keep separate, and ones he didn't want Carly to see. Even though he still had a couple of days before leaving, he didn't want to leave anything to chance. There was nothing worse than needing something that was hundreds of miles away.

First, he placed his black sweat suit with a hoodie in the bag to act as a cushion, then his night vision goggles and binoculars. Adding several burner phones, he suddenly felt tired but satisfied—even more than expected—with what he'd accomplished. Yawning, tomorrow is another day and closer to San Francisco and Carly.

Chapter 38

When Carly opened the front door, she was standing before him, wearing a pink see-through negligee. As James opened his mouth to speak—his heart racing—she asked mischievously, "Are you ready for dessert?"

"More than ready," James answered, sweeping her up, kicking the door closed, and carrying her to the bedroom. The last words spoken before the bedroom door closed, "God, you're beautiful."

When their breathing slowed, James asked, "Can you tell how much I missed you?"

"Yes, I wish we didn't live so far apart." Smiling widely, Carly added, "I'm thinking; we could do this every day."

"I don't think my body could survive this every day, but I'd definitely give it my best shot."

Changing the subject, Carly asked, "How long will you be staying?"

"I need to be back at work in Los Angeles Monday morning."

"That soon? That means you'll need to leave Sunday," she replied with a pout.

"Didn't you tell me you had a bunch of vacation days left?" James asked.

"I did . . . I do. When you said you were coming, I asked for next week off. I thought you'd stay as long as last time," she responded in a dejected manner

Thoughts rushing through his mind, James said, "So, you'll be working tomorrow and Friday."

"Yes, I'm afraid so. I tried to get those days off too, but we're right in the middle of Activity Days. It's the biggest event of the year for the Boys and Girls Club and its supporters. As you can imagine, I've been really busy. I don't know what to do. Can't you stay longer?"

"How about this idea," James offered. "You go to work tomorrow and Friday, and I'll finish up my investigation while you're working. I still haven't decided whether to tell Gabriel and Michelle Walker my reason for being in San Francisco, but I do want to see how they're doing. Now for my idea, why don't you come back to Los Angeles with me?"

Carefully following every word since hearing, "How about this idea," Carly stammered, "Really?"

"I could show you the sights, take you to the beach, show you the fun spots, and . . . ."

"But don't you need to work?" she interrupted.

"Yes, but we'd have the whole week together plus weekends. If I'm sent out of town—probably not—but you could even go with me."

Caught by surprise and even though she already knew her answer, she needed a moment to consider her response. "Can I think about it?" Carly asked.

"Sure, but I'd really like you to come. If you don't

want to, I'll probably cry, throw a tantrum, and curl up in a ball."

Smiling, Carly answered quickly, "No problem. I deal with that type of behavior every day at work."

"Uh oh, you're wise to me," James answered before kissing her tenderly.

"Okay, I want to go back with you. Gosh, I've got a lot to do to get ready. I've never packed for a trip before."

"Keep in mind it's warmer and lots more casual . . . like flip flops and shorts. Hum, on second thought, I should keep you away from the beach. Seeing you in a swim suit around all those surfer dudes, I'd get too jealous."

"Then I won't wear a suit," she said seriously.

"Carly . . . ?"

"You were kidding . . . right?"

"Bingo. You can wear whatever you want. You are beautiful, and I love you. I just want you to relax, wear what you want, do what you want, have fun, and be happy."

"Can I go to the beach naked?" Carly asked, unable to keep from laughing.

"I'm talking about doing whatever . . . as long as it's legal. Besides, you'd create a riot."

"All kidding aside, there are so many decisions to make on what to take. It sounds really complicated . . . even scary. I've never been out of San Francisco before. I mean since arriving here years ago."

When James looked at her, she looked far away in

thought. "Carly, don't worry about anything. That's what I'm here for."

"Look at my hands . . . they're shaking,"

Pulling Carly close and wrapping his arms around her, James said, "Sweetheart, if you feel this is too much for you, we can do it another time. I don't want you to do anything out of your comfort zone."

"No, I want to. I think I'm shaking because I'm so excited. Would you hold me until we go to sleep? Nothing calms me down like snuggling in your arms."

THURSDAY

Thursday morning was unusually rushed for Carly. She needed to be at work earlier than usual but still prepared breakfast before leaving. In spite of James telling her not to bother, he ate two eggs, two sausage patties, and two English muffins with strawberry jelly. After gulping down a large glass of orange juice, he commented, "Who knew you'd be the perfect girlfriend . . . beautiful, smart, and can cook."

"Am I your girlfriend?" she questioned.

"Do you want to be?" James asked.

Her hands rolled up into fists and resting on her hips, Carly asked, "Are you answering my question with a question?"

"Busted . . . you caught me. I would be proud to have you as my girlfriend."

"Me too but better for you to be my boyfriend," she

quipped before kissing him goodbye.

*   *   *   *

James nonchalantly walked around the area close to Lehmann's building, using his binoculars to read the sign next to the open warehouse entrance. While thinking holy crap, he carefully read the sign twice:

CLOSED FRIDAY THROUGH SUNDAY

(for Maintenance)
Reopening Monday 10:00 A.M.
(Sorry for any inconvenience)

Surer than ever about Friday night's gathering, James looked for the best spot to park his car tomorrow—the best place to observe people entering the parking structure and the most direct route in and out by foot. Having a momentary sinking feeling, what if the gathering was scheduled for Saturday or even Sunday? Chastising himself for even going there with any thoughts along that line, he needed to only concentrate on Friday.

It was good news to see a trash dumpster beside the warehouse entrance. However, since it was on rollers, he couldn't be sure it would be there during nighttime hours. He could check back after dark, but not sure what excuse he'd give Carly. Since he now considered the dumpster an additional spot for a smoke bomb, he decided not worry about it either way. Again, he returned to thinking about being gone Friday night and coming up with a reasonable excuse to tell Carly. Would it be better to tell her the truth? Still not sure, he was right back where he'd always been when thinking about what to say to her. One way or the other, he had to make up his mind soon on how to handle it with Carly.

Having already decided where to position the smoke bombs, he'd removed a couple of large rocks from Carly's property, placing them in the trunk of his car beside his black duffle bag.

Before leaving Los Angeles, he'd had a lengthy conversation with Janet, promising not to use inflammatory smoke bombs and thus eliminating any possible threat of fire. He continued to be impressed with Janet. Whether or not the operation they'd discussed took place, he'd always be indebted to her for her help and guidance.

Not mentioning the particulars of how it was accomplished—other than a drone was involved— he'd learned no exits were found on the backside of the building, and only one narrow exit door was located on the left side of the warehouse. As the warehouse elevator only went to the second floor, it was a no brainer that the only way out for Lehmann and the group from the third floor would be through the parking garage.

James couldn't help but wonder if the attendees realized what a precarious position they could be in if confronted with a real emergency, or did they not care about the risk, or did the fortress like surroundings make them feel more secure? Regardless—and Janet agreed—there was no way the fire department would ever sign off on such a blatant disregard for safety unless there was some hidden agenda.

After Janet and he finalized plans for Friday night, she'd talked about her children and how disgusted she'd been after learning of Carly's plight and her feelings about Lehmann. He smiled when remembering her words about what she'd personally do to someone who would harm her children. It was more than just the words; it was about the feelings behind the extreme details of the hurt she'd put on such a person.

Janet's last remarks before the conversation ended, "You get the operation in motion, and the rest will be taken care of."

When he asked, "What exactly will happen?"

Her answer was a simple one . . . "Watch and see."

Finishing up his final assessment of Lehmann's building and the surrounding area, James returned to Carly's house within a half hour of Carly's arrival. After thanking him for taking care of the girls, she seemed tired and distracted. When he offered to take her to dinner, she readily agreed and appeared relieved.

Throughout the meal, she incessantly talked about outfits to wear each day, places to visit, and things to do. Even though he tried to calmly answer her questions and reassure her insecurities, he was inwardly preoccupied with what he needed to do the following day, continuing to contemplate different possibilities, along with good and bad scenarios.

Before falling to sleep, Carly told him Charlotte had offered to watch Maggie and Penny but wanted to take care of them at her house. When she asked, "Can we drop them off on our way," James answered with a mumble . . . followed immediately by snoring.

Chapter 39

FRIDAY

Hesitating to mention Jennifer's name—knowing it brought back sad memories—James told Carly about having a meeting tonight to finalize Jennifer's investigation. Not exactly truthful, he was relieved when Carly didn't ask for more information like: what, when, or where. Fearful she might still ask for specifics and not wanting to worry her, James hurriedly brought up the possibility of being gone when she got home from work . . . even being as late as eleven o'clock before returning.

Obviously fixated on getting ready for her trip to Los Angeles, Carly quickly answered, "That's okay. I'll be busy doing laundry and packing. If convenient, call me if you'd like a snack when you get home," she added sweetly.

Carly's leaving early for a second day in a row gave James the opportunity he needed to run errands and get gas. When she offered to prepare breakfast, James assured her he'd pick something up while out.

Unbeknownst to Carly, his main reason for getting an early start was to watch for Lehmann when he arrived at the warehouse. It would be a long day and a late night, but hopefully a productive conclusion to an investigation that would never be fully complete without finding Jennifer. He'd decided not to talk to the Walkers until after tonight's covert operation.

James was in position and watching the building by 7:30 AM. Closing in on nine o'clock, he began to wonder if Lehmann had already arrived, would be coming in much later in the day, or perhaps waiting until the evening hours to show up. However, at exactly 9:00 o'clock, Lehmann arrived in tandem with another vehicle. He recognized the first car—a silver Mercedes—as Lehmann's and assumed his associate or someone closely involved was following in a black SUV. Smirking and unable to see through the dark tinted windows, he remembered the witness being picked up at a Vegas hotel by a black SUV. As each vehicle stopped, a hand extended forward—most likely to enter a code—into a metal module located to the side of the garage entrance. Once the door opened—wondering if it opened for a set amount of time—both vehicles proceeded inside and the door closed immediately. Aware of the module's existence, he'd been unable to safely get a closer look for fear of being noticed. In any event he now knew for certain the module activated the garage door. He wondered if there was also a security camera involved. Making a note of the second vehicle's license number—already having Lehmann's—he waited to see if either came back out. After a half hour of no activity, James left to get something to eat.

*   *   *   *

Lehmann and Gordon began their familiar routine on the day of The Club's San Francisco party. They both agreed not to think about or talk about the aftermath of their last hosted party and to concentrate solely on tonight's festivities. Methodically checking off items on a list of things to do, both were busy in their own areas of expertise. Gordon was preoccupied with room preparations, while Lehmann double-checked the credentials and estimated time of each member's expected arrival. Although busy with preparations during the week, each had necessary last minute tasks to complete.

Because more objects would be available for fewer attendees this year, Gordon and Lehmann would need to take turns watching the extra or perhaps unused commodities. Never having this situation before, the handlers insisted on delivering the total number requested, fearing not being paid the amount previously agreed upon. Thus, it was necessary to set up a large portable enclosure to corral the extra human objects until chosen, not chosen, or chosen for additional times.

Their prime commodity—the German's request— was scheduled to arrive one hour before the other captives and several hours before the members were scheduled to arrive. Because she would not be offered to the general attendees, she would be locked away in a separate bedroom. Since crying, wailing, and whimpering sounds were heard before, during, and after a party, her pleas for help would not be considered out of the ordinary. They had agreed not to administer drugs to her because of the German's request not to compromise his enjoyment.

Because of this year's implementation of personal videos—available for members to take with them—they'd both worked diligently on this new arrangement. Their original plan was to place some sort of backing around the beds to block out the surroundings but because of set-up and take-down difficulties, they'd decided to have opaque curtains installed around all of the beds . . . similar to privacy curtains surrounding hospital beds. If the bedroom was not used for video purposes, the curtains would remain against the walls beside the head of the bed. It was up to the individual's preference whether to choose a bedroom or the large round couch and whether or not to allow others to watch their experience or join in. Because of the German's fantasy, a video would not be placed in his particular bedroom. After he was finished and exited, the room would again be locked and not opened until later after everyone had vacated the property.

Parties usually began with watching videos, drinking, personal drug usage, and becoming acquainted with their desired objects. Per Lehmann's instructions and to speed the process along, special requested objects had been labeled by those responsible for their capture and imprisonment.

Arrangements had been made for the human objects to arrive no earlier than five o'clock and no later than six o'clock. Members were to arrive between seven and eight o'clock; no one would be admitted after eight o'clock with no exceptions.

While Gordon double-checked his briefcase to make sure he'd brought the various sprays and medications to administer to the captives if necessary, Lehmann put on his favorite video. As he watched the same film on all screens at the same time, he began to feel a fresh excitement of what was going to transpire there shortly. Afraid of becoming distracted from the necessary jobs at hand, he abruptly turned the video off. Gordon noticed the young frolicking images on the screens before saying, "Patience . . . our time is coming soon." Laughing, Gordon responded, "I needed to see if the main video feed was working properly."

Leaving together in Lehmann's car, Gordon and Lehmann left for a late lunch before picking up their orders of miscellaneous appetizers and hors d'oeuvres from two different specialty shops. Trays of sliced Italian prosciutto, Moroccan spiced salmon, Mexican carnitas, Bavarian beef, lobster, and shrimp were carefully stacked above unique cheeses from around the world. Before closing the lid to the cooler, Lehmann added the most expensive item . . . a large container of imported caviar. After placing several boxes of assorted crackers beside the cooler, he closed the trunk lid.

Returning to the third floor and placing the food items in the refrigerators below the bar's counter; Lehmann opened a rare bottle of Louis XIII Cognac. "Let's toast to our vigilance in becoming prepared and our readiness to receive the play toys and The Club members. Above all, we're looking forward to another successful party." As their glassed clanked together, Lehmann sighed, and Gordon smiled.

*   *   *   *

James hated the waiting and watching time of surveillance work. Feeling antsy, he casually paced back and forth numerous times in different directions from his vantage point—sometimes covering a longer or wider path.

He'd followed Lehmann's car when it left the premises with another person; a person he assumed was his partner or associate. Lehmann parked at a restaurant two miles away, and they were inside for approximately forty-five minutes. When they exited the parking lot, James tracked them as they stopped at two separate delicatessens to pick up items which were placed into the trunk of Lehmann's car. After their last stop, he followed them back to Lehmann's building . . . arriving at exactly 3:34 PM.

Having no idea when others would arrive, James decided it would probably be a good time to grab a quick bite and use the restroom. He also used the opportunity to change clothes. Once in dark clothing, he transferred the smoke bombs into the larger of the two backpacks normally kept in his car. Finally, he placed the compact bolt cutters into the same backpack.

After grabbing two burner phones and a can of spray paint from the trunk, he drove back to the same vicinity . . . relieved to find the exact parking spot as before. Noticing the fog was beginning to settle in, he knew it would get dark earlier than expected.

Constantly looking around to make sure no one was keying in on him, he strolled casually around. Wearing the backpack and holding his notebook, he hoped—if noticed—he'd look like an older college student . . . perhaps gathering information for a class project. He was surprised by the lack of street traffic on a Friday afternoon. Reconsidering, it was most likely due to the warehouse's location within the commercial district.

Within minutes of being back in place, a lone grey double-cab pickup with tinted windows stopped at the module. While quickly jotting down the license number, he saw the driver's side window slide down and waited for a hand to extend outward. When no hand appeared, James surmised a camera or verbal communication was used to identify the driver. Guessing the person responsible for admitting access must have been satisfied, because the door opened and the pickup proceeded inward. Finding the pickup's appearance odd—as there was nothing in the truck bed to suggest a delivery—he placed a question mark beside the license number and the vehicle's description. Expecting more vehicles to follow, he was disappointed when it became quiet again.

Within an hour, two black vans arrived together. It was difficult to see the license plate of the first van . . . blocked by the van following closely behind. They each stopped at the security module; the door not opening until both vehicles were cleared.

James made the following entry into his notepad: transporting objects or party goers (?). Now what, he questioned? His gut told him to continue to wait and see if more cars arrived. Surely, Lehmann's yearly event would involve more than a pickup and two vans.

Totally dark with no visible moon and his patience running out; James started to walk around for probably the eighth time . . . having lost count. Before leaving and looking back a final time, a black town car appeared. Pulling the hoodie up and around his face, he thought . . . here goes.

A string of automobiles—limos, town cars, and one Rolls-Royce—were lined up to enter the structure, seemingly converging all at once. Pushing the button on his watch to light up the dial, he quickly glanced down . . . 7:20 PM. There was a delay at the module, as only one vehicle was allowed in at a time . . . the door closing after each entry. James remembered seeing the parking area on the video and wondering why so many parking spaces for so few employees. Now it made sense.

Adjusting his night vision goggles, he quietly skirted

the parameter of the area . . . what he'd later refer to as the staging area. He was glad his sweatpants were made similar to cargo pants, consisting of several different sized pockets. While surveying the surroundings, he took a closer look at the narrow exit door on the warehouse side. It was difficult to see from the fence but planned to place one of the smoke bombs near the door . . . just in case someone tried to escape from there. Although impossible to get to the warehouse from the third floor, it was still a door to the outside and shouldn't be completely ignored. He hoped the lock on the gate wasn't wired to a security system . . . if indeed, one existed for the outside.

Having gone over his plan of attack many times—judging the pros and cons and making sure he had everything necessary to pull this off—he wanted to give the party goers time to get into full operation. While knowing the delay would jeopardize more innocent children, his ultimate goal was to remove any doubts and catch the perverts during their sickening actions.

His best guess was to start one hour after the last car arrived . . . hopefully knowing when that would be. At almost eight o'clock, James watched and waited for a half hour with no additional automobiles appearing at the garage entrance. Practicing static sounds one last time, he decided it was now or never.

Using one of the burner phones, James called 911 with his rehearsed statement. When the dispatcher answered, "911 . . . what's your emergency?"

"I was driving by this big building and heard a boom

then saw black smoke coming out. I'm not sure but maybe heard kids screaming."

"Sir, what is your location?"

"I don't know the address or street name. I'm calling from the corner. Let me see . . . I'm about a block away at Tyler and Second."

Doing his best to sound panicked, "You need to send somebody quick . . . the fire department . . . quick."

"Could I have your name?" she asked in a calm manner, before adding, "Fire engines are already on their way. What is your name, Sir?"

"Can't hear . . . sskkhhhh."

"You're breaking up . . . your name please?"

"Sskkhhhh . . . goin' to help."

Hearing sirens in the distance, James ran over and picked up the biggest of the set-aside rocks, heaving it through the warehouse window. Surprised when no alarm went off, he began tossing in three smoke bombs. Hearing the sirens closer, he watched as smoke wafted back out of the broken window and escaped through the air vents. Pulling the bolt cutters out, he ran over to the gate, cut the lock, ran to the side door, and set off a smaller purchased smoke bomb. Lastly, he sprayed the module's screen with black paint and placed his last smoke bomb at the corner of the building closest to the garage door. Out of breath, he took cover. He watched the smoke billowing from the front and sides of the building, hoping the bombs were still emitting smoke when the fire trucks arrived.

Within a few minutes—maybe four from his 911 call—not only fire trucks were onsite, but police cars with flashing lights accompanied them. He sensed they must have been prepped and ready . . . thank you Janet. Since not hearing security alarms when the window was broken or when the gate lock was broken, it was hard to believe Lehmann wouldn't have a security system in place, especially to protect the expensive items on the second floor showroom.

Just like Janet suggested, he would stay put, fade into the background, and "watch and see." True to her word, the area was filled with more police cars than fire trucks. Obviously understanding the true situation, the personnel concentrated on the garage side of the building. Not having a clear shot of what was going on; he did hear more glass breaking before hearing someone shout, "All clear."

Feeling his heart beating and having a better angle on the garage side activities, two firemen were busy cutting out a section of the metal roll up door.

*   *   *   *

While a few of the drivers waiting inside the garage were sleeping in their vehicles, others were busy talking and laughing, playing dice, or listening to rap music. Unaware of glass shattering, their first hint of a problem was hearing the sound of a saw chewing through the metal door. In conjunction with the sawing noise, a bullhorn proclaimed, "Is anyone inside? Help is on the way."

Panicking and not knowing how to escape, one of the drivers ran to the elevator and pushed the alarm button. Lehmann's voice came through the intercom asking, "What the hell do you want?"

"There's a fire outside. The building's on fire. I can see smoke coming in through a hole in the door."

"What hole in the door?" Not waiting for an answer, "Get the cars lined up and ready to leave. You know where the button is to open the door," Lehmann answered quickly.

"No . . . I don't."

"It's the green button on the wall . . . on the right side . . . you idiot."

*　　*　　*　　*

As James watched the hole in the door getting larger, it was difficult to remain in the background. While the operation seemed to be moving in slow motion, he wanted to rush in with the responders and catch Lehmann. Frustrated and shifting his weight from side to side, the garage door suddenly began to roll up. Immediately, firefighters—but mostly police personnel—converged inside the garage. While mass chaos erupted, James glanced up to see a helicopter circling above, and to his right a news truck appeared.

Doing his best to watch what was happening and stay out of sight was proving almost impossible to do.

Within an hour or so, a few of the police cars began leaving, replaced by four police transport vans and two ambulances. Several men—maybe ten—looking like they'd dressed hurriedly, were led out first in handcuffs. James watched carefully for Lehmann or his associate, thinking maybe they were still being questioned. As the handcuffed men were being loaded into a police van, a second group of ten or so—also handcuffed—was led out. Since most were dressed in uniforms, he assumed they were drivers. Still not seeing Lehmann, he decided to take a look at both sides and the back of the building. Was it possible another outside door was missed by the drone? Was it possible Lehmann was hiding away in a secret unknown room on the third floor?

Because the attention was directed to the front of the building, he felt confident to walk around the confusion before passing through the unlocked gate. Not wanting to be seen and finding the area extremely dark, he adjusted his night goggles and proceeded toward the side door, noticing the smoke bomb had already dissipated. Curious, he stopped and tried the door. As expected, it was locked. Moving past the door—maybe fifteen steps away—he heard a familiar creaking noise behind him. Stopping and looking around, he saw the door slowly opening outward.

Naturally, his first thought; a policeman was checking to see where the door led. However and to his utter surprise, Lehmann and the guy who was with him at lunch walked cautiously outside into the darkness.

Lehmann had his arms wrapped around a computer console, holding it tightly against his chest.

His new dilemma . . . what should he do? Standing completely still against the building and fairly certain they couldn't see him; James watched to see which way they would go. They hesitated and seemed to whisper to each other before changing positions . . . Lehmann moving to the rear before both taking short cautious steps toward the gate. Once passing through the gate, James knew they'd be able to skirt detection and blend into the night. Hell, with Lehmann's money, they could easily escape and be out of the country tonight.

Reaching under his sweat top, James pulled his gun from its holster. Taking a deep breath, he crept up behind Lehmann. When they stopped inches away from the closed gate, James said, "You got a key to the lock?"

They froze like deer caught in the headlights. Standing paralyzed in place, Lehmann questioned, "How much to look the other way?"

"Are you trying to bribe an officer of the law?" James asked with authority.

When Lehmann started to turn around, James said, "Don't move. This is the deal . . . you both are going to go through the gate and walk slowly to the group of police officers to your left."

When neither moved, James placed his revolver against Lehmann's lower back before saying, "You might tell your partner you have a loaded gun to your back and to walk forward very carefully."

"Gordon, you heard him," Lehmann responded.

Of all that transpired that night; the mental image that would stay with James forever was the look on Lehmann's face when the arresting officer turned him around to place him in handcuffs. As they stared at each other, Lehmann's mouth dropped open. It was priceless.

*   *   *   *

Carly's eyes grew wider and wider as she grappled with what James was telling her. "Are you okay?" she finally asked.

"I'm drained, but we finally got him. I'm not certain what the police found inside the third floor, but it must have been horrendous."

"You must be exhausted. Do you want to go to bed?" Carly asked.

"Not yet . . . I'm too keyed up. You know, at one time tonight, I considered shooting Lehmann. Carly, I'm sorry I couldn't find Jennifer."

Momentarily unable to speak, Carly felt tears running down her face. Clearing her throat, she finally said a simple, "Thank you."

Before she could say more, Carly's phone rang. Surprised anyone would be calling so late, she hesitantly answered, "Hello."

"Carly, this is Janet Bigelow . . . ah, Charlotte's niece."

"Hi, Janet," Carly answered, wondering what was wrong.

"Sorry to call so late. By any chance, is James there?"

"Yes, just a moment," answered with relief, assuming Charlotte was okay.

James took the phone from Carly and said, "Hi, Janet . . . is everything okay?"

"Better than okay. I planned to call you tomorrow but couldn't go to bed without thanking you."

"I was going to call you tomorrow too. Janet, you're my hero. I don't need to know how you did it but thank you."

"I've gotten some information already and wanted to share it with you. What they found was a child's worst nightmare. Don't say anything to Carly—well, that's up to you—but they found one little girl unconscious. They believe she was tortured, strangled, and left for dead. She'd been raped savagely, so they'll be able to connect DNA to the responsible person. She's in a coma . . . poor child."

"So awful," was all James could say."

Janet took a noticeable big breath before continuing. "This could never have happened without your relentless pursuit of that bastard. Oh yeah, I think the press also got some great photos of the Fire Commander in handcuffs."

Abruptly changing the subject, Janet made the comment, "Aunt Charlotte says you and Carly are going to Los Angeles tomorrow. I won't hold you up any longer. Have a safe trip."

Thanks for the call, and I promise to take good care of Carly."

"I know you will . . . bye."

After disconnecting, he'd forgotten to ask Janet if she knew how Lehmann got from the third floor to the warehouse. Oh well, he was sure they'd talk again soon.

Chapter 40

By the time Carly woke James, she'd fed the dogs, packed their dog food, put their water and food bowls in the doggie traveling bag, and gathered their toys together in one spot. She'd also gotten dressed, packed her night clothes, put on her makeup, and packed her makeup container into her suitcase. Lastly, she'd fixed breakfast.

As Carly patted James on the shoulder, she said, "Wake up sleepy-head."

Confused, James sat up abruptly and said, "What?"

"It's after eight and you wanted to be on the road no later than nine. I wasn't sure if you meant from here or from Charlotte's."

"That's the best sleep I've had in a long time. I was dreaming about chasing spies through the airport. Guess I'll never know if I caught them."

Leaning over and kissing James on the cheek, Carly replied, "I'm thinking you would. I've made burritos for breakfast. I thought they'd be fast and easy."

"Speaking of fast and easy . . . how about jumping back in bed?" James asked.

Laughing, Carly shook her head before responding, "Not this morning. We'll have plenty of time for getting in and out of bed later."

"Okay, but I'll hold you to that," James quipped on his way to shower and dress.

On the drive to Charlotte's, James openly discussed his involvement in the previous night's activities. "It almost feels like it's unreal . . . like a dream with a good ending." Carly stayed mostly quiet but sometimes had him stop talking, so she could ask a question.

As quickly and efficiently as they could with two excited and jumping dogs, James and Carly hurried into Charlotte's house. After greeting them, Charlotte said, "Look on the dining room table. I'll take the dogs out to the backyard."

Spread out on the table was the morning newspaper. In big bold letters, the headline read: **CHILD SEX CLUB BUSTED**. In smaller letters but still bolded: **Fire Commander and Dignitaries Arrested.**

Charlotte came back in and patted James on the back before saying, "Janet said this wouldn't have happened without you. Thank you from the bottom of my heart."

"You're welcome, but it wouldn't have happened without Janet. You should be very proud of her," he answered sincerely . . . meaning every word of his comment.

Looking away from the newspaper and staring at James questioningly, Carly jumped into the conversation saying, "The department had been tipped off before the raid. Was that you?"

"Maybe," he answered shyly.

Glancing toward Charlotte, Carly asked, "We're running late. Can we take the paper with us, so I can finish it on the trip?" Without waiting for an answer, Carly added, "I haven't looked at all the photos yet."

"Sure and don't worry about Penny and Maggie. They're already feeling at home in the backyard. They can sleep in your old bedroom."

Saying their goodbyes, Carly and James were finally on their way to Los Angeles. As they talked about the passing towns and scenery, Carly was enjoying every mile along the way. They discussed their likes and dislikes, and finally what they were going to do while she was in Los Angeles.

They stopped for lunch about halfway to Los Angeles in a town called Morro Bay. While sitting at a restaurant table over-looking the Morro Bay Rock, Carly offered, "I feel like the luckiest girl in the whole world. I don't think I can ever make you as happy as you've made me, but I'll spend the rest of my life trying . . . if you want me to?"

Taking her hand in his, James replied, "Carly, I want to be with you always. Besides, you've already made me the happiest man alive."

Before starting the car, James said, "I need to call Gabriel. I'm not sure if he's seen the paper, but I owe him an explanation. Dialing Gabriel's number, a message picked up. When hearing the beep, "Gabriel and Michelle . . . this is James Allen. I wanted to talk to you about my real reason for visiting San Francisco. Perhaps you've seen the paper this morning. I'm on my way back to Los Angeles and will call again. Hope you are both doing well."

Disconnecting the call, James had an instinctive urge to call his dad and tell him what happened last night. No, he would talk to him later . . . having spent enough time on slime-bag Lehmann and his disgusting group. Right now, it was all about enjoying the trip to Los Angeles with Carly and embracing the many new beginnings they would hopefully—no, definitely—share together.

True love isn't easy to find, so whether you seek it out or stumble upon it . . . it's always worth the journey!

U. S. AND INTERNATIONAL STATISTICS

- Two girls for every boy are victims of human trafficking for labor, sex, or organ collection. Ages usually range from one to eighteen years old.
- Children from different races, ethnic groups, and religions are taken from cities and rural areas throughout the world. Some legally or smuggled by kidnappers, pimps, and professional brokers. Many are sold by their own families.
- 50% of two to four million trafficked are estimated to be children.
- 76% of transactions for sex with underage girls starts on the internet. Two million children are subjected to sexual abuse in the sex trade business. Sex trade is considered a 32 Billion a year industry.
- Young girls exploited, especially virgins. Children are lured by good jobs, educational opportunities, and supposed loving families. Young children used for hard labor, begging, sexual exploitation, and servitude. Average life span of an abused child is 7 years, attributed to malnutrition, overdose, and suicide.
- Human trafficking is the world's fastest growing criminal industry.
- Most common form of human trafficking is sexual exploitation.

- Human trafficking is a global multi-billion dollar enterprise.
- Estimated 24.9 million people trapped in forced labor via human trafficking worldwide

  Figures compiled as of July 31, 2017 from:
    - International Labor Organization
    - Ark of Hope for Children
    - Polaris Project
    - United Nations Office of Statistics
    - Erase Child Trafficking
    - Human Trafficking by the Numbers

Made in the USA
Las Vegas, NV
22 October 2023

79542651R00197